THE GERMAN CLUB

THE GERMAN CLUB

PATRICK OSTER

Distributed by
Argo Navis Author Services
www.argonavisdigital.com

Print ISBN: 978-07867-5602-5
ebook ISBN: 978-07867-5603-2

Distributed by Argo Navis Author Services

CONTENTS

ABOUT THE AUTHOR

Patrick Oster is an award-winning journalist who has covered the White House, the State Department and the CIA. He has been a foreign correspondent in Latin America and Europe, covering the fall of the Berlin Wall and the creation of the European Union. A lawyer, he is managing editor for legal news for Bloomberg News. He is the author of "The Mexicans: A Personal Portrait of a People" and the comic thriller "The Commuter." More details about him can be found at www.patrickoster.com.

Leipzig, Oct. 9, 1989 — More than 70,000 East Germans staged a protest tonight, ignoring threats of military reprisals as they demanded democratic and economic reforms to mirror changes in the Soviet Union under President Mikhail Gorbachev.

Under orders from Communist Party General Secretary Erich Honecker, local doctors had stockpiled body bags, blood plasma and makeshift operating tables in the great hall of the city to deal with protest casualties. Local officials ignored the order to punish protesters, joining instead in a call for peace signed by Kurt Masur, conductor of the city's famed Gewandhaus Orchestra, among other dignitaries.

The push for what some called "socialism with a human face" followed the visit the week before by Gorbachev to East Berlin, where more than 1,000 persons were arrested after shouts of support for his policies of *perestroika* and *glasnost* as alternatives to armed confrontation with the West. Soviet tanks, once the implied threat behind any Honecker demand to quell unrest, were seen blocking entrances of East German military compounds near Leipzig before the protest.

Some eastern European countries with Communist governments have opened their borders, letting East German visitors freely travel west in a way otherwise blocked by the Berlin Wall. The Leipzig protesters demanded a similar easing of travel restrictions.

"This cannot last," said one protester, who asked not to be named. "With the borders open, something's going to happen. Something soon."

1

Friday, October 27, 1989, 11:30 p.m., West Berlin.

The man who called himself Willy was a Berliner, a true native of the divided city, not one of the countless hordes who had come to inhale its exotic, permissive air in search of fun or fortune. He found such interlopers — the draft dodgers, the artists, the Turkish guest workers — amusing enough. They gave the city a bit of its old cabaret color and flair. But they had nothing to do with him. Berlin was not really theirs. It just used them, as he did.

These strangers lived on the city's trendy surface. They had no clue of the edgy life that coursed underground. They did not know its forbidden flavors, like the smoky tang of danger and death that penetrated Willy's shadowy work. They welcomed news of superpower peace overtures and the growing atmosphere of relaxed occupation in the city. Willy reveled in its continuing intrigues. He called *all* the city home and roamed where he pleased, ignoring the formalities of border controls and so-called military sectors. The Russian Sector, the American Sector — even geographic names like East and West Berlin — were just fictions of bothersome occupiers, as far as he was concerned. Even the Wall was irrelevant if you knew its weak points, as he did.

For him, those 97 miles of concrete and barbed wire —The Antifascist Protection Rampart, as those in charge in the east called it — was just a 30-year-old appendix waiting to be surgically removed some day. In the meantime, it did him and his confederates no real harm. In fact, he earned a bit more in his line of work because of his ability to pass openly through its military checkpoints or stealthily through its handy unofficial passages, as he had earlier on that cold October night.

"Where the hell is it?" he said in accented English, betraying his impatience and a hint of his Berlin origins. "They were supposed to be here an hour ago."

Anyone close to him could have detected the sound of molar-grinding pistachios, the remains of which lay to either side of his feet. It wasn't good tradecraft to make the muffled noise or leave traces of the shells, but he was addicted, as he was first to admit.

"Patience, Willy," said his companion, whose *Hochdeutsch* was grammatically flawless but nonetheless betrayed his origins, which were recognizably American. "Our guy says they'll come to the warehouse to switch to the van. As long as we watch the van, we're OK."

"What if it's all a decoy? What if we're sitting here with our thumbs up our asses while they drive the body across some other way?"

His employer, whose name was David, let out a long sigh.

"Then we'll catch them at one of the checkpoints," the American said. "It would be messier, but we can still stop them. Our people know what to look for."

The response didn't do much for Willy's fuming mood.

"You're such a worrier, Willy. Sometimes I think you're getting too old for this."

The American flashed a taunting smile. Willy harrumphed but otherwise ignored the needling. He knew things his taunter didn't and so bided his time.

"Something coming," a message in English crackled over Willy's car radio.

"Told you," the American said.

Willy hauled his beefy frame out of the black Mercedes S-car and began the short walk down the street of abandoned buildings toward a boarded-up warehouse. The American stayed behind. Officially he wasn't supposed to be anywhere near the operation.

The warehouse was in what some called the American sector. Most just said it was Kreuzberg, a rundown enclave of Turkish *gastarbeiters*, drug addicts, vegetarians, homosexuals, punk rockers and assorted others Willy wouldn't have pissed on if they'd been on fire. No one officially lived on the street where the warehouse was located. A few bombed-out hulks that had been large houses before the war stood nearby as fossilized reminders of what had happened to the once great city when the Thousand-Year Reich ended after a dozen years. Inside one, two squatters, the only remaining residents of the street, had been rousted from the comfort of their candle-lit, urine-soaked sleeping quarters. After that, there were no lights to be seen in the surrounding area, including the street lamps, which Willy's men had disconnected.

Dressed in black, Willy blended in well with the grit and grime of his surroundings, an inky, leather-clad cat against a new-moon sky. The warehouse was dark too. Two of Willy's men had hidden themselves in the dimness of a loft where crates and shadows would conceal their movements even when the lights were switched on. Their job was to disarm the driver and his helper and make the encounter look like a robbery. Willy was armed with a 9-mm pistol. He was an extremely accurate shot with either hand. If pressed, he would admit to being a shade better with his left, the hand that comfortably held the gun that night.

The men in the loft had been instructed to wait until everyone had emerged from the long-awaited truck, then pounce. If someone stayed in the truck, the men were to grab the person who got out and use him as a hostage to get his partner out of the vehicle. With Willy still in the shadows behind a buttress of the warehouse, a truck with an M registration — Munich — lumbered up to the sliding front door. The vehicle's headlights had been shut off before it came down the street. Only the strains of its diesel engine gave Willy a warning of its presence.

A slim young man slipped out of the truck cab on the passenger side. He looked around. Seeing no one, he undid the door's recently picked padlock with a key that hung from a chain around his neck. The tall youth, paid well to break a few laws, groped for the light switch to the right and flicked it on, spilling a harsh white glare across the concrete floor but little illumination elsewhere. Like a ground controller dealing with a jumbo jet, he guided the truck into the vast warehouse through the tight entranceway. Mission accomplished, he raced to the back of the truck to bolt the front door.

Outside, Willy waited. With no traffic on the street, he became acutely aware of what little noise there was. The autumn wind had picked up, making whistles out of the warehouse's saggy rain gutters. A weather vane on a nearby house creaked against its rust. To the trained ear, there were muffled sounds of rifle fire. That was not part of the plan. Willy streaked to the warehouse door, not immediately sure what to do once he opened it.

The American had heard the noises over the car radio and hurried down the sidewalk. Willy sensed footfalls and extended his pistol toward their sound. Thanks to excellent night vision, he uncocked his weapon just before the American ran into its muzzle.

"I heard shots," Willy said.

"May have been my boys. I put a couple of extra shooters in there."

"And you didn't tell me? You're lucky my guys didn't shoot yours." Willy considered the shootings, then asked, "Does the ambassador know what you're up to?"

The American smiled and said, "When your ambassador used to run the CIA, not to mention your president, who knows."

The sound of a bolt being slid back from inside interrupted the banter. The door opened slightly, exposing the American as Willy stayed to the side in the dark.

"I guess it's safe," Willy said. "No one shot you." Willy waited a moment then called out "Horst?"

"Ja," came the reply from inside.

Willy entered the warehouse with the American right behind him. Horst slid the door closed and bolted it again. In the center of the warehouse, the two men were lying face down. A thick reddish-black liquid oozed from neat holes in their heads, forming shallow pools on the oil-stained floor.

"Get those two into the truck and hose down the floor," the American said, taking control of the operation.

Two men with sniper rifles stood in the shadows as Willy's team cleaned up. The American took out a pack of Marlboros and lit up a cigarette.

"We need to get this sorted out fast," the American said after giving in to a vice he was trying to quit.

"Perhaps we should get the body out of the truck before we put the departeds' remains in there."

The American gave Willy a hard stare.

"Good idea."

Horst got the truck keys from the ignition and found one that opened the rear door. Inside were a dozen drums, the size of oil barrels.

"What the fuck?" the American said. "Where's the body?"

"I'll take a look," Willy said.

Willy hoisted himself into the back and used a crowbar he found dangling inside to pry open a barrel top, sending the lid clattering to the truck's wooden floor bed.

"Someone got a flashlight?" Willy asked.

Willy's other man unclipped an L-shaped military-issue one from the side of his webbed belt and tossed it to his boss. Willy aimed a beam at the murky liquid in the open barrel. His face pinched together in disgust.

"What is it?" the American asked.

"Looks like old cooking grease." Willy sniffed the surface. "Smells like it too. They recycle this shit on the other side, if you can believe it."

"Anything in it?"

Willy shot the American an irritated look.

"Get me a stick or something," he said to no one in particular.

Horst found a broom, and Willy stuck the handle inside the contents of the barrel.

"Nothing in this one that I can see."

"Hurry up and check the rest. I don't want to stay in this place any longer than I have to. Dead bodies and a diplomatic career do not mix."

"It's less of a liability in your real job."

"Shut up and get on with it!"

Willy continued his work with the crowbar and broom handle. He found nothing in the next four. In the sixth, he didn't need the broom to tell what a tangle of human hair on the surface meant.

"Jackpot," he said in a flat tone.

"Wolf?" the American asked.

"Tell you in a minute. It's definitely somebody. Or at least part of somebody."

Willy began stripping down to his underwear, ignoring the cold of the unheated warehouse as he carefully folded his expensive leather jacket and pants out of harm's way. Willy undid his paratrooper shoes, stuffing his socks into them. Down to his black bikini briefs, he plunged his arms into the drum of interest and hauled out what remained of a body.

"Jesus, they shot away half his head," the American said.

"Burned his fingerprints off too from the look of it."

Willy examined the fingers carefully.

"Blowtorch, I'd say. Either they didn't want us to know who he was or they wanted him to tell them something very badly."

"I wish I'd had that chance," the American said. "Anything in his pants pockets?"

Willy checked, his oiled chest hair glistening in the incandescent light. He found nothing including clothing labels, a belt or shoes.

"We'll have the lab boys check everything, including clothing sizes, likely origin and the cut and thread count," Willy said. "Wolf was particular about what he wore. He had expensive tastes."

"Aside from the clothes, we have any chance to be sure it was Wolf?"

"Couple of teeth broken off in his mouth. One's a molar with some dental work. That should help." A pause. "You have his dental records?"

The American shook his head, then said: "You should be able to get them from his dentist's office over the weekend. I'll get you the address."

"You need anything from his apartment as long as we're breaking and entering?"

"Don't go anywhere near there. We checked it last week right after he disappeared. By now someone may be watching his place. I don't want them to think we're too interested in Wolf."

"And who would *they* be?"

"I wish I knew. That's why I would have liked to have had a session with Wolf before the guys who did this."

"Won't they think you were interested in him when their truck doesn't show up?"

The American shook his head.

"This truck is going to have a terrible accident. I've got another team outside."

Willy put his thumb between the index and middle fingers of his right hand and gave the American the European version of the finger.

"Like I said, you should have told me. Someone might have gotten shot."

"It probably wouldn't have been you."

Willy found some old rags in a closet in a corner of the warehouse and wiped the cooking grease off his body as best he could. He sniffed his chest once he'd gotten his shirt back on.

"I stink," he said as he watched his men put the two bodies in the truck and wrap the oily corpse in a plastic tarp next to the van the dead men had intended to use to hide their tracks.

"Wipe everything down, and leave their van here like no one ever came for it," the American said.

Willy flashed a half-hearted Nazi salute in mock obedience. He grabbed a walkie-talkie out of one of his team's duffle bags and told his outside men that he'd meet them at a garage rendezvous after he showered and changed clothes. They went into action, putting the corpse into a van of their own and drove the dead men's truck toward its fiery destiny. Willy gave the warehouse one last look to see if anything had been forgotten. He switched off the light, using one of the oily rags to wipe off any fingerprints, a precaution he took with the padlock after locking the front door.

"I'll drop you off," he told the American.

"Just leave me near the Ku'damm. I'll get a cab home in case anyone is watching my place."

As Willy pulled away toward Berlin's center of nightlife, another man sitting in a second-story room a thousand yards away flicked off a monitor connected to an electronic listening device in the warehouse. He exhaled and said: "Christ, that's not the way it was supposed to happen."

"Too late to worry about that," said his more calm colleague, who was still monitoring the street in front of the warehouse through night-vision binoculars. "The question now is: do you think it worked?"

"I certainly hope so. I'd hate to think two men died for nothing."

*****

Saturday, October 28, 10:00 a.m., Bonn.

One of Willy's men took the teeth from the warehouse body and flew to Bonn the next day. In the evening, the office of a dentist in that city had unscheduled visitors. Records of a certain Wolf Springer were removed from a filing cabinet. A dentist with an interest in off-the-books dollar payments examined the molar in question and pronounced it a match for one of Springer's, while making no conclusion about the other teeth, which had not benefited from dental work.

Willy reported by phone to the American in Berlin on the match. The American was ambivalent about the finding.

"Tooth matches, clothes do too, but they seem a little big for the body."

"So what does that mean?"

"It means we appear to have questions only a dead man can answer."

"So we're stuck?"

"Maybe not. I have an idea. If Wolf is still alive, I think I have an irresistible way to flush him out. And if he's dead, my plan still works."

*****

After that conversation, Willy made a call to one of the two men who'd monitored the events at the Kreuzberg warehouse from down the street.

"He bought the molar," he said. "The dentist said it belonged to Wolf. But Price is still suspicious. Something about the clothes."

"The clothes! Forget that! What happened? You were supposed to knock those two drivers out and tie them up, not murder them."

"Hey, not my idea. Price had his own guys inside. Seems like their orders were shoot to kill. Guess he didn't want any witnesses."

"Well, the drivers were just some hired criminals, but still I don't like the idea that our people got murdered, so you better watch yourself. They won't be happy if they figure out you're really working for us."

2

Monday, October 30, 10:00 a.m., Chicago.

When the call came in, Homer Thornton's scalpel had begun its journey from throat to vulva and was about to split Sherry Willard's navel in half. The clangy ring of the black wall rotary-dial phone ricocheted around the ceramic-tile walls of the autopsy room. The jarring sound startled Ritter's new partner, Doreen Lavin, who got up from her observation post atop a wobbly wooden stool next to the examination table and answered the phone after its fourth ring.

Ritter seemed not to notice, which wasn't surprising, given his mood. To outward appearances, he was frozen in a stare at the corpse of the once beautiful young woman lying before him. One might have guessed that he was grappling with the obvious: who had done her in—and why. He'd been thinking about that at the beginning of the exam and had some suspicions about both — hoping he was wrong. But he had more on his mind.

As Doreen listened to the caller, a somber line from the poet Heine popped into Ritter's head, perhaps the product of his reading Great Books at the University of Chicago before taking a pre-graduation detour into police work. Something about how sleep is good but death is better and best of all is never to have been born. The poem might have been his dark take on what had happened to Sherry Willard, but it could have as easily been triggered by the awful state of his own life.

As much as he was trying to focus on matters at hand, pesky thoughts of a week-old domestic scene at his northwest side apartment poked painfully into his thoughts. Back came a blow-by-blow account of an hour-long contretemps that had ended his marriage of almost 25 years as best he could tell. That battle between professional and personal thoughts probably explained why Doreen, a rising star just five years out of the police academy, had to tell Ritter twice that the call was for him.

"Some guy from the State Department, Matt," she said.

Snapped back to the present for a second, Ritter grew angry as he guessed it was probably a joke call from one of the guys at the precinct or from some weirdo who'd seen his name in the newspaper and was trying to play with his head, which wasn't in the best shape that morning. He'd had too much to drink the night before, a habit that seemed to be linked to fights with his wife, Anita.

The last thing he needed at that moment was someone messing with him. He shoved the call out of his consciousness almost as quickly as it had entered. Back came his gloomy focus on his wife and his life along with a scant possibility that things, however briefly, might get a little brighter in a couple of days. He reminded himself that that Monday was closer to Wednesday than Sunday had been, and on that looming midweek October date, he was scheduled to take some sorely needed time off. He wanted to make sure nothing interfered with that.

After his championship bout with his wife the week before, he'd realized that he hadn't taken any vacation since the Christmas holidays of 1987, when he hadn't gone anywhere. He'd decided after that epiphany that he needed some time to get his bearings and decompress. He didn't even mind that some of his vacation would have to be spent getting his crummy new apartment in order. At least there, there would be no one yammering at him. No boss, no wife, no members of the public clamoring for action on the latest unsolved murder.

He was stuck in a dive because Anita had insisted he move out after she'd demanded a separation during that last shouting match. Her only olive branch was to suggest they meet with a marriage counselor to see if there was some way to patch things up. Ritter had said sure. At that point he would have agreed to almost anything, but he thought it was a waste of time. It was over.

The Sherry Willard case unfortunately was far from over, and given Thorton's initial findings, Ritter was getting the sinking feeling that it might threaten his days off if he didn't do something. Thornton had done a quick exam at the crime scene and told Ritter that poison was a possibility. Plus rape. That was exactly the combination Ritter hadn't wanted to hear. He'd had two other rape-poison cases in the previous year. Three was a trend. Three might mean a serial killer. Three might mean daily press conferences and round-the-clock shifts. And everyone looking at him.

After the first crime, The Sun-Times had dubbed the guy the Rat Poison Rapist, because that was the substance the murderer had used to kill the victim, Wanda Lupinski. With a plastic funnel jammed in her mouth, she'd been forced to drink lemonade laced with the stuff, then raped as she died a painful death tied to a bed with her own panty-hose in a vacant bungalow near Logan Circle. Six months after Lupin-ski, there'd been another rape-murder, and poison was again the cause, though a different kind. In that second one, the woman had been raped after she was dead, the autopsy showed. Ritter, nowhere on the first case, had used the differences to tell reporters the crimes weren't neces-sarily linked.

"Different poisons, guys, and could be a necrophiliac," he'd said, even though he and the local FBI profiler didn't believe that.

Now Sherry Willard's death would probably bring a connection back to the first case — rape while still alive — and everyone would be in a panic, even though the guy seemed to be working on a steady six-month murder schedule. Ritter hadn't caught the guy in a year, and most likely would not catch him in the next couple of days unless the killer made some mistake, which, up to then, he hadn't. Stumped and exhausted,

Ritter had arranged with Thornton not to hurry the autopsy. Ritter figured if he had any chance to catch the guy, it would happen a lot faster if he got some rest.

"Next Monday at the earliest," Thornton told Ritter and Doreen, in a stagey voice, when Ritter asked when the results would be in. "We're swamped."

Ritter figured Doreen could work the case as a standard murder while he was off, getting background on who Sherry Willard was, where she'd been just before her death and who her acquaintances were. He'd keep in touch by phone. But that plan would go out the window if it became a serial-killer case.

Captain Malone would insist that Ritter run it because he was supposed to be the department's best homicide detective. At least that's what the chief had told him the last time he'd cracked a big murder case. But the department's best had no clue how to catch the Rat Poison guy after all those months, so Ritter was in no hurry to look like an idiot when the mayor, the chief, his boss and scads of reporters began asking him what he planned to do, as they surely would.

As Ritter sorted through the case's possibilities, Doc Thornton, who typically kept morgue talk light, was probing around the various organs of Sherry Willard, a small-breasted brunette who seemed to have nothing in common with the other poison victims other than her gender and a Chicago address.

"Bears are coming back, looks like," Thornton said. "You see the game?"

"Nah. Don't have my TV hooked up yet. Just moved."

"Heard about that. How long you married?"

"About 25."

"Well, at least the Bears won. Five and three now."

Doreen cleared her throat loudly enough so that both men turned toward her.

"Should I tell the guy to call back?" she asked.

Ritter sighed at the prospect of dealing with the call. He slid off his stool and ambled toward the phone. When he got there, he just stared at the handset sitting on top of the wall unit for a while. He found himself thinking that at the end of the year, he could take the 25-and-out route and retire with a pretty nice pension. Before the breakup with his wife, it wasn't an option he'd been considering, but its appeal was sneaking up on him as a newly separated husband who was about ten pounds fatter than he wanted to be at age 50.

Maybe it was time for a clean break, for something different. Go back to school and get his degree. That sort of thing. He nodded as the appeal of retirement sank in, but first he had to deal with whatever numbnuts was on the phone. Shouldn't take long, he figured. He put the receiver to his ear and barked out a simple "Yeah?"

After a brief delay, a man with a nasal, educated voice asked "Matthew Ritter?"

"Who wants to know?"

The man identified himself as Clyde D. Havermann of the U.S. State Department in Washington, D.C., consular-services division. Havermann said he needed to verify Ritter's home address, Social Security number and mother's maiden name. Ritter cut him off without telling him anything.

"Who's this really?" Ritter asked.

Havermann began anew, undeterred in his mission, even using his middle initial again as if there might be some other Clyde Havermann. He pressed on to explain that consular services dealt with, among other things, bodies found on foreign soil "that might be of interest to American citizens."

That stopped Ritter for a moment. Maybe the call wasn't a prank. He wondered if the call might be official, perhaps about a body of interest to the Chicago Police Department, but Havermann quickly made it clear that this was more of a "personal" call. Havermann's circuitous route to the point began to irritate Ritter, who, marriage aside, was also in a bad mood because he'd given up smoking while dieting after moving into his North Clark Street place. Part of his clean-break thinking.

Havermann droned on about what his unit did and the services it provided. Ritter tuned him out as he thought about how little he had going to make his fresh start. All his worldly possessions had fit into his unmarked police car when he'd moved out of the apartment he'd shared with his wife: some books, a set of free weights, a speed-bag from his Golden Gloves days, and a stereo system and speakers he'd built himself from tubes and catalog components.

He'd left behind a spinet piano that Anita insisted on keeping even though she hardly played. He played well when he was in the mood. That was one legacy Grandma Helga had left him. She'd adopted the strict-instructress school of parenting after his parents both died, and among her orders were piano lessons with a proper professor. There wasn't much chance Georg Solti would ask Ritter to solo with the Chicago Symphony Orchestra that fall, but he could do the instrumental part for some Schubert lieder if some budding Dietrich Fischer-Dieskau knew the words. He was sad — angry really — about the piano but reminded himself there was no room for it at his third-floor walkup anyway.

Ritter suddenly noticed Clyde D. Havermann was asking him in a loud voice, "Are you there, Mr. Ritter? Mr. Ritter?"

"I'm here, Clyde. Now suppose you just cut to the chase and tell me what the hell this is all about. Whose body are we talking about?"

Ritter jingled the change in his left pants pocket as he waited for an answer from Havermann, who took a moment to reply.

"It's about your brother," Havermann finally said.

Ritter stopped playing with the change and said, with a distinct edge in his voice,

"Is this some kind of joke?"

That outburst got the attention of Doreen, who'd been eavesdropping while trying to seem engrossed in the autopsy. Ritter noticed her staring at him and twirled his index finger around his right ear as if to say he was dealing with some kook. Doreen nodded as if she sympathized.

"Not at all," Havermann said. "I'm sorry to inform you that your brother has died and that you are named as his next-of-kin."

"Un huh," Ritter said in a flat tone. "So what happened to him?"

"It says here that he was, uh, murdered."

"Un huh," Ritter said again, keeping a calm demeanor.

"The form doesn't say how. It just says 'Murder' under the 'Cause of Death' heading. That's a bit unusual, I must say. Typically it gives some detail like 'shot' or something. But I'm sure you can get the details from our people in the Federal Republic."

"The Federal Republic?"

"Of Germany."

"That the one that's ours or theirs?"

"Ours. Your brother died in West Germany. Or at least that is where his body was found. Which makes sense because he was a West German citizen. But then you must know that."

"Right," Ritter said, stretching out the word.

Havermann cleared his throat and returned to his mission.

"Your brother's attorney has arranged a round-trip plane ticket for you from the funds of his estate."

"There's an estate?"

"Yes. You have a reservation on a flight this evening, if that is convenient. The ticket is being held at the airport. O'Hare, it says here. Vice Consul Richard Davies or his representative will meet you when you land."

"*Tonight?*"

"If that's not convenient, you can change it."

"And it's all paid for, you say?"

"Absolutely."

Havermann gave Ritter the airline reservation details and a contact telephone number.

"Can I put you on hold?" Ritter asked, doing just that before Havermann could respond.

Ritter dialed the number and confirmed that there was a plane ticket, first class, waiting for him on a late evening flight to Frankfurt and that a car would take him from there to Bonn. He focused for a moment on the blinking phone light that represented Mr. Clyde D. Havermann, of the U.S. State Department consular division.

For a lot of reasons, the story about a murder in Germany made no sense, but Ritter had developed a nagging hunch there was something going on that he should look into, and hunches in his time in homicide work had always served him well.

Ritter punched the phone button and changed his tone with Havermann. The way he looked at it, he had some time coming. He toyed with the idea of taking off a day early, getting on that plane and telling Malone he'd be back for the autopsy report. If someone wanted to give him a free trip to Europe, why not? How better to get away from it all than to go to another country? Fixing up his apartment could wait. It had for a week. There was nothing to keep him in Chicago except crap.

Besides, he'd never been to West Germany, and if the trip turned out to be a joke, he'd have a big laugh with the joker and thank him for the freebie over a stein of beer. As he saw it, there was no down side to taking up the offer, and more than anything, it would give him something he dearly wanted. He wanted out. He just wanted out.

Ritter apologized to Havermann for having been abrupt at the beginning of the call. He adopted a matter-of-fact pose he used while working a case.

"You caught me in the middle of something at work, Mr. Havermann. I wasn't paying as much attention as I should have. Could we go over this one more time?"

"Of course," Havermann said, sounding as upbeat as he'd been at the start.

Havermann repeated what he'd said. Ritter, still wavering a bit on what to do, listened without interruption for several minutes before finally interjecting: "You sure you got the right Matthew Ritter?"

Silence on the other end for a moment.

"I believe so."

Havermann went over some new material: Ritter's home address, at least the one he'd shared with Anita in their Jefferson Park neighborhood, his police rank, his January 1, 1939, date of birth, his mother's name (Greta), his father's name (Rudolph), the names of his four grandparents, three of whom he'd never met. Ritter confirmed them all. Havermann, almost triumphant, said in a Q.E.D. tone, "Then there can be no mistake. You are the Matthew R. Ritter we are looking for."

And who exactly was that, Ritter asked himself, thinking of the parents he never knew and boyhood questions never answered by the taciturn grandmother who'd reared him. As Havermann prattled on, Ritter traveled back in memory, only half listening to what he'd have to do in Germany to deal with his brother's body. The only thing he caught was that all would be explained by Vice Consul Davies when Ritter arrived.

Ritter looked at his watch. It was ten in the morning. He had time to get to the bank and get some money out of a vacation fund for a trip he and Anita would not be taking. He had a passport somewhere in an unpacked box at his new place. If he took the evening flight, he'd be in Bonn by Tuesday morning. Plenty of time to check things out and be back for the autopsy report the following Monday.

Ritter hung up and walked back toward what was left of Sherry Willard. Doreen was staring at him, as if waiting for some explanation for the long phone call.

"I need a little favor," Ritter said, knowing there was nothing small about it.

"Sure," she said, straightening the jacket of her blue pants suit as if about to undergo rifle inspection.

"Can you take over the case for a couple of days? I need to go out of town."

"Absolutely!" Doreen said, sounding a little too eager for Ritter's taste.

"And I need you to sub for me this morning with Captain Malone. He needs an update on the autopsy. Tell him we won't get the report till next Monday, so there's not much I can do anyway. And there won't be any press conferences that I'd need to deal with, so no worries there."

"Well, if there are, should I do them?"

Ritter smiled at the beware-what-you-wish-for prospect.

"That will be up to the captain. Tell him I'll be back, Monday but I need to start my little vacation a day early."

"Why?"

"Death in the family."

"Sorry to hear. Anybody close?"

"My brother."

"I didn't even know you had a brother."

"Neither did I."

3

Tuesday, October 31, 8:30 a.m., Frankfurt

Ritter had never been able to sleep well on planes. He was logy when the 747 pulled up at the gate Tuesday morning in Frankfurt. He'd picked at the airline dinner and skipped the stale rolls of the continental breakfast. Most of his nourishment during the flight came from peanuts and three double Scotches. First class merited single malt, and he took advantage of a drink he usually didn't get to buy on a cop's pay.

He'd hoped the drinks might make him drowsy enough to sleep. They hadn't, so after listening to the plane's classical selections for a while, he wound up reading. Ritter had grabbed a few old paperbacks from his moving boxes, things he'd bought while in college. He'd chosen some short stories by Ring Lardner and a novel by Nelson Algren, fellow Chicagoans. Both had made him even more morose.

He switched off the reading light after a few hours and tried to lull his six-foot-three frame to sleep. With the seat next to him empty, he quietly hummed a drunken lullaby, but it was no use. The alcohol created a tightness around his head like an invisible steel band. By the time the plane landed, the pain was worse.

As he trudged through the airport with his carry-on toward passport control, he found he was picking up threads of conversations in a language he knew but didn't use much. Grandma Helga had absolute rules: German in the home and English everywhere else. Aside from the language and his interest in the country's classical composers, Ritter's German heritage wasn't a big part of who he was. Boxing and the Bears had been as important as Bach and Brahms in Ritter's Second City upbringing.

He'd taken some German literature courses at the U of C. He still read a novel in German now and then without having to look up many words. That didn't mean he got all of what Günter Grass was peddling, but he at least enjoyed his story lines. As far as Ritter was concerned, he was just an American from Chicago, which he pronounced Sha-caw-gah, like a native.

He knew he was a German-American, which was the most common type of hyphenated-American — and the most assimilated. But he didn't think about that much. He'd go to an Oktoberfest every once in a while, but it was more for the beer than to revel in things German. He couldn't name a pal who was a fellow Kraut, which is what Captain Malone called Germans. Ritter took no offense. A German identity and World War II guilt didn't seem to apply to him. In talking about German-Americans, Ritter usually said "them" not "us."

He hadn't thought about that attitude much before landing back in the fatherland, as his grandmother used to call Germany. Why were German-Americans so invisible as an ethnic group, he found himself asking as he stood in the passport line? Maybe it was because they weren't pushy about their heritage once they got to the United States. Having to explain about Nazis and what happened to the Jews might have had something to do with the more recent immigrants. And why hadn't anyone noticed that the Supreme Commander of Allied forces in Europe during World War II was a German-American? Eisenhower. Hewer of iron.

At the front of the passport line at last, he thought maybe fellow German-Americans Babe Ruth and Lou Gehrig had probably helped pave the way. Good old George Herman Ruth Jr. Nobody asked *him* which side he was on during the war.

The uniformed immigration officer saw Ritter's name on the passport, looked at his face and dropped right into German.

"*Sind Sie zum ersten Mal in Frankfurt?*" he asked.

"Yeah, first time," Ritter said in English, realizing later what had happened.

"What is the purpose of your visit," the officer asked, switching to a lightly accented English.

"Just tourism," Ritter said, not wanting to get into details about a murder and a body.

"Will you be staying long?"

"*Ich bleibe....*" Ritter heard himself begin before cutting himself off and saying,

"Just a few days."

The officer smiled and stamped the passport. Ritter, with only his carry-on, spotted the *ausgang* sign and headed toward the exit. A man holding up a sign that said "Ritter" lowered it and strode toward him.

"Mr. Ritter?" he asked.

"Yeah. You Davies?"

"No," said the man, who was not much taller than five feet. "Permit me. I am Werner. Your driver. Mr. Davies is awaiting us."

Werner insisted on carrying Ritter's bag. Ritter resisted at first.

"It's my job," Werner finally said, which won him control of the suitcase.

Ritter was uneasy about the arrangement. He'd never even had a cleaning lady, so any master-servant relationship was uncomfortable. In the end, he let Werner take the bag because he was tired, and his head was still hurting.

In the parking lot, Werner stopped at a metallic black Mercedes and put the carryon in the trunk. He opened the right rear passenger door for Ritter, who tried the front passenger one only to find it locked. With little energy for another tussle over protocol, Ritter got into the back and sank into the soft leather seats.

Werner was soon on the autobahn following the signs to Bonn. The weather was common for Central Europe for late October. The fog-covered horizon was a palette of grays, making it difficult to distinguish tree bark from low-hanging rain clouds.

"It will be winter soon," Werner said, pronouncing the season as if it began with a "v," the way Ritter's grandmother had.

"How long will it take to get to Bonn?" Ritter asked, not remembering the conversion rate for miles and kilometers.

"Not long."

That sounded long enough for a brief nap. Ritter closed his eyes, but he had no more luck sleeping than on the plane. The only way he really fell asleep quickly was lying on his stomach and that just wasn't possible in the car. He managed to daydream a bit and found himself remembering German lullabies like *Guten Abend, gute Nacht* that his grandmother had sung to him at bedtime. After a while, he gave up on a nap, opened his eyes and noticed that trees seemed to be whizzing by at a tremendous clip.

"How fast are we going, Werner?" he asked.

"About 200 kilometers per hour," Werner said.

Ritter knew miles were longer and so the speed was something less than 200, but he suddenly wanted to know how much.

"What is that in miles?" he asked.

Werner looked at the small numbers on the speedometer under the ones that indicated kilometers.

"Looks like about 125," he said.

Ritter let that sink in, then asked: "Is there any speed limit over here?"

"Only in parts of the autobahn where people crash all the time. Then we knock it down to about 130. Kilometers, that is."

Werner noticed the look on Ritter's face through the rear-view mirror.

"Nothing to worry about. This is a very safe car, and these roads are built for high speeds. Lots of banking and smooth surfaces. Not like those washboard things you find in the East. You could lose a filling if you drove this fast over there."

"Good to know, but I'm not in that much of a hurry."

Werner smiled into the mirror.

"Mr. Davies said he'd like to see you as soon as possible."

The Mercedes gobbled up more kilometers at the same pace till the signs for Bonn got bigger. Werner slowed down and got off at one marked "Bad Godesberg."

"I thought we were going to Bonn," Ritter said.

"People say Bonn, but the embassy is here. Lots of others too."

A few minutes later, Werner turned the car into a long driveway and made a left behind a long glass-and-concrete building that was part of a sprawling complex on the Rhine. In a previous epoch, the largest U.S. embassy had been in Saigon, and later it would be in Baghdad, reflecting the hot spots of the day. But in late 1989, as the United States, the Soviet Union and Europe all sensed they were in the endgame of the Cold War with no one sure of the precise outcome, the center of the American diplomatic universe was in what the most famous spy novelist had called a small town in Germany.

The president at the time had been the head of the Central Intelligence Agency and so had the big bluff man who was then the ambassador to West Germany, so diplomacy was not the only activity conducted under the roofs of the complex, which had more than their fair share of satellite dishes and antennae. Inside, if one knew where to look, were secure rooms that kept the diplomats up to date with the latest findings of signal and human intelligence. Diplomats who had access to such rooms had missions greater than their lowly official titles conveyed.

After a very thorough security check involving mirrors and a trunk check, the Mercedes was waved though. Werner parked next to a number of other expensive cars, all made in Germany.

"You can leave your bag in the trunk for now. I'll show you the way to Mr. Davies's office, and after your meeting, I'll take you wherever you need to go."

"Where would that be?"

Werner smiled.

"I haven't been told."

Davies had a corner office with lots of windows He was shorter than Ritter by a couple of inches but fit and looked as if he could handle himself in a fight. It was a routine Ritter had picked up as a young boxer, using the advice of his trainer to gauge arm reach, balance, awareness and other attributes of opponents that might cause him pain.

"Call me Rick," Davies said after the introduction by Werner.

At that point, after a transcontinental flight, a hair-raising ride in a Mercedes and an invitation to sit down in what appeared to be a genuine U.S. government office, complete with the picture of the president on the wall, Ritter decided he was not the victim of a transcontinental prank. Beyond that, he had no idea of what he'd gotten himself into with his impulsive journey.

"I have some papers for you to sign," Davies said, laying some documents out on his desk.

Ritter made no move to read or sign them, and Davies broke the silence by asking, "Will you be taking your brother's body back to the States or burying him here?"

"I'm not even sure I have a brother, *Rick*."

Davies blinked his eyes.

"I beg your pardon?"

"As far as I know, I have no brother."

Davies cleared his throat and tidied up the papers, which were already in perfect order.

"You are Matthew R. Ritter, are you not?"

"Yeah, I went over that with that Havermann guy, but in the 50 years I've been alive, no one ever said I had a brother."

Davies picked up one of the documents.

"Your mother's maiden name was Greta Vogel, who died when you were about six, and your father was Rudolph Springer. Correct?"

"Springer? No. My father's name was Ritter like mine….Maybe that's the problem."

Davies nodded his head as if taking that response in.

"That's not what it says here. When your mother separated from your father in, uh, 1939, shortly after you were born in Berlin…."

"That's not right either. I was born in Chicago. You could look it up."

"We have."

Davies handed over a copy of a document titled "Change of Name" that had been issued by the Cook County clerk's office. The signature at the bottom was in the elegant script he'd seen on other things his mother had signed. Ritter saw that "Mattheus Springer" had become "Matthew Ritter."

"I don't know how she did it, but she also listed your place of birth as Chicago, whereas we know very certainly that Mattheus Springer was born in Berlin."

Davies handed Ritter a copy of a Nazi-era Berlin birth certificate, including infant hand and feet prints, which seemed to be in order. Ritter felt too groggy and tired to make any final decision about his past based on documents he'd never seen.

"Mind if I hang on to these?" he asked.

"Be my guest. We have copies."

What was clear to him suddenly was his grandmother's pattern of avoiding talk about his father or any family members in Germany.

"Oh, Mattheus," she would say. "Your father died in the war, and so did everyone in our family who stayed there. It's just the two of us now."

He eventually gave up trying to find out more. When she died in his third year of college, there was no one else to ask — and no one else to stay in school for.

"It's an interesting choice," Davies said, breaking up Ritter's train of thought.

"What is?"

"Ritter. As you probably know….You speak German, right?"

"Yeah. Not a lot of chance to practice, but somewhere in here are years of talking to my grandmother," Ritter said, pointing to his right temple with his index finger. "And I used it in college."

"Then you probably know Ritter means knight, a title like a knight in shining armor."

"Don't feel too shiny after that plane trip."

Davies smiled.

"And Springer means knight too — the chess piece that can jump — spring —over the others."

"I knew that first one. Not much of a chess player, though."

"It will all come back after a few days. You'll be speaking like a real Berliner before you know it, just like your grandmother."

"I don't plan on being here that long, but I should be able to order a beer without too much trouble."

Ritter's timeframe appeared to take Davies by surprise.

"You'll need a little time, if only for the formalities. You'll need to identify him as the next-of-kin. We've arranged a private autopsy."

"I'm not going to be much help there. I have no idea what he looked like."

"It's just a formality. But in Germany, formalities count."

"What's that involve?"

"The first thing you need to do is go to Berlin to see the body, and that will take a little time."

"Berlin? What's the body doing there?"

"We're not really sure. That's where Wolf was found."

Ritter nodded his head.

"That's his name? Wolf?"

"Yes. Wolfgang Springer."

"Uh huh….Any more information on how he died?"

"Some sort of mugging, I think. The consular people in Berlin handled the particulars."

Ritter was tired but the detective in him suddenly came awake.

"If he was mugged, how did your people make the ID? Didn't the muggers take his wallet?"

Davies paused.

"I can't really say. Maybe they took the cash in it and left the wallet. You can inquire in Berlin. I'll arrange a ticket for you for tonight, and you can get a good night's sleep in a hotel before you view the body tomorrow. I have a man there to help you out."

Ritter thought about what cash he had on hand and asked: "Is this on me or does my brother's lawyer have some more spending money in the little slush fund?"

"I believe there's more. I'll make the arrangements. He has a power of attorney over your brother's affairs until the estate is settled. That's how he found out about you Your name was among your brother's papers"

"My brother knew about me?"

"I guess. I'm only telling you what I was told."

"Funny he never contacted me."

"I'm afraid I can't explain that. Perhaps he'd just learned the truth."

Ritter thought about that.

"Perhaps." Ritter waited a moment then asked, "When did he die anyway?"

"Ah, sometime Thursday, I believe."

Ritter considered that.

"And the lawyer was able to contact you, and you were able to gather all these documents over a weekend before that Havermann guy called me Monday morning?

Davies cleared his throat.

"Well, I think it was early Thursday, German time. And the lawyer found most of the documents. And, of course, there is Germany efficiency."

Davies smiled at his last remark. Ritter didn't.

"There is a flight about eight," Davies said, pressing ahead. 'Werner can drive you from your hotel."

"I don't have a hotel."

Davies smiled again.

"We have a few rooms booked nearby for just such occasions. People often need a little rest, given the ordeal."

I'd settle for some straight answers, Ritter thought, but he said instead: "Sure, that'd be great. I'm bushed."

Ritter signed the documents Davies had on his desk.

"Perfect," Davies said, examining each page.

He put the documents in a folder and held out his hand for Ritter to shake. Ritter hesitated, then took it.

"If you like, I can book a hotel near the Ku'damm in Berlin. It's quiet but close to the action."

Ritter laughed lightly.

"I'm not sure I'll have time for any action, but the quiet part sounds good."

"Well, if you change your mind, along the Kurfürstendamm you'll find all kinds of night spots, two miles of glitz and glitter, sin and sex. Even transvestite shows, if that is of any interest."

"Not since I stopping working vice."

Davies walked Ritter to the Mercedes.

"The Dreesen, Werner," he told the driver. "And later to the Bonn-Cologne airport. Mr. Ritter has a Berlin flight at eight."

Used to police-car protocol, Ritter again tried the front passenger door and found it open this time. Werner looked uncomfortable but stayed silent. Before he could pull away, Ritter hit the push button to lower the passenger window.

"One thing, Rick."

"Yes?"

"You said the autopsy was private, right?"

"Yes."

"Isn't that a little unusual? I mean why isn't it at the morgue."

Davies flashed the same smug smile.

"In Berlin, anything is possible."

4

Tuesday, October 31, 5:00 p.m., Bonn

The hotel was on Rheinstrasse in Bonn itself, and as the street name indicated, it was right on the river. Ritter tried to take a nap again but had no luck falling asleep. About five in the afternoon, he went down the lobby to have a beer. Werner was sitting in a wing-back chair reading Der Spiegel and popped up when Ritter appeared.

"I didn't want to be late, so I came early, Herr Ritter," he said.

"Yeah, extra German. But it's just Matt. Forget that Herr stuff."

"As you wish, *Matt*," Werner said, making a quick nod with his head and what seemed like a light heel click.

"You want a beer, Werner?" Ritter asked.

"Not on duty, but maybe a *mineralwasser*....and if you want a beer, we could go to a better place than this. Something down near the central square. I could give you a little tour on the way. We have plenty of time before your flight."

Ritter agreed and got his bag from his room so they wouldn't have to come back to the hotel. Werner took off down Rheinstrasse and ticked off some of the highlights of the town, which many tourists found underwhelming. There wasn't much to see if you didn't have business with the parliament, the chancellor or the president.

Zealots of Bonn, which had been a Roman town, could boast about the remnants of the largest fort of any legion or the Sterntor, a gate that was built with the remnants of a medieval city wall. The town had been part of the French Empire, then was turned over to the King of Prussia before it became part of the German Empire in the 19th Century. For most of that time, it had remained historically irrelevant.

After World War II, however, Bonn came into its own. Berlin was in ruins. Germans held out for eventual reunification and some semblance of a return to greatness, so large logical cities such as Hamburg and Frankfurt were rejected as a capital for West Germany. Potentially too permanent. Bonn was picked as something provisional — and not far from Cologne, where West Germany's first chancellor, Konrad Adenauer, had been mayor.

Some said Bonn could point with pride to being the birthplace of Ludwig Van Beethoven, whose house could be seen on Bonngasse, near the market place, not far from the rococo Old Town Hall. There was also a Beethoven Monument in Münsterplatz near the Bonn Minster, one of Germany oldest churches, Werner droned on, as Ritter began to feel sleepy at last.

"I guess it's not too exciting a place," Werner said as Ritter began to doze off.

"I'm sure it has hidden charms."

"Not really. Unless you are in government, it's pretty boring. And even then it can be pretty awful unless you are at the very top" Werner paused. "You know the joke about Bonn?"

"Don't think so."

"We Germans say that B-O-N-N stands for *Bundeshauptstadt ohne nennenswertes Nachtleben.*"

Ritter translated in his head and smiled. Federal capital without noteworthy nightlife. Ritter thought of that other joke about German humor being no laughing matter.

"Even our Beethoven claim to fame is a bit flawed. I have a cousin who's a Belgian — a Flemish speaker. He says we shouldn't even brag much about the master because Beethoven is a Flemish name. His grandfather, after whom Beethoven was named, was called Lodewijk van Beethoven. That's Flemish for Ludwig."

"And the great man is buried in Vienna, if I recall. That's what my piano teacher said."

"Yes. A bit of a sore point. But we have Schumann!"

Ritter looked over tolerantly at Werner, and said: "Well, that almost makes up for it."

*****

As Werner was completing his city tour, two men were catching up in an embassy room designed to keep their conversation private.

"You think your little scheme is going to work?" asked the larger of the two men, privately referred to as Triple X by those who worked for him, a play on his extra-large girth. His real name was Algernon, but few knew that. All his IDs and business cards just said "Gerry."

"It better work or someone will eventually take a look at why Price's guys killed those two people in Berlin," said Rick Davies, who was facing the large man as he stood in front of the equipment that was the heart of the embassy's communication center.

"You buy his explanation that it was self-defense?"

"I want to buy it because if I don't, someone is going to prison, and I fear it will not only be Price but me and maybe you."

Gerry drew his jowly face close to Davies as his eyes narrowed.

"I gave no authority to use deadly force. If anyone inquires, that responsibility is on you. Price is your goon as is that crazy Willy. Dogs and fleas, Richard. Remember the adage. Next time be more careful about your associates."

Davies thought about arguing the point, but instead just said: "He was told to use best judgment, given the situation. It was supposed to look like an armed robbery, not a murder."

"Your problem, not mine."

"What does the ambassador say?"

"Nothing, because I haven't told him….We're in the midst of an investigation, so any report is premature. On the other hand, if you find me Wolf Springer, and we get a few answers, the bad news of two killings might go down more easily if we present it with the intelligence of what the West Germans and the Soviets are really up to."

"Understood."

"I hope I never have to tell him anything because I think he's in denial here. Did you read his last cable to Washington?"

"Of course."

"I liked that part about 'no one believes reunification is the first order of business on the German-German agenda.'" Gerry paused. "That's very comforting except for that intercepted phone call from Moscow involving someone who sounded an awful lot like our dear missing friend, Wolf."

Gerry picked up a sheet of paper with an analyst's voice-pattern assessment of the call, which had been made shortly after the ambassador's Oct. 25 cable and Wolf Springer's sudden disappearance.

"We have a deal," the person speaking had said at one point during the short call from a hotel just off Red Square to a private club in West Berlin.

"Could be something; could be nothing," Davies said.

"And it could be that your little agent, who wasn't supposed to be in Moscow, wasn't really working for us."

"Aware," Davies said, sounding defensive. "Completely aware."

"Which would mean everything he told us was crap."

"Some things panned out."

"You know the game: feed the other side crumbs while you slip the poison in."

"I still can't see anything that's obviously bogus in hindsight."

"What about that club the call went to? Any clues there?"

"Bunch of do-gooders, as far as we can tell. Promoting all things German. Lots of VIPs on the list. Even the chancellor. The deal referred to on the tape could just be some bullshit conference they want to hold."

"Or something a lot more serious. We need to find out who took that call."

"That's doable, but if that body that Price and his men found in the oil barrel was Wolf, we may never find out what he was up to."

"Have you tossed his apartment?"

"Thoroughly. We got nothing. If he was keeping files or codes for someone else, he must have stored them elsewhere. Maybe at his office."

"A bit risky to break in there to find out."

"There might be a way — with the right burglar."

"You think the West German government might be in on whatever Wolf was doing with the Russians?"

"Given his standing in the polls, the chancellor probably sees reunification as a neat way to save his career. But would he screw us and sell out to the Russians? I just don't know."

"Wouldn't you do it to get half your country back?"

Davies smiled.

"I would, but then I'm unscrupulous."

*****

Willy, the man Gerry thought was crazy, had given his own report of the incident when two men had been shot as they were attempting to transport a body across Berlin. The man listening to his report didn't work for the U.S. embassy or any part of the U.S. government. In terms of loyalty, neither did Willy.

Once a lowly officer in German intelligence, Willy's boss sat in an expensively appointed office in a building in Bavaria, thinking not of the billions he'd accumulated since the end of World War II but of why an incident in a warehouse in West Berlin's Kreuzberg district had gone so wrong.

Willy set the scene for the rendezvous and summed up the plan to let the Americans recover a body hidden in a drum of recycled cooking oil. The billionaire and Willy listened to a tape recording of the incident.

Willy's boss recoiled a bit when he heard the two muffled shots ring out. Then the warehouse door could be heard grinding open along metal runners.

"The two are dead at this point, and this is David Price coming up," Willy told his boss. "Officially a diplomat but really a spook. Arrogant. And dangerous."

"Get those two into the truck and hose down the floor," Price was heard saying. "We need to get this sorted out fast."

Willy told his boss he'd taken over the job of searching the truck and eventually found a body with much of its head blown away and its fingerprints burned off.

"Blowtorch, I'd say," Willy could be heard saying on the tape. "Either they didn't want us to know who he was or they wanted him to tell them something very badly."

Willy turned off the tape.

"We talked about who was responsible for the body. Price has no clue if it was the East Germans or their Soviet bosses or someone else. He certainly doesn't know it was us. And he's not sure if Wolf was a double agent."

"Arrogance and incompetence are such a deadly combination," Wolf's boss said.

He lit up a cigarillo, a small German cigar shaped like a cigarette. After taking a few puffs, he offered one to Willy, who declined politely.

"Now that I've listened to the tape, I still can't fathom why Price would order his shooters to assassinate those men."

"Perhaps he didn't want any loose ends. Plus Price is a bit of a psychopath when it comes to the KGB or the East Germans. They shot his girlfriend on the other side a couple of years ago when she was helping someone escape."

"Maybe. No real loss, anyway. They were just some criminals we hired, so his anger was misdirected. They were just supposed to get robbed and maybe knocked out."

"On the other hand, it may show just how desperate the Americans have become to find out what Wolf was up to."

"If those two died to keep that secret, maybe it wasn't such a fiasco after all."

The billionaire tossed the half-smoked cigarillo into a glass ashtray that was otherwise unblemished.

"What happened with the dental records?"

"We stole them and, surprise, the molar matched Wolf's."

"So that settled it ?"

"No. They didn't like everything about the clothes. Price thought they were too big."

"They were Wolf's!"

"Price is a suspicious bastard."

*****

Tuesday, October 31, 9:30 p.m., West Berlin

As Willy's briefing drew to an end, Werner was still blathering on about the wonders of Bonn. He took so long that Ritter never did get his beer because he needed to check in for his flight by the time Werner's tour was finished.

The almost full PanAm flight got into Tegel right on time. Lots of business people returning from the capital, Ritter guessed. He picked up his bag and looked around for the man who was supposed to meet him. He was expecting to see someone holding up a little sign with his name on it. He didn't know what Davies's colleague looked like and figured the ignorance was mutual. It turned out, there was no sign, but a tall, self-assured man with chiseled features came up to him directly and asked, "Mr. Ritter?"

How did he know what I look like, Ritter wondered, spitting out a "Yeah" in response.

"David Price," said the well-tanned man, dressed in khaki pants, penny loafers and a cranberry crew neck wool sweater. "*Willkommen.*"

"*Danke* to you."

Price tried to take Ritter's bag. This time Ritter didn't let it go. Price seemed surprised but made no protest.

"Your first time in Berlin?"

"Sorta. I just learned I was born here, but my memory is a little fuzzy on that."

Price didn't pursue the remark.

"Well, it's a wonderful city. Especially now."

"Now?"

"Big changes in the East. Honecker's gone…."

"Who's that?" Ritter interrupted.

"Erich Honecker, the East German leader….There's pressure for reform over there. Just a couple of days ago they gave amnesty to everyone who'd fled west. And yesterday a bunch of dissident leaders read the riot act to the local Communist Party chief and the East Berlin mayor over at City Hall. And nobody was arrested. They even showed snippets of the protest on *Aktuelle Kamera,* the main evening news program.

Something big is going to happen. That's for sure. Maybe at the protest march on Saturday."

"I think I read something about it. But foreign affairs isn't really my thing."

"You should have been here a few weeks ago when Gorbachev came for the 40th anniversary celebration. People were in Alexanderplatz yelling 'Gorby!' and 'Freedom!' like he was some sort of Abe Lincoln."

"Sorry I missed that. I was trying to catch a serial killer and just couldn't get away."

Price gave Ritter a long look but let the snideness slide.

"Of course, what could be coming is a crackdown, even with Honecker gone," Price said. "Everybody's pushing for something."

"Us too?"

Price laughed.

"The United States wants what's good for Germany. And NATO."

"Sounds like the official position. What's the real deal?"

"That plan is above my pay grade. But you could be in for quite a show while you're here."

"Not exactly a pleasure trip."

"Guess not."

Price dropped the happy patter and changed the subject. "Had anything to eat?"

"Just a few nibbles on the plane."

"I know a great place for a late supper if you're awake enough."

"Somehow I feel like I should be eating breakfast."

The restaurant was a chic bistro off the Ku'damm, an expensive hangout for artists, writers and others trying to get attention. The menu was mostly Greek — stuffed grape leaves, moussaka and the like. But the place might as well have been in Southern California, given the goat cheese, sun-dried tomatoes and extra virgin olive oil among its dishes' ingredients.

"It's not on the menu, but they can do a veal chop that'll knock your socks off,"

Price said as he scanned the crowd, which included two leggy women in matching fur mini skirts and a transvestite in a scanty black cocktail dress.

"Fine," Ritter said, just glad to be out of the rain that had started suddenly on the way over. "But just that and a salad."

"And a beer. You have to have a beer. You're in Germany."

Beer didn't fit into Ritter's new diet regimen, but he didn't protest.

"I love this city," Price said, ogling the women in mini skirts. "It's so alive….and it's so easy to get laid." Price laughed as his own assessment. "The rest of Germany is like a morgue."

"I thought officially this wasn't part of Germany."

"Very good. Most Americans don't know that. Even after all these years, it's still an Allied occupied city."

The waiter brought the beers. Price immediately quaffed a few ounces.

"West Germany claims Berlin as a state, but it has 'temporarily' suspended jurisdiction over it from its 'provisional' capital in Bonn."

Ritter, not that interested in the history lesson, took a slug of beer.

"East Berlin officially does not exist," Price continued, not noticing he'd lost his audience. "Nor does East Germany for that matter. West Germany has an embassy in East Berlin, but they don't call it that. It's a *ständige Vertretung*, a permanent mission."

"Fascinating," said Ritter, taking his beer down to the halfway point.

"We play the same games. Officially West Berlin is the American, French and British sectors. East Berlin is the Russian sector.…When you come right down to it, we run this place. We're the law, although we try to give more and more day-to-day stuff to the Germans. After all, they are footing the bill for our soldiers over here."

"No kidding," Ritter said, taking another sip and checking out the two skirts himself.

"We tap phones, open mail, jail people whenever we want," Price said, sounding pleased at the sound of his own voice. "We control which planes fly in an out. And we have final say over whether Berlin ever becomes one city again — or Germany one country, for that matter."

Ritter finished his beer and put his empty glass back on the table with a thud.

"For most people, the Russian sector is East Berlin, and East Berlin is the capital of East Germany, which usually does pretty well in the Olympics," Ritter said.

"They like to call it the German Democratic Republic. Bit of a joke, really."

"I see you are a font of information. How you on bodies?"

Price looked perplexed.

"My brother's body — what do you know about it?"

Price paused.

"I know where it is and that we're going to see it tomorrow."

Ritter dropped into his nonthreatening mode of interrogation, as if Price were a crime suspect he wanted to put at ease.

"What have you found out so far?"

"Not much. They're not doing the autopsy until just before we arrive. We'll just have to wait, I guess."

"Is the medical examiner German or one of yours — since you guys run everything."

"I think he's private."

"Uh huh."

The salads came, then the veal chops. Price wolfed his meal down without much break in his running commentary on the wonders of Berlin. Like a living Baedeker, he ticked off the basics in an apparent effort to make Ritter's stay more enjoyable. Ritter wondered if it was just a filibuster to avoid talking about Ritter's brother.

Ritter learned Berlin — at least the three Allied sectors — had about two million people and that the population was holding steady thanks to the robust birthrate of about 125,000 Turkish guest workers. East Berlin had about a million inhabitants. West Berlin was walled in both from East Berlin and the surrounding countryside of East Germany, making it a West German island.

The enclosure gave West Berlin a claustrophobic feel for tourists, Price said, but the locals knew that a third of the city was open space, mostly water and woods out in the city's Spandau, Wannsee and Gatow sections.

"There's even a little village, Lübars, up in the northern part, where you can see farmland," Price said.

Price passed on the coffee and skipped dessert, as did Ritter. Price called for *die Rechnung*. Ritter didn't protest when Price paid the bill. The rain had stopped, and they strolled toward the Ku'damm. A brisk wind had kicked up. Some icy drops fell on Ritter's face. He felt chilled after the cozy heat of the restaurant. Price, almost glowing, didn't seem to mind the weather.

"There'll be people out here till two, three in the morning," Price said, picking up his travelogue.

"I may be one of them," Ritter said. "I had a nap in Bonn. I'm not exactly ready for bed again."

"If you want a walk to tire yourself out, you could head toward what the locals call the Gaping Tooth."

"What's that?"

"The old Kaiser Wilhelm Memorial Church. It's a bombed-out ruin they keep as a memento of the war. Berliners call it the Gaping Tooth because it sort of looks like one."

Price look up at the clearing sky.

"They have a way with words," he said.

Price told Ritter he'd pick him up at 9:30 a.m. Ritter set out for the old church, having nothing better to do till he could view his brother's body. Or somebody's body. He looked at the old building a moment, then headed back down the Ku'damm. Warmed a bit by the walking, he strolled past the famous street's expensive boutiques, jam-packed restaurants and tacky sex clubs. As he crossed the street, his hands in the pockets of his trench coat, the traffic lanes were slick with a film of black water from the rain. The lights overhead — gaudy reds, greens and yellow of billboards and restaurant signs — splashed ribbons of shimmering color on the road.

He walked on, deep in thought, enjoying none of the pleasures of the city that had besotted Price. He fled the hubbub of the thoroughfare and turned down a side street, eager for a moment of peace to sort out things that seemed nonsensical. He found himself on Liebnizstrasse, which took him to a line of the S-Bahn, the city's above-ground rail system.

He was engrossed in sorting out all that Havermann, Davies and Price had told him when he became aware of two extra sets of footfalls in the shadows behind him. In his own time zone, in his own town, he might have anticipated the iron grips he suddenly felt on each of his elbows and wrists. Without the fatigue of his flight and a beer more than he needed, he might even have been able to focus more on what the two men were shouting to him in Berlin-accented German. But on that cold, wet night in West Berlin, with his mind already confused, all that he could remember was that they kept shouting "Wolf!"

Two more sets of feet grew louder behind him, and there was shouting from a distance. Ritter wasn't immediately sure if it was help or more trouble on the way. Before he could puzzle that out, one of his abductors slammed the butt of a gun into the back of Ritter's head. By the time the two plainclothes West German policemen got to the scene, Ritter's body was crumpled on the sidewalk and his attackers were 50 yards away.

Ritter, who'd taken his share of blows to the head in the ring, was only out for a few moments. He came to in a swiftly moving car. In his mental haze, he picked out just a few words — *rechts* and *links* — as a man in a passenger seat told the driver which way to turn.

"Where are we going?" he finally asked in German as his aching head cleared and he massaged the back of it.

"To the hospital," the man in the passenger seat said in English. "You've had a nasty blow."

"You guys police?"

"Ja," the driver said. "Lucky we came along. Those muggers might have killed you....Did they get your wallet?"

"I don't think they were after my wallet....They kept talking about my brother — or at least someone named Wolf. I wasn't completely focused."

Neither officer said anything for a while. Then the driver added: "Maybe you just misunderstood. We have a lot of muggers around here,"

At the emergency room, a young intern gave Ritter some pills to relieve the aching. The doctor wanted to take some X-rays to see if there had been a fracture or concussion, but Ritter waved him off.

"I've taken worse."

While Ritter was still sitting on the examination table, Price burst into the room.

"I heard about the muggers," he said. "I came right over."

Ritter took that in and said, "You really do run things in this town if you heard about it this fast."

"Any attack on an American, and we get a call," Price said, a little defensively. "I'm the duty officer tonight so I was the one called."

"Uh huh."

"Did they take your wallet or say anything?"

"As I told the plainclothes guys, I don't think they were after my wallet. They could have had that pretty easily."

"So what did they want?"

"They wanted to talk about Wolf. In fact, I think they called me Wolf, if I got it right."

"Wolf?"

"Yeah. Do I look anything like my brother?"

"I don't really know. I haven't seen his body myself yet....They say anything else?"

"Don't know. It happened kinda fast, and I'm still in jet-lag mode a bit. But they were definitely Berliners. I recognized the accent."

Price bit his lower lip as if not sure what to say next. Finally he asked the question most people might have posed first in such a situation.

"You going to be all right?"

Ritter smiled at the belated concern.

"The doc said take two aspirin and call him in the morning."

*****

While Ritter was still in the hospital, Willy, back in West Berlin, made several calls, including one to a chalet in the Black Forest.

"Word is there were about 300,000 out in the streets in Leipzig," he reported. "Some nice placards made the television videos."

"Like what?"

"*Wir sind das Volk!*" Willy said. "Has a nice ring to it, no? We are the people."

The man on the other end thought about that for a moment and said. "See if you can get some of our people at the Nicholas Church to change it a bit."

"To what?"

"'*Wir sind ein Volk!*'" We are *one* people.

*****

Wednesday, November 1, 2:00 a.m., East Berlin

In a large drab office on Normannenstrasse, an official of the *Ministerium für Staatssicherheit,* the formal name of the state security police that most just called the Stasi, interrogated two street thugs in his employ after their hasty return from a side street off West Berlin's Ku'damm.

"What is that smell?" the official asked.

The two thugs looked at each other, but neither responded at first. Finally, the smaller and junior member of the duo, a man with a pockmarked face, said, "Perhaps it's the gel, colonel."

"The gel?"

The larger of the two heavies, whose name was Rudiger Hahn, cleared his throat and said, "I use a special hair gel....for operations. A good luck thing."

The colonel, whose first name was Heinz, squinted at Hahn's coiled, curly hair and asked: "What kind of gel?"

"Gelignite."

The colonel's eyes widened.

"Keeps me on my toes," Hahn continued. "If I screw up, I might blow up."

The colonel took in the bizarre explanation, then got back to the dressing down.

"Well, obviously it's not working because you *did* screw up, and unfortunately you didn't blow up."

"The police turned up unexpectedly," said Hahn.

"I thought you were to grab him quietly," said the colonel, who was seated behind a scuffed wooden desk in a swivel chair upholstered in plastic that was officially called "East German leather."

"That was the plan," said Hahn, who fixed his eyes — one blue, one cloudy — on the red, black and gold shield of the agency that hung on the wall behind the colonel's desk. "We were on a deserted street, but then the West Berlin police came running out of nowhere."

"Do you think they followed you — or him?"

"I don't know, but if they were tracking him, that would explain things."

"So first he was supposedly dead. Now you've seen him with an American diplomat, who let him go after dinner, and then he was driven away in a West German police car after you smashed his head with a gun butt?"

Hahn, who'd left his cloudy eye untreated over the years because he'd found it scared prisoners, let out a long breath and dropped his view from the wall to the colonel.

"Correct."

The colonel smiled thinly as he toyed with a sheathed knife he used as a letter opener and occasionally for more deadly purposes in the interrogation rooms below his office. "Not very comforting that we seem to be the only ones who can't have a little chat with him, is it?"

"No."

The colonel stopped popping the knife in and out of its sheath and tossed it on top of his desk. The motto of his agency was visible on the handle: *Schild und Schwert der Partei.* The Shield and Sword of the Party.

"And what about that autopsy tomorrow?"

"Whoever that body is, we're going to find out. We were told it's Wolf. But that doesn't seem possible now."

The colonel dismissed the two, and after they'd left, the officer's superior, a party official named Erich, came into the room from his observation post, an enlarged closet full of monitoring equipment.

"So what do you make of that?" the colonel asked his boss.

"Thanks to those two idiots, we still have not solved our most pressing problem."

"Which is?"

"Making sure that Wolf didn't betray us in a way that will stop us from dealing with all this unrest. If he left us some trap, we may all be out of jobs — and perhaps a lot worse."

"Well, there may be some innocent explanation to all the paranoia and rumors about him. And if that's what we find, whether he's dead or not, then we had a good run with him. A direct pipeline to what the foreign ministry was thinking and what Moscow was telling them. And maybe he goes back to work for us."

"Assuming he wasn't feeding us garbage for years."

"A lot of it came true."

"That's the way we would have played him as a double. Sacrifice some data amid all the disinformation. Our problem now is: we're not sure if he was a double, and many of our plans for survival are based on assumptions from his intelligence about what the West Germans and

Moscow are likely to do. If that's all a lie, we'll be lucky if we wind up in some federation with the West as junior partners."

"Has the Politburo given up on the idea that East Germany can survive?"

"Tossing out Honecker may have given us a slim chance for that. But we still need to appease people with some travel reforms and other concessions. Maybe even elections. 'Socialism with a heart,' we're calling it."

"And if that doesn't work?"

"A two-state federation is the backup."

"And reunification?"

"Don't even think that or we may wind up with nooses around our throats. A unified government will get its hands on our files. And if they do, you and I and the whole leadership will go to prison if we're not killed by angry mobs after they find out what we've been up to for the last forty years."

*****

Wednesday, November 1, 9:30 A.M., West Berlin
Price was sitting in the lobby reading the International Herald Tribune when Ritter came out of the hotel restaurant after breakfast. Ritter had kept the fare light, passing up the buffet for yogurt, black Douwe Egberts coffee and a glass of fresh orange juice. If he kept up the discipline, Ritter thought, he might even lose a few pounds before he got back to the real world of serial killers and divorce.

"Sleep OK?" Price asked.

"Fair," Ritter said. "Woke up about three and didn't really go back to sleep. Another day and I'll be adjusted — just in time to go home and feel screwed up again."

"You going home tomorrow?"

"Probably. Depends on today."

"Don't follow you."

"Will any of the cops investigating my brother's murder be at the autopsy?"

"Really don't know. Why?"

"I'm a little curious about who killed him....You know how it is when it's family."

As Ritter and Price headed for the autopsy, the weather was normal for Central Europe in the fall. Rainy. Cold. Generally miserable. From the light in the sky, it might have been five in the afternoon, but it was 9:45 a.m. Ritter decided he would have fared better in Chicago for that time of year.

In Berlin, fall had only glided down the Spree a few weeks before, after a warm summer. Temperatures had dropped suddenly into the 50s, then the 40s. On the way to the autopsy, Ritter spotted a bank weather sign that said the temperature was 4 degrees.

He did a double take before recalling that meant 4 Celsius. He remembered that 32 Fahrenheit was 0 for Celsius, but the rest of the conversion formula eluded him — like a lot of things since arriving in Europe.

If he'd come a little earlier from Bonn, he would have seen the sun pop out for a while the afternoon before, giving Berliners a false hope of a resurgence of nice weather. But when November dawned, they were greeted with a damp, penetrating cold that had ridden into town under a misty camouflage of morning fog. As he left the hotel headed for Price's car, Ritter regretted that he didn't have a sweater to put on under his sports jacket and trench coat. Unable to settle the Celsius temperature puzzle, Ritter just concluded it was pretty cold for the first day of November and so was he.

The autopsy site was a multi-car garage in Kreuzberg, not far from where Willy and Price's assassins had stolen a corpse a few days before. Without explanation, Price turned his Audi sedan down Oranienstrasse. The bars and clubs of the seedy street had finally closed.

Snatches of damp newspaper scudded down the byways of the neighborhood, pushed by a blustery north wind.

Ritter noticed a few drugged-out derelicts slumped in doorways, oblivious to the weather. An old woman, swaddled in scarves and sweaters, was being tugged down the street by a small Schnauzer. A Turkish woman in black babushka had a small, reluctant boy in tow as she trudged toward Friedrichstrasse.

There were signs in Turkish, Arabic and English in addition to the usual German ones. On a wall outside a dance club, Ritter saw graffiti that said: "Raus mit dem Schweine-Schwanz System."

"Down with the swinish penis system," Price translated without request, adding "Feminists," as if that explained it all.

Over the years, Ritter had seen places like Kreuzberg in Chicago. Old Town in the early days. New Town, Uptown. Pick a decade, pick a street. Close your eyes and it would be the same. The outs yelling at the ins, the new at the old, the hip at the square. Price turned off Oranienstrasse, drove a few blocks and pulled the car over to the curb.

"Here we are," he said.

Price walked toward the garage and jammed his thumb onto a small black buzzer to the side of a sliding, wooden door.

"This is the coroner's office?" Ritter asked.

"We wanted a little privacy."

No one answered, so Price rang again. The buzzer inside could clearly be heard.

After a moment more, Ritter suggested Price just try the door.

"Maybe somebody's gone to the bathroom" Ritter said.

"Maybe. But let me go first."

Price just smiled and pulled the garage's large sliding door to the right. The scene inside was not unlike what it had been in the garage after Price's men had done their worst. Two men lay face down on the concrete floor. Ritter noticed no shot or knife wounds in their backs and figured they'd been dealt with face to face. He wondered if either might be alive to identify their attackers but also quickly remembered he was not in Chicago and had no authority to turn the bodies over or force anyone to answer any questions.

"Fuck!" Price said as he turned over the first body.

"Try not to move or touch anything till the police get here," Ritter said, slipping back into work mode.

"Huh?" Price said, having lost his in-charge tone of voice.

"The evidence. You don't want to screw it up before the police get here."

"Oh, yeah," Price said.

"You know this guy?" Ritter said pointing to the man Price had turned over.

"He works for us sometimes."

"How about the other one?"

Price looked at the face of the second man, which was turned sideways.

"Medical examiner, I guess….Never seen him before."

"But not my brother."

"No. Definitely not."

Ritter paused then said, "I thought you said you didn't know what my brother looked like."

Price cleared his throat, then said, "I don't. But that guy's obviously just been killed, and your brother has been dead for a couple of days."

"Right," Ritter said, drawing out the word.

Ritter looked around the garage for other clues to what had happened to the two men, likely just minutes before. He saw a table with a long grease slick on it and a dark red patch of something at one end. Price was going through the pockets of the dead man he knew. Ritter used the opportunity to take out a handkerchief to mop up a little of the red substance. He also plucked a strand of dark brown hair from the tabletop.

It was a violation of his own rules of evidence to mess with the crime scene. But something told him that there would be no police investigation of the murders just as there had been no official autopsy as far as he could tell. We run this place, Price had said. Ritter was beginning to understand that boast.

After Ritter had folded the handkerchief carefully and put it back in his jacket pocket, he shouted over to Price: "Looks like my brother's body might have been over here. There's something that looks like blood on the table….Was he wounded badly?"

Price came over to confirm what Ritter had found.

"I don't see how this could have happened," Price said, ignoring Ritter's question.

"Any reason why somebody would want to snatch my brother's body?"

Price didn't answer, staring blankly at the table and the stains on it.

"Any valuables on that guy you searched?"

Price inhaled deeply and let out a long breath.

"No. Nothing. Pockets were empty."

Ritter sniffed the warehouse air, trying to place an unfamiliar odor.

"What is that," he said, making of point of sniffing loudly. "I think I smelled that before."

Price seemed distracted but said almost automatically, "Could be gelignite."

"Gelignite?"

"Well, probably not. The IRA like the stuff but not too many other groups, and I don't think this place is of interest to anyone Irish."

Price said he had to make some calls to people who would deal with the bodies and make a thorough search of the warehouse. He hustled Ritter out of the building and sealed the outside door with a padlock he'd found inside. He said he'd be in touch with Ritter as soon as he knew anything. He recovered some of his composure and apologized for what he said must be "a traumatic experience." Ritter said he wasn't too broken up since he wasn't completely sure he had a brother. Price didn't show any surprise at the remark. Perhaps Davies had briefed Price on Ritter's skepticism, Ritter thought.

Ritter went back to his hotel. He wanted to call his partner, but it was only 10:45 a.m. in Berlin. It would be before sunup in Chicago. He decided he'd better wait to brief her and get a status report on the serial killer. He tried to catch a few winks but couldn't sleep. A cable service gave him some CNN headline news and an awful satellite channel with American TV shows from the 50s and 60s. Ritter switched to a Berlin station that had news on. The lead story was about how 50,000 East Germans had fled to the West since Hungary had torn down the Iron Curtain and let vacationers escape west via Austria. More were on the way from East Germany, the West Berlin anchor said.

Other stories were local. Ritter listened to increasingly familiar words. As they washed over him, the rough edges of the language he'd used regularly as a child with his grandmother began to smooth out. A lot of what he'd forgotten began coming back.

About two, Ritter went down to the dining room for lunch. Before he went in, he bought a thick German paperback dictionary in the hotel gift shop. He wanted to look up a few words he'd heard on the television but hadn't understood. They turned out to be slangy, modern words that his grandmother never used and that he hadn't run across in the German novels he'd read in college. Mauerkrankheit. Gastarbeiter. Freischwebende Intellektuelle. Wall disease. Guest worker. Free-floating intellectual.

Price hadn't called by the time Ritter had finished his lunch of *Kalbsbraten* and French fries, so at four o'clock Ritter dialed Doreen.

"*Guten Morgen*," Ritter said.

"Who's this?"

"Matt."

"Really?"

"At least what's left of me," Ritter said, rubbing the back of his head.

"You OK?"

"Yeah, but I had a close encounter with some muggers — or at least two guys who wanted me to think they were muggers."

"Muggers? Am I missing something?"

"Not as much as I am. Still a bit in the dark."

"You gonna be home by tomorrow? Malone is having kittens about the delay in the coroner's report."

"Don't think so. Sorta got a situation here….Somebody snatched my brother's body."

"You got to be kidding."

"Wish I were. I need a little more time to straighten things out."

"Malone's gonna blow a gasket."

"Remind him I'm on vacation. My first one in a couple of years. And add that somebody clobbered me in the head with the back of a pistol….I might have a concussion."

"Really?"

"Well the pistol bit is true. Got a bump on the back of my head that's feels like a cantaloupe….Play that up."

"OK"

"One other thing."

"What?"

"You remember that Berlin cop you helped a couple of months back? He was investigating some terrorist murder?"

"Sure. The Red Army Faction case."

"You remember his name?"

"Becker. Günter Becker."

Ritter found several Beckers in the West Berlin phone book. The first was a bartender. Then he got lucky. The second was a policeman, the right policeman, who'd just arrived home. Ritter said he was in Berlin on family business and had promised Doreen he'd stop by to say hello. Becker said he had some time first thing in the morning and gave Ritter his office address and direct phone number.

Ritter had wanted to explain to Becker what he was really after, but he remembered Price's remark about being able to tap phones and open mail. Ritter decided it would be safer to explain things in the privacy of Becker's office and hope he wasn't one of those working for Price.

*****

Thursday, November 2, 9:30 A.M., West Berlin

Ritter was right on time for the appointment. He wasn't German in a lot of ways, but he was a stickler for punctuality. It was one of the things that drove him crazy about his wife. He'd be in the car, looking at his watch as the time approached for a party or the start of a movie, and she'd still be upstairs finishing her makeup. Ritter sometimes wondered how they'd ever wound up together.

As he headed toward Becker's office, he found himself hoping that the old adage was true that a cop was a cop no matter where you go. He needed a favor, the sort only a cop could give. Becker turned out to be an affable man in his fifties who looked like he enjoyed a good rump steak now and again. After the usual pleasantries, Ritter explained why he was really in town. Becker listened attentively, as Ritter ticked off the bizarre events since Clyde D. Havermann's telephone call. Ritter included his "mugging" and mentioned that his attackers had called him "Wolf." He told Becker about the dead bodies and his brother's missing corpse.

"I know all this must sound a little weird," Ritter said. "But all I'm really trying to do is to find out if I have — or had — a brother, and if I did, I'd like to find out who killed him."

Becker, whose English was excellent, said that sounded perfectly reasonable under the circumstances. He promised to try to find out what he could.

"Appreciate the help. I think people at the embassy are lying to me. I just don't know why."

Satisfied that he'd found a sympathetic ear, Ritter reached into his sport jacket and pulled out his handkerchief.

"You may want this," he said.

Ritter unfolded the hanky with the brown hair strand inside and handed the evidence to Becker.

"There was some red stuff on the table where my brother's body was supposedly laid out waiting for the autopsy. I think it was blood. I mopped up some of it. And there's a hair sample folded inside."

"An autopsy in a garage is very irregular," Becker said.

"That's what I thought."

Ritter got into a cab after the meeting and went back to Kreuzberg. He got his bearings after he saw the "swinish penis system" graffiti. He made a few false tries down side streets before spotting the autopsy site. In German, he told the driver, "*Bitte warten Sie ein paar Minuten hier.*"

The driver agreed to wait.

The garage was still padlocked, but Ritter noticed a dirty window to the right and above the sliding front door. He looked around and saw a large wooden box standing in front of an adjoining building. He dragged it over and stood on it to look inside. The window panes were caked with damp road dust. Ritter wiped a circle of the dirt off with the heel of his right hand and peered inside. The place was empty, picked clean. No bodies. Not even the table with the spot of blood on it. Figures, Ritter told himself, glad he'd tampered with the evidence. Ritter moved the box back to where it had been and took the taxi back to his hotel. He found a message from Becker. Ritter called back from a public phone, playing it safe.

"I found no report of a death of a Wolf Springer or even a Wolf Ritter," Becker said. "I even checked with people outside Berlin….And we have nothing on those two at the garage."

"Doesn't that seem a little strange?"

"Yes, unless…."

"Unless I'm imagining it all?"

"Well, I didn't mean to…."

"No, I understand. I might feel the same way....How about the blood. I didn't imagine that, did I?"

Becker laughed.

"No. It was O-positive....I don't know if that helps....Pretty common."

"It may," Ritter said, knowing that was his blood type, a type he might share with a brother. "You still have that hair sample and handkerchief?"

"Yes."

"Would you mind sending them back to my partner in Chicago? I may want to have someone take a further look at them."

"Well, uh...."

"I mean since you have no report of a crime, it shouldn't be a problem. They're not really evidence, right?"

Becker cleared his throat.

"I guess not."

"By the way, that garage where the autopsy was to be held is empty now. No bodies, so you probably won't be getting a report later. But if you do, you already have the lab test on the blood sample, and, if you're worried, you can cut the hair strand in half and keep part. That's all you'll need for the lab."

Ritter gave Becker the address of the garage, just in case he might get curious. He thanked him and offered to return the favor some day. He thought about promising not to bother Becker again but decided not to. He had a hunch he might be calling back.

Ritter packed his bag and checked out of his hotel. He wasn't sure when the next flight back to Bonn was, but he figured there'd be one soon since it was a workday. By four o'clock, Ritter had landed and was in a taxi on the autobahn, speeding toward Bonn. When he got to the embassy, Davies's secretary said he'd already left. He had an early tennis match with a friend at a nearby indoor court, she said. Ritter managed to pry the address out of her, arguing it was urgent and that Davies shouldn't mind since he'd already given him his unlisted home phone number.

Ritter got another cab and was at the tennis club by five-thirty. Davies was just coming off a court with a lithe blonde dressed in tennis whites and a blue headband. Davies gave Ritter a confused look and quickly mumbled something to his partner, who strode off toward the women's locker room, looking irritated. Davies composed himself and greeted Ritter with the same glad-handing welcome as when they'd first met. Ritter was considerably cooler this time. His hulking frame leaned toward the smaller Davies. Ritter grabbed a handful of Davies cotton tennis shirt and pulled the diplomat's worried face toward his.

"You got some explaining to do, pal," Ritter said.

5

Thursday, November 2, 4:30 p.m., Bad Godesberg

"What's this all about," Davis said, his voice sounding constricted.

"I've had a very bad day." Ritter's left eyebrow arched as he leaned even closer to Davies. "A bad weekend really. Somebody stole my brother's body — or somebody's body. Two people got killed in the process. I got a lump on the back of my head the size of Cleveland, and people are lying to me." Ritter's eyes narrowed. "People like you."

"I don't know what you're talking about," Davies said, making a brushing move with his left hand that got Ritter to let go of his shirt.

"Don't you, dickhead?" Ritter said, staying in Davies face. "You said my brother was killed in West Berlin, but the police there have no record of that. They also never heard of those two stiffs in the garage where you were going to have a rather unusual private autopsy, even though your buddy Price said he'd call the police."

Ritter delivered the last point while poking his thick right index finger into Davies's chest, mimicking what Captain Malone had done to him on more than one occasion when he'd been displeased. Davies didn't protest, seeming distracted by the sudden attention another American tennis player had taken in the loud conversation.

"We can't talk about this here," Davies said. "Let me change, and we'll talk in my car."

Ritter nodded and backed away from Davies. The diplomat looked relieved and headed for the locker room, with Ritter right on his heels. Ritter sat on the bench in front of Davies's locker. He smiled when Davies headed to the shower with his tennis outfit still on. Davies came back a few minutes later, clothed in a towel and looking angrily at Ritter as he worked the combination on his locker. He took out his street clothes but stopped before dropping his towel to change.

"Do you mind?" he asked Ritter.

"Not at all."

Davis changed without further protest, giving Ritter the rear view of his body as he did. They walked silently to Davies's car. Once inside, Davies, more composed with his street clothes on, finally said, "It wasn't supposed to happen this way."

"What was supposed to happen? Was I supposed to be dumber?"

"Of course not….You weren't supposed to get involved this way. Certainly not hurt. We'd hoped it would all go very quietly, that you'd just claim your brother's body and that would be that."

Ritter took that in.

"So what was supposed to be happening in the background while I was bumbling about?"

"I can't tell you everything. I shouldn't even be telling you this much, but I guess I can say your brother was involved in some very sensitive matters concerning the United States and the Soviet Union. He was a high official in the German foreign ministry."

Ritter made a fist and hit Davies's left shoulder with short, power jab that staggered the diplomat.

"Anything else you forgot to tell me?"

"I was under strict orders to keep my comments to a minimum….This is *classified*."

Ritter grabbed Davies's new shirt and pulled the smaller man toward him again.

"You better tell me *something*. Remember: I don't have to follow the usual police interrogation rules over here. You won't be getting a Miranda warning before I pop you."

Davies hesitated, then said: "I, I can only say that your brother's death is not being investigated through the normal channels because of the sensitivity of the matter."

"You saying *somebody* is investigating?"

"Of course. It's a murder."

Ritter nodded his head and let go of Davies's shirt as he considered that. Davies went on without more prodding from Ritter.

"In West Germany, there are many police agencies that can handle the matter. I assure you we'll get to the bottom of it, but we have to do it in a discreet way."

"So you mean you don't want the local cops going through his papers?"

"Exactly."

Davies cleared his throat.

"Maybe we can work together," he said.

"I work better alone."

Davies paused.

"At least let me give you some names of people you might want to talk to."

Ritter wasn't sure what to make of the sudden offer of help but took the short list of names Davies scribbled out for him.

After Ritter left, Davies called the embassy from his club. An overweight man in a windowless room filled with electronic equipment answered. Davies relayed what had happened.

"What did you tell him?"

"A bunch of lies. An Oscar-winning performance, if I do say so myself. I think he bought it."

*****

On the ring road that surrounds Moscow, other lies were being told in the back of a black Russian Zil. Its fender flags snapped in the wind as it zoomed through a reserved lane toward its destination, a comfortable dacha an hour away, if traffic allowed. There, away from the prying eyes and ears that plagued offices in the Kremlin, the limo's passengers would be able to converse about weighty matters of state in a more relaxed atmosphere, hydrated by some excellent vodka then chilling in the dacha's Western-manufactured deep freezer. Getting a start on the weekend, the two limo passengers had almost finished a bottle of the clear liquid from the vehicle's onboard stock.

The 7.7-liter limousine had been swept for bugs before the two government officials had left for the day, so the banter, with a little help from the alcohol, had been candid, salted with expletives and criticisms and jokes about colleagues. Shortly after leaving the ring road, the talk turned more serious.

"You think that idiot Krenz and the rest of the leadership finally get it now that Honecker is out, Faddey?" asked the more senior of the two, an economic adviser to the party general secretary.

"They're putting off the inevitable, Slava," said his colleague, whose Russian surname masked the Volga German lineage of his mother's side of the family.

"If they don't change East Germany themselves — and soon — the people will change it for them. We don't want that." The senior officer downed another shot of vodka. "We've arranged for something more rational, more controlled."

The junior official, whose German side of the family the Grefs dated to Catherine the Great, considered his response.

"I've heard rumors of a treaty."

The senior adviser laughed.

"Not exactly a treaty. More of a secret understanding, and you should keep those rumors to yourself if you know what's good for you."

"You think it will work?"

"It will if the East Germans do what they're told to keep people happy. Otherwise their borders are going to disintegrate."

"Krenz told Gorbachev that he gets it, but I'm not so sure. I think he just wants to stay in power."

"The one thing he should get is that our troops are going to stay in their barracks if there are any protests."

Faddey tried to commit his superior's conversation to memory through the vodka fog. He didn't want to make any mistakes when he reported it to one of his real bosses, a man named Frank, who managed a club located not far from the Schloss Charlottenburg in West Berlin.

*****

Thursday, November 2, 7:00 p.m., Bad Godesberg

Heidi Springer lived on a quiet street of stucco houses whose fronts had dulled into the dirty pastels common in Bad Godesberg. Thick-trunked trees lined the sidewalks. Their leaves had faded from early autumn's burnt orange, cadmium and vermilion to November's rusty brown. Most of the trees' finery had fallen and lay scattered on the ground. A few dead leaves stuck stubbornly to branches made suddenly black by a late dusk.

Ritter's trench coat had a lining, but the cold night air, drawing dampness from the nearby Rhine, made quick work of his American clothing. What he really needed, he thought, as he jammed his hands into the coat's pockets, was a wool overcoat. Doubleweight. And some gloves.

It was not the first time he'd considered the heavier clothing option. Chicago winters were usually bitter. But his previous partner, Bernie, had once chided him when he talked about buying an overcoat, saying it would ruin his detective image.

"People expect a homicide cop to look like Columbo," Bernie had said. "Trench coat. And a little rumpled." In Bernie's view, shared by others on the squad, wool topcoats were for captains. Even then, Bernie said, if Ritter ever became a captain, he'd be considered by those below him as "highfallutin" for wearing one.

Despite the cold he felt, Ritter chuckled fondly at the memory of Bernie, the man Doreen had replaced, as he mounted the steps to his sister-in-law's house. Sister-in-law. That sounded so strange, but as his brother's wife, that's what she was. Or at least that was Davies's story.

A prim, tidy woman of about forty-five, dressed in a cardigan, wool skirt and expensive daytime pumps answered the door. Her brown hair was pulled back in a chignon. She wore minimal makeup on a face that turned harsh at the sight of Ritter.

"Why, Wolf, what brings you here? Bored already?"

Ritter was momentarily at a loss, not only because she'd blurted out her chilly welcome in rapid German but also because he'd again been mistaken for his brother.

"I'm not Wolf," he said in German.

Heidi said nothing immediately, crossing her arms over her breasts as she surveyed the man in doorway.

"I don't know what sort of nonsense you're up to, but I won't have it. Go back to your little friend and stop bothering me....Unless she's thrown you out. Is that it? You've come crawling back?"

"Wolf's dead," Ritter said, switching to English, hoping that would get her attention. "I'm his brother Matt. From Chicago."

Heidi squinted at Ritter in the gauzy light of her front doorstep. She studied his hair and clothes. After her inspection, she invited Ritter in.

"If this is some sort of sick joke...." she said after Ritter stood in her foyer.

"I assure you it's not."

Ritter pulled out his detective shield and showed it to her. She examined the badge carefully and said quietly "A policeman?"

"Yeah."

With the credential still in her hands, she added, "But it says here that your name is Ritter."

"It's a long story….And I don't know all of it myself."

Heidi motioned for Ritter to go into a sitting room that was at the front of her house. They sat down on firm, facing couches that had stiff, oatmeal-colored slipcovers on them. Ritter pulled out the photocopies of his birth certificate and name change, his passport and even his Visa card to back up his tale. Heidi looked them over and handed them back.

"Is he really dead, then?" she asked in English, the bitterness gone from her voice.

"That's what I'm told," Ritter said, sticking to English, which he figured was a comfortable idiom for the wife of a German diplomat. "I still haven't seen the body. I don't even know what he looks like. Until recently I didn't even know I had a brother."

The remark produced a surprised look on Heidi's face. She got up from her couch and went to a side table. From one of the brass-handled drawers she brought back a framed photograph and handed it to Ritter.

"He looks like you," she said.

Ritter had expected some resemblance after Heidi's mistaken response at the door and the angry remarks of his attackers in West Berlin. But he had not anticipated how close the resemblance would be. The black hair, graying at the temples, was the same as were the hazel eyes, the high cheekbones, the strong nose and the bushy eyebrows. All the same. Precisely the same.

Wolf's hair was cut a bit shorter, and he looked ten pounds lighter. But other than that, Wolf was his spitting image.

"How old was Wolf?" Ritter asked.

"Fifty."

"Uh huh," Ritter said as his brain raced to the logical conclusion. "Birthday is January 1?"

"Yes." Her brow furrowed as she took in what Ritter was asking. "Twins?"

"Guess so."

"And you didn't know?"

"Not till a couple of days ago."

She took in a long breath and let it out.

"How bizarre. He never said a word. But then that was very typical of Wolf. Secretive. And a brooder."

Must run in the family, Ritter thought.

"That why you two split up?" Ritter asked.

"Split up? Oh, you mean separated."

"Yeah," Ritter said somewhat absent-mindedly as he thought about why Davies hadn't mentioned Wolf's marital status before giving him his wife's name. Even more puzzling: why hadn't Davies informed Heidi of Wolf's death?

"It was a lot of things," Heidi said, bringing Ritter back into the moment. "We'd been married twenty years. He was always absorbed in his work. Traveled a lot, so I was alone quite often."

"Sounds familiar."

"I eventually started a life of my own. I have an art gallery."

Ritter looked at the paintings and lithographs on the walls of the room.

"Was Wolf interested in art?

Heidi laughed lightly.

"Not really. He preferred literature and classical music. Any serious music really."

"Weird. I'm a little into opera myself."

"Maybe it's genetic."

"Don't think so. Just my grandmother's making me go all the time. It didn't take at first, but eventually I got it. And the Lyric in Chicago is pretty good."

Ritter spotted a baby grand in a corner of the room.

"Did Wolf play?"

"No. That's mine. He was just a listener….How about you?"

"When I can find a piano. Took some lessons as a kid. Grandma Helga saw to that."

Neither said anything for a while as thoughts swirled in their heads.

"What was he like?" Ritter finally asked.

Heidi laughed.

"You may be asking the wrong person. He became a stranger to me, so much so that I finally suggested the separation. I thought it might shock him into something. But he just said yes and moved out."

Ritter found himself thinking of his own situation with Anita.

"It was foolish of me," Heidi said. "Wolf didn't like to be backed into a corner."

As the conversation went on, Ritter learned that Heidi and Wolf had met at university. They moved to Bonn after Wolf accepted a junior-level job in the foreign ministry.

"At school, he was a ruthless competitor," she said. "He hates to lose….Hated to lose, I guess I should say. And he thought he was a lot more competent than he actually was. He had to be in control, so sometimes he deluded himself into thinking he was."

"Is that an objective assessment?" Ritter asked, a smile on his face.

Heidi smiled back.

"Probably not, but he would always try to do everything himself. He thought he was a genius when it came to cars, but he ruined a couple of ours over the years with his 'repairs.'"

"I'm no mechanic myself."

"I remember once he tried to fix a toilet rather than calling a plumber. We didn't get the stink out of the house for months."

"Sounds like my brother could be a bit of a jerk."

"Maybe I'm being too harsh."

Heidi turned interrogator, and Ritter found himself having to answer questions about his own marriage. Ritter changed the subject and asked when she'd last seen Wolf.

"He moved out about a year ago and didn't come back except once when he'd discovered he'd left a favorite tennis racket."

"Did he leave any papers? Bank statements, appointment books, that sort of thing?"

Heidi shook her head

"He took everything with him to his new place. It's not far from here. I can give you the address….but I don't have a key."

Heidi looked around the room as if mentally checking for any other remnant of her husband.

"I'm afraid I removed most traces of him here….About three months ago, I had the place redone….I wanted to get on with my life."

Ritter wondered why Davies had bothered to give him Heidi's name if she was so out of touch. Unless that was exactly why he'd given it up.

Heidi suddenly got up from the couch.

"There might be one thing."

She asked Ritter to follow her. She led him to a windowless storage room on the upper floor of the house. Against one wall was a large wooden trunk that looked as if it might have been used on some ancient sea voyage. The clasp was open, and Heidi undid two latches on either side of the trunk's front. On top was a newish album, which she handed to Ritter.

"It starts with our wedding and eventually peters out. Wolf wasn't much for photos….I kept it because it was more mine than his."

Ritter flipped through the pages, which began with Wolf in a morning suit and Heidi, a little thinner, in an elegant white dress with camellias in her hair. Not a propitious choice of flower, Ritter thought as a snippet La Traviata passed through his head.

"It gets a little disorganized as it goes on. I wasn't as diligent about the photos as we got older."

"You made a beautiful couple," was all Ritter could think to say.

Heidi sighed.

"Well, we both got older. Wolf got grayer and a little heavier….though not much. He stayed pretty fit with tennis and mountain climbing and the like. He did laps in our local pool. Even in the wintertime. He was a little vain about his looks."

Heidi guided Ritter through the book as they stood under the harsh overhead light in the storeroom. There were the happy vacations, the beer-garden poses with improbably large steins at some long-ago Oktoberfest, images of a skiing trip to Switzerland. Ritter saw a life very different from his own, but in some ways, it was the same except for the geography. There were no pictures of children. The circle of friends seemed small and always changing. From the photos, it appeared it had been a life of just two people for two decades. Change the city, and the core of it could have been Ritter's life. A romantic beginning, a demanding job followed by long bouts of silence.

The last picture was a birthday party dated four years earlier.

"When my business got going, I found I didn't have much time to update this."

Heidi looked away and her eyes fell on another, older book. She reached over, grabbed it and opened its pages.

"This one belonged to Wolf's grandmother….Your grandmother. I hadn't realized he'd left it behind. She was your father's mother, the one who brought him up."

"My mother's mother did the same for me," Ritter said, feeling the hair on the back of his neck standing up.

"I haven't looked at this one in years. It's mostly pre-war stuff, so there's not much of Wolf in it. And nothing of you that I remember."

She went to the last page of the album.

"This was Wolf with your grandmother."

The date on the photo said "Berlin, 1940." Wolf in a baby buggy and his grandmother were in front of a house.

"That was her house. After the war, they moved to Frankfurt. She thought it would be the new capital."

"Is that where Wolf grew up?"

"Yes. Not a very pretty place, but that's where the money went, and Bonn was just up the road."

Heidi flipped through the musty pages until she found a photo of a tall, pretty woman in a flowery summer dress. The woman, appearing pregnant, was smiling and hugging the waist of a handsome man in a military uniform.

"Your parents."

Ritter had only a slight recollection of his mother. She had died just after the war had ended. There had only been one grainy photo of her in his grandmother's apartment. He lingered on the precious new image, which was dated"October 1938."

It was a sunny day in the picture. In the background were mountains with alpine trees and plants. His parents looked happy. What the hell had happened that next year? Why had his mother gone to the States with him and left his father and brother behind?

"Did Wolf ever talk about why our parents had separated?"

"No. They'd both been dead a long time by the time I met him. He just said they'd split up. It happened to a lot of people one way or another. I never thought much about it."

Ritter asked if he could borrow the albums for a while. Heidi agreed. At her doorway, he asked if anyone else among Wolf's friends might know what he was up to in his final days.

"Well, there is one person."

"Who's that?"

"His mistress."

6

Thursday, November 2, 10:00 p.m., Bonn

By the time Ritter got to Ulrike Fischer's ground-floor apartment, it was late for an unannounced visit by a stranger. But such visits had often proved fruitful for a homicide detective looking for an unguarded response. The presence of someone who looked exactly like Fischer's lover might make the visit even more productive, Ritter had decided. He pushed the doorbell, then had the sudden fear that the police, sophisticated about such matters, might have notified Wolf's mistress that he was dead, while leaving his ex-wife in the dark. He thought about walking away to avoid any shock, but before he could, he heard the door deadbolt scrape back and the brass handle turn.

His opening lines raced through his head. "I understand you were friends with my brother." was one. Is that all she was? He certainly wasn't going to call her Wolf's "mistress," the term Heidi had used. To some, that implied she was some sort of kept woman. He would stay away from "lover" for obvious reasons. Girlfriend? Wolf was fifty. If Ulrike was in her thirties or forties, would she want to be called a girl in post feminist times? After twenty-five years of marriage, Ritter was so out of date on the terminology of dating that he decided to stick with the safest term of all — friend — when the time came. But all his careful mental planning proved irrelevant. The door opened and a woman with luminous green eyes and a svelte figure yelled *"Liebling!"* just before she threw her arms around Ritter's neck and kissed him, using more tongue than he was used to. Anita was not a tongue person, and she'd never called him "Darling!"

Ulrike pushed her pelvis against Ritter's. He knew he should break off the embrace and explain the mix-up, but he found himself taking his time, perhaps a reaction to breasts pressing into his chest and the image of a woman dressed in a leather skirt and form-fitting ribbed sweater. He hadn't put his arms around her to return the emotion, and he finally brought his hands up to her shoulder and gently pushed her back.

"I'm not Wolf," he said in slow but perfect German. "I'm his brother Matt."

Ulrike blinked and protectively stepped back into her apartment.

"Is this some kind of joke?" she asked in a replay of Heidi's reaction.

"Not at all."

Ulrike looked beyond Ritter, as if searching for something.

"Where is he anyway? I've been worried sick. No one's heard from him in days."

Ritter had been searching for the words to break the news. In the end, he just tackled the matter straight on.

"That's what I came to talk to you about. It appears he's dead. At least that's what I've been told."

Ulrike pivoted to avoid showing her face and took a step back, knocking a small framed picture off the side wall. It plummeted to the tiled entryway, shattering the glass that protected the image of a ski chalet. Ritter lunged forward to help Ulrike clean up the mess, but she reacted badly.

"Stay where you are!" she yelled, tears brimming in her eyes. "I don't know who you are, but if you don't leave immediately, I'll call the police."

"I am the police," Ritter said.

He reached inside his jacket and pulled out his credentials.

Ulrike's anger turned to confusion as she looked at Ritter's detective shield.

"You're an American."

She wiped the beginnings of tears in one eye with the back of her left hand and continued to examine Ritter's badge.

"And this says your name is Ritter....I thought you said you were Wolf's brother."

It was the conversation with Heidi all over again.

"I am. My mother changed her name and mine after we left Germany in 1939. Wolf and I were split up....I didn't know till a couple of days ago."

"I, I never heard him talk about a brother."

She asked to look at Ritter's credentials once more, and he showed them.

"This is probably just some twisted prank."

"And somehow I just happen to look like Wolf's twin brother?"

Ulrike sniffed.

"Your hair is different now that I look it at. It's longer....And you're *fatter.*"

Ritter laughed. Ulrike didn't. Ritter tried a new tack.

"You're probably right about the fat part. But I do have documents to show I am who I say I am. And you can check with the U.S. embassy. They're the ones who called me in the first place about his death."

"The Americans? Why would they be the ones?"

"Next of kin, I guess. I'm still trying to figure that out."

Ulrike paused, then said, "I want to see the body."

Ritter cleared his throat.

"So do I, but there's a complication. It seems to have disappeared."

Ulrike's look turned harsher.

"I'm not an idiot, you know."

"No one said you were," Ritter said, thinking that whatever the vulnerable, mercurial and angry woman before him was, she was not stupid. He found himself envying his brother. "Perhaps I should come back later....I'll be in town for a while."

Ulrike said nothing at first, then asked: "Where are you staying?"

Ritter considered the question a positive sign. It sounded like she wanted to know how to contact him.

"I don't have a hotel. I just flew in from Berlin."

"Berlin?"

"That's where they say Wolf died. Was murdered actually."

Ulrike's shoulders slumped, and she let out a breath. She looked at the floor and was shaking her head back and forth. Then she stiffened and said quietly, "I don't want to hear any more of this….Please just go."

Ritter decided it wasn't the time to argue.

"All right."

He started to leave, then turned back, hoping to recapture the brief positive moment. He had the name of the hotel Davies had arranged, but, grasping for a connection, he said: "If you have a recommendation on a place to stay, I'd appreciate it."

Ulrike was miles away but finally muttered: "The Bristol. On Prinz-Albertstrasse."

"I'll check back tomorrow."

Ritter pulled out the business card Davies had given him and wrote down the diplomat's name and office number. He ripped out the page from his detective's notebook and handed it to her.

"That guy will confirm what I said."

Ulrike looked at the name but said nothing. Ritter opened the door and let himself out. When the shadow in front of him disappeared as he walked away, he knew she'd closed the door.

*****

Friday, November 3, 8:45 a.m., Bonn

After he'd finished breakfast the next day in the hotel dining room, Ritter got a call at the Bristol. He hoped it was Ulrike, but it was Becker.

"*Guten Morgen*! I had a little trouble tracking you down till the overnight hotel registrations came through."

"Americans get a little nervous when the police start keeping data like that."

"It's not so extreme. We already have credit-card statements, phone-call records, bank-account access."

"Well, we're probably a little old-fashioned, but unless we've committed a crime, we pretty much think what we are doing isn't the business of the police. Particularly late at night in a hotel."

"It's just a matter of time before you change. We've got terrorists now. Security cameras, more government eavesdropping on phone calls. It's coming. In fact, from what I know, it's already here."

Becker cut off the lecture and laid out what he'd learned "unofficially" about the various bodies Ritter had asked about.

"There is rumor going around that a body was found shortly after your brother was supposedly murdered, but it came in from Munich. Berlin was just where it was sent."

"Why would someone bother to move it?"

"I don't know. What I'm told is that certain people were looking in West Berlin for a truck with Munich registration last week. That is all I can say."

"Why?"

"Because that is all I know....though I do have one guess for you."

"What?"

"That your host at the embassy is not really some low-level diplomat. Ask him what agency he really works for."

By noon, Ritter hadn't heard from Ulrike and considered going back to her place. But he had a couple of things he needed to do first. Lunch was one. He had a quick one, just some *sauerbraten* and glass of pilsner. With the hour about right, he called Chicago after that, hoping to catch Captain Malone at the beginning of the day before his daily production of bile had reached the anger zone.

"Malone," he heard his boss grunt into the phone.

Ritter winced at the sound, even though he had the protection of thousands of miles of land and sea between him and his boss.

"It's Matt Ritter, Captain."

"Well, well. The Prodigal Son. I hope you're calling from O'Hare or that stink hole you moved into on Clark."

Ritter cleared his throat.

"Not exactly. Got a couple more complications with my brother's body."

"So I heard. Still missing, is it?"

Ritter explained what he'd learned about his brother as Malone offered back responses like "Right." and "Sure." that Ritter interpreted to mean "Bullshit."

"I'm shooting to get back there on Monday for the autopsy report, but there's an outside chance, it might be a little later."

"Later? If I find out that this is just some boondoggle to get you some European vacation while I'm having to deal with the latest murders, you'll be back doing vertical patrol."

Ritter didn't really think Malone would send him back to a beat of riding housing projects elevators and having to dodge the occasional fusillade of bullets while stepping out onto a floor, but he knew he was risking something bad by staying in Germany too long. He went into fast damage control.

"Doreen's very capable. She can get things started, and I'll finish up when I get back."

"And what if it's poison and we have a serial killer case on our hands?"

Ritter thought quickly.

"Having a female detective out front on a crime against women might be good for the department's image."

"Reporters are going to ask where the hell our No. 1 homicide cop is."

"Tell them family emergency — and that I'll be back shortly."

"I see you got it all figured out."

"Hey, I'm not making this stuff up."

Ritter gave Malone Rick Davies's name as a way his boss could check out his story.

"I'm not running up departmental phone bills making international calls. Next time I talk to you it better be in my office. And it better be before we have another poison murder. Stop lollygagging over there in the sun and get your ass back here ASAP."

"The sun hasn't been out since I got here."

"Well I wouldn't know if it's been out here either because I never got out of this frickin' office."

Malone slammed down the phone, making Ritter flinch on the receiving end of the insult. He waited a while before calling Doreen, who was not so early a riser. He caught her at home. Her voice sounded a little groggy, pre-coffee.

"I hope you're calling to tell me you're back," she said. "Malone is making my life hell. I hadn't realized what you have to put up with."

"The price of fame, young lady. You just need to develop a thick skin."

"So you'll be back Monday for the report, right?"

"Maybe not."

"Oh, god."

"Don't worry. You can handle it. If it's poison, do the traces on the sources like Bernie and I did on the last one. Call him if you need advice. He's just sitting at home down in his woodshop. He'll be happy to hear from you."

"What if there's a press conference?"

"Put on your game face. Keep your answers short. If you don't think you should tell the public something, like that evidence we held back on the other two cases, don't tell the reporters. If you don't know, say the department is looking into it. If they ask how long it will take to catch him, just say as soon as possible. And one other thing: Don't tell them the kind of poison. We don't want wackos coming in and saying they did it. Not knowing what to say about the type of poison will keep the kooks out."

Ritter tried to think of any other advice to help Doreen out long-distance.

"Hey, and if it's something like belladonna or strychnine or anything rare, check the Chicago Public Library and libraries in Cook County to see who may have checked out books on poisons."

Doreen was silent for a moment.

"I thought I wanted this, but I'm not so sure now."

"Piece of cake, kid."

"I guess."

"Good girl."

"So what's the holdup over there?"

"Things got a little more complicated than I expected, but I got a guy from the CIA who's helping me sort it out. At least I think he's CIA."

"The CIA!"

"Yeah, I know it sounds wacky, but I hope it won't be too much longer....By the way, did you get a package from your pal Becker?"

"Not yet."

"Probably tomorrow. It's got blood and a hair sample in it. You'll also get one from me with some instructions for the lab."

"This official or personal?"

Ritter cleared his throat.

"Gotcha."

7

Friday, November 3, 4:00 p.m., Bad Godesberg.

After the call to Malone, Ritter had one more thing to get out of the way, based on what Becker had told him. Payback. He took a cab to the embassy, which was about 30 minutes away via Adenauerallee. By 4:30, his taxi was turning left onto a curvy street called Deichmanns, where the sprawling complex was located. Ritter played it cool. When he got to the lobby, he just told the receptionist he'd like to see Mr. Richard Davies. She was all smiles at first as she dialed the number, but then Ritter saw her scrunch her eyes a bit and tighten her nose as she listened to whoever was on the other end of the line. Ritter figured it was Davies, who probably was none too cheery after he learned who was looking for him.

Ritter wondered if Davies had asked the receptionist if the man in the lobby looked as if he wanted to kill someone. Ritter couldn't really blame Davies for that sort of reaction after the way he'd treated him the last time. Ritter clasped his hands behind his back as he waited, hoping that sort of body language would seem nonhostile.

"Mr. Davies will be right down," the receptionist said as she cradled the phone.

With bodyguards? Ritter wondered.

Ritter continued to hold his temper as he paced around the lobby, feigning an interest in the posters and pictures on the wall. The marine guard in the bulletproof glass security booth seemed to be giving Ritter more than average attention. Ritter tried to avoid eye contact. He didn't want any trouble. At least not in the lobby.

A few minutes later, Davies emerged from one of the elevators. He looked hesitant at first but showed no overt hostility. His stride became more confident as he walked toward Ritter. Eventually, he gave off a hint of a smile. Perhaps he'd decided that he and Ritter had worked things out after the confrontation at the tennis club, Ritter thought. He gave Davies no indication that things were completely otherwise.

"Good to see you again," Davies said, holding out his hand.

"Yeah. Hi," Ritter said as if suddenly distracted from his review of the lobby's artwork.

"Any luck with your brother's wife?" Davies asked.

"A little, but I think it'd be better if we discussed it in your office. Ritter shot a glance at the receptionist and the marine guard. "You know, given the situation."

Davies pondered the request a couple of beats before agreeing.

"I can only give you 15 minutes. I have a meeting with the ambassador."

"Shouldn't take that long. Learned a couple of things from Heidi and got a couple of questions. I'll be out of your hair before you know it."

Davies escorted Ritter to the elevator. After the doors closed, he said, "Oh, by the way, I had a call from a Fraulein Fischer. She said she was a friend of your brother's. She wanted to check you out."

Was it possible that Davies, with all his resources, didn't know Wolf had a mistress, Ritter wondered. Unlikely, he thought, but he played along.

"Yeah, I gave her your number. Heidi put me on to her, but she wasn't too cooperative. She seemed very suspicious. Didn't believe Wolf was dead."

"She didn't believe you were his brother either, but I put her straight."

"Appreciate it. She didn't seem to know much, but you never know."

The elevator door opened, and Davies showed Ritter the way to his office. As they entered the room, he asked: "So what did Heidi have to say?"

"She was a bit out of touch. Separated, you know."

Davies waited a moment, then said, "No, not really. I'm not the one looking into the case in depth. My job was just to get you here."

"Uh huh."

Davies headed to the chair behind his desk and had his back to Ritter, who flicked the door closed with one leg and moved up quickly behind the diplomat. He grabbed him around the neck and snapped one of Davies's arms behind his back. He shoved Davies against a wall, flattening his right cheek against the gypsum board.

"I need a little information."

"If you don't let me go, I'll call security," Davies managed to say through his twisted mouth."

"Not before I break your arm. Or maybe your writing hand. You know how long a hand takes to heal? Lots of little bones in there. You wouldn't be playing tennis for quite a while."

Davies tried to wriggle free but couldn't and finally said, "What do you want?"

"Good boy," Ritter said, not letting up the pressure on Davies's arm. "I know you need me for something. Otherwise you wouldn't have dragged me over here, but the question is: what?"

"Your brother died. You are next of kin. That was it. Honest."

Ritter ratcheted up the pressure another notch on Davies's arm, eliciting a yelp from his captive.

"I'm having trouble thinking of you and honesty at the same time. What I'm pretty sure of is that you know all about my brother and his mistress and my mom and dad, and I know you're going to tell me what I want or you're going to be very sorry."

"I told you everything I could the last time, except the classified stuff, and I can't tell you that. It'd be illegal."

"So's my breaking your arm, but I don't see what could be classified about why you didn't tell Heidi about Wolf's death since she was his wife."

"Ex-wife."

"Not really. Just separated, a little something you neglected to tell me when you were being so helpful in giving me her name."

Davies let out a breath of exasperation at his predicament.

"It was up to the Germans to tell her. My job was to tell you. You're the American in this. I have no jurisdiction over her."

"I thought you were working with the Germans on this. Isn't that what you said?"

"You have to realize that when allies work together, they don't always tell each other everything. You think I would have sent you over there if I'd known she hadn't been told?"

"Maybe. If you wanted to buy some time, but even if I grant you your bullshit explanation about Heidi, you want to tell me why you for-got to say Wolf was my *twin* brother?"

Ritter notched up the pressure on Davies one more turn.

"You're killing me," Davies said.

Ritter let out a light laugh.

"Nah. That comes later.…Unless you talk."

"I thought Havermann told you that when he called you in Chicago."

"You got an answer for everything, don't you?"

Ritter mashed the heel of his size 13 right shoe onto the top Davies right foot.

"Stop!"

"Broken foot bones are another one you want to avoid. They never really heal."

"I've told you all I know."

"Don't think so. I think Mr. Clyde D. Havermann is a very particular individual and would not have forgotten to tell me I had an identical twin. I think he just didn't know. But you knew, and you wanted to toss me out there in Berlin like chum to the sharks to see who might think I was my brother. And that's not something the vice consul's office would do. That would be another agency. That's what I think."

Ritter slammed his left fist into Davies's kidney, just as he'd done dozens of times in his boxing days to weaken opponents. Davies's body slumped a bit in quiet pain. Ritter sensed a moment of weakness and played a hunch.

"Another thing, Ricky Boy. My brother wasn't killed in Berlin. He was killed in Munich, and his body was dumped in Berlin. I'd like to know why."

"Who told you that?" Davies asked, mustering some anger through the pain.

"I thought you might have known."

"You can't prove a thing."

Ritter laughed.

"You talk like we're going to trial or something. This is just you and me. Don't go all Perry Mason on me."

Ritter was enjoying himself, but decided to switch tactics. He let Davies go and twirled him around, keeping the diplomat physically trapped between himself and the wall.

"I can see you're not going to be much help, so maybe I'll just go home. Got a real murder to solve back there, and you're just wasting my time over here. I'm sure a smart guy like you can figure out whatever he needs without me."

Davies smoothed out his clothes and regained his composure.

"You wouldn't do that."

"Why not?"

"Because you want to find out who killed your brother as much as we do."

"Maybe, you're right — if I had some leads I might stick around, but I got nothing, and I got more important things to attend to back home, including a boss who wants my head on a plate. Besides, this isn't my turf. I have no authority over here."

Davies looked at Ritter for a moment, then said, "Maybe we can work something out."

Davies slipped away from the wall and headed to his desk. He opened a drawer, and Ritter reached over and grabbed his arm, not sure what Davies was getting. It turned out to be a file.

"I'm going to tell you something, but it has to remain between us. I could get in a lot of trouble if anyone found out."

Ritter put up two fingers of his right hand.

"Scout's honor."

Davies thumped the closed file with his right fist.

"Your brother worked for us."

Ritter looked confused.

"I thought you said he was a West German diplomat."

"He was. That's the point."

"You mean he worked as a spy?"

"We call them agents in place."

"Why do we need to spy on the West Germans? I thought they were our friends."

"Don't be naïve. Everybody spies on everybody. The Israelis spy on us. The British spy on the French, and we spy on the Germans."

Ritter snorted out a laugh.

"Information is the name of the game," Davies continued. "Always has been. Governments don't like surprises. Surprises can get you killed. Up to now everyone has wanted to know mostly about missiles, but soon it will be economic and technical data. The Cold War is ending."

"What's that got to do with me?

"As I told you, Wolf was working on some sensitive matters involving the United States and the Soviet Union. He was going to tell us what he'd found out, when he was killed. Apparently in Munich."

"And you have no idea what he found out?"

"No. Other than it probably had something to do with Germany."

"Pretty vague conclusion for a guy with a world-class intelligence agency behind him."

Davies made no direct admission about his employer, saying only: "There's an awful lot of guesswork that goes on in what we do."

"So what's your guess?"

Davies paused.

"If I had to guess, the Krauts are up to something. Something with the Russians."

"Something big enough to kill Wolf over?"

"That's what worries those of us who remember the Hitler-Stalin pact. That came out of nowhere and seemed completely illogical. They were archenemies. Then suddenly allies. And something like that *isn't* so illogical with the current coalition government in Bonn." Davies paused then asked: "You follow German politics?"

"Not at all."

"Well, all you need to know is that the left holds a lot of sway here now, and Gorbachev is a big hero for all his reform talk....You know who Gorbachev is, right?"

"Yeah, that much I learned on TV. What I don't get is how is someone like me going to help someone like you? Other than being bait."

"I assure you that was never our intention."

Ritter's eyes narrowed.

"Don't make me hit you again, Rick."

"All right, you were bait. I'll admit that, but we never planned that you'd get mugged. We just couldn't risk telling you the truth. You might have said no."

"Good guess."

"We just wanted to see who'd come out of the woodwork and then follow them. Could be left, could be right, could be the East Germans, could be the Soviets. We were in the dark. Still are."

Ritter nodded his head, considering the evidence.

"So why did — whoever — ship the body to Berlin?"

"Don't know. And we don't know who killed him. Maybe he was left for dead, and the East Germans or the Soviets found the body and wanted to make a positive ID. He was pretty shot up. Based on the cargo in the truck we grabbed, it appears it was headed to East Berlin."

Ritter was sure there was a little truth amid what was probably mostly lies, but the detective in him wanted to find out which was which, so he decided to surprise Davies.

"So now what?"

Davies eyes widened.

"You mean you'll help?"

"As long as I can come back and pound the crap out of you if I find you're lying to me again."

Davies cleared his throat.

"Fair enough."

"Look, I'm not doing this because I like you all of a sudden or out of patriotism. You have your agenda. I have mine. I want to find out who killed my brother. You help me, maybe I help you."

Davies considered the offer and nodded.

"What do you need?"

"Some answers. If you had to guess, who killed Wolf?"

"The KGB," Davies said without hesitation.

Ritter's head moved back as if distancing itself from something unpleasant.

"You gotta be kidding."

"That's what it looks like. Too sophisticated an operation for anyone else. Maybe the East Germans were along for the ride, but the Soviets were likely running the show."

"Just when I thought this could not get any stranger." Ritter paused to think about his next remark, then said: "So if I wanted to help you, what would that involve, other than being bait?"

"Being bait is one of the best things you could do."

"Bait's baloney. I can't fool anyone that I'm Wolf for more than a few minutes. I'm heavier. He had shorter hair. Better clothes."

"That can all be handled."

"What'd you have in mind?"

"You had any experience with burglary?"

"Only on the arresting side."

"Well, this is more like sneaking in than breaking in."

"Sneaking into what?"

"The West German foreign ministry....to Wolf's office."

Ritter told Davies that he'd think about his lunatic idea. And he meant it. His own plan was pretty much nonexistent. He could go to Munich and ask at hotels and other places whether some guy who looks exactly like him had been grabbed by guys with bulges under their suit-coat armpits. Beyond that, he had to admit that interrogating the KGB for some answers was not high on his list of skills.

He did have Ulrike. At least he hoped he did. Maybe there was something at Wolf's apartment. She might have a key, so there'd be no burglary involved with that plan. He decided to head back to his hotel to check for messages.

As Ritter got into a cab in front of the embassy, Davies watched him through partially closed venetian blinds. His overweight boss, who was also using diplomatic cover to hide his real job, was doing the same.

"We almost broke in," Gerry said. "I thought he might kill you."

"Good you didn't. He may be a thug, but he's no murderer. That's why I put up with it."

"You think he bought it?"

"I think so. There are kernels of truth in what I said. Plus I told him I wasn't sure what was going on, so anything anyone else tells him won't seem like a lie."

"You think he'll do the foreign ministry job?"

"I think so. He wants to find out what happened to his brother. And he's a detective. He wants to solve the puzzle. And I've made doing that irresistible."

8

Saturday, November 4, 10:30 a.m., Bonn.

When Ritter got back to his hotel, he found a message from Ulrike. It just said she was on the road and to call in the morning. On the telephone, the next day, she was cool but not hostile. She said she was going to help. She didn't explain her decision other than to say: "I guess I want to find out what happened."

Half an hour later she called from the lobby of Ritter's hotel. He came down and found she'd put her long hair into a single, loosely woven braid that hung down to the middle of her back like long brown corn silk. Ritter was sure she was still upset about Wolf's death, but to him she looked radiant. She had on a belted, black raincoat, appropriate for the misty day they had to work with. She was wearing black leather cowboy boots with faded jeans tucked into the tops. A white, button-down broadcloth man's shirt poked out from the open neck of her coat. Ritter found himself distracted in a pleasant way. If Ulrike was making similar assessments of Ritter, she showed no signs. She shook hands firmly, as if they were about to commence a business deal.

"Where shall we start?" she asked crisply. "Questions first or do you want me to take you somewhere?"

Ritter didn't hesitate in asking: "You have a key to Wolf's place?"

Ulrike paused, then said: "Yes."

She never did say if she was Wolf's lover or mistress or girlfriend, so Ritter wasn't sure what he was supposed to call her. From the way

91

she'd kissed him when they'd first met, he knew what the relationship had been, and she knew he knew. He just called her Ulrike and left it at that.

She had a red Volkswagen sports coupe. Ritter found the front bucket seats cramped for his legs. Over his creaky knees, he took in the soggy Bonn landscape as Ulrike drove to Wolf's place. She drove with skill and speed, snicking the shift lever from gear to gear with professional ease. Ritter had a lot of questions for her, but he edged into things, chitchatting in a way that didn't really help solve the mystery about Wolf.

"What's that?" Ritter asked as they passed a large building with red letters on the top.

"Headquarters of the chancellor's party."

"Chancellor's like the prime minister, right?"

"Yes. Head of government."

"Conservative? Liberal?"

"Conservative. Pretty stodgy. "

"Somebody must like him if he's the chancellor."

"Not as many as you'd think. The only reason he's in charge of the government is he has the support of another party — which used to be with the opposition."

"They switched sides?"

"And they might switch back. The far right is suddenly winning elections."

"You mean like neo-Nazis?"

"Not really."

Ulrike gave Ritter a sarcastic smile to show her own view of the group's politics.

"You seem to know a lot about it," Ritter said.

"It's my job. I'm a journalist. I thought you knew. That's why I was on the road. I had an assignment."

"I was just told you were a friend of Wolf's."

"A *friend?* By whom?"

"His wife."

Ulrike said nothing for a moment, then replied, "Really?.. What did she say?"

Ritter cleared his throat.

"That you might be more up-to-date on Wolf than she was."

"That's what you're interested in? What he was doing when he was killed?"

"I'm interested in anything that'll tell me who killed him and why."

"Why would that be of concern to the Chicago police?"

"I'm interested because he was my brother."

Ulrike didn't look like she bought that explanation fully. Ritter didn't argue as he scanned the drab, neat houses they were passing.

"Besides, I'm not real impressed with the way the case is being investigated. It just offends me as a cop."

Ulrike twirled her head toward Ritter.

"What do you mean?"

"Something's not right. The police in Berlin don't even have a record of Wolf's death."

Ulrike hit the brakes too hard for a stop at a red light.

"If you want my opinion," she said, "I don't think he's dead. I would know."

"Somebody was dead. And at least two people died trying to protect his body."

"That makes no sense!" Ulrike said, slamming the heel of her right hand against the wooden steering wheel of her car. "Why would anyone want to kill him?"

Ritter considered how much he should tell Ulrike about what Davies had said. He owed Davies nothing, but if Ulrike knew too much, she might be in more danger than he'd already put her in. On the other hand, if she realized he was holding out on her, she might stop helping him. It was a lousy choice, but he decided to tell her the truth — at least as it had been told to him. Before he could speak, a horn blared behind them. The light had turned green. Ulrike put the car in gear and peeled away.

"Wolf was apparently working on some sensitive diplomatic matters," Ritter said as Ulrike picked up speed.

"What could possibly have been so important that somebody would have killed him?"

"Don't know exactly. Had something to do with the Soviet Union and Germany. The U.S. embassy thinks the KGB may have killed him to stop him from passing the information on to the U.S."

Ulrike looked over a Ritter with an accusing stare.

"Are you saying Wolf was working for the Americans?"

"That's what they say, but I think you'd better keep that to yourself. A couple of guys who were probably KGB already tried to punch my lights since I got here."

Ritter rubbed the back of his still sore head.

"That's preposterous. There's détente between East and West these days. Everybody knows that."

"Apparently the intelligence boys didn't get the word. In fact, I think we'd better be careful what we say in public. Talking in a moving car is probably OK. But let's be careful at Wolf's place."

"I suppose you think were being followed, too."

Ritter turned and checked the cars behind them.

"Not impossible. I get the feeling people have been following me since I got here."

"Aaaargh."

Ulrike pulled the car over to the curb. She turned in her seat toward Ritter and ticked off her points with her fingers.

"CIA, KGB, missing bodies, Wolf's a spy. You expect me to believe this garbage?"

"I'm just telling you what I've been told. I've got to say it seems a little weird to me too, but their story is all I've got to work with. That and you."

"Me? I don't know a damn thing! And if I did, I'm not sure I'd tell you."

"I know it must seem a little strange…."

"Strange! You come to my door late at night posing as your brother…."

"I never said I was Wolf."

"You took advantage of me!"

"Yeah, well." Ritter looked sheepish. "You caught me by surprise." Ritter flashed an impish grin.

"It's not funny." Ulrike showed a hint of a smile. "You're no gentleman."

"That's something I've rarely been accused of."

Ulrike's smile widened a bit.

"You were a real stinker."

*****

Wolf's apartment was on the top floor of a five-story, stone-and-glass building. Wolf's hallway had off-white walls and brushed-brass door fittings. Ritter found it had Prussian charm: functional design with elevators that ran on time.

Ritter stopped Ulrike before she inserted Wolf's key in the lock. He rummaged in his trench coat pocket for an item he'd dug out of his bag that morning. He aimed the mini-flashlight at the keyhole of the lock, peering at it intently as Ulrike looked on. From another pocket, he took out a small magnifying glass that was part of a kit he brought to crime scenes in Chicago. With a practiced flick, he swiveled the magnifier out of its leather case and moved it back and forth over the keyhole until things came into focus.

"What are you doing?" Ulrike asked.

"Somebody's been picking this lock" Ritter pointed at the door. "See those little scratches?"

Ritter handed the magnifier to Ulrike, who took a look.

"Who?"

"Maybe we'll find out inside. Let me go first."

Wolf's flat was warmer in style than the exterior of the building and the hallway. The hand-set parquet floor was the color of mature tobacco. On it, lay an assortment of small rugs, their cobalts, indigos and blood reds the products of dye vats in Teheran and Kabul.

Two walls, covered with raw silk, the color of linen, had prints and paintings on them. Overhead, track lighting illuminated each work, focusing brightness where it was needed while creating no harsh glares anywhere else. Another wall was filled with bookcases, each section of which had its own tubular light fixture to display the volumes.

The only other pieces of furniture were two modern, brown leather chairs, a matching love seat and an old wooden trunk that served as a coffee table.

"Someone has been here," Ulrike said, as she and Ritter did a cautious search of the apartment's rooms. "I just feel it."

As they searched, Ritter noticed Ulrike was looking wistfully at what she saw as if visiting a childhood bedroom.

"Nice place," Ritter said after they found no one lurking inside.

Ulrike didn't respond, taking off her coat and tossing it over one of the leather chairs. Ritter did the same. She moved to the bookcases and ran her fingers over some of the titles.

"He liked books," she said, slipping into the past tense.

Ritter made an examination of his own. Most of the titles were in German. He translated in his head: "The Tin Drum," "The Clown," "Group Portrait with a Lady," "The Lost Honor of Katharina Blum." About what he expected. Boll and Grass and a few other moderns, names he'd heard as a university student many years before. There were some well-thumbed texts by other authors of the so-called Gruppe '47, post-war titles Ritter remembered from his studies.

A slim volume titled "Wie Deutsch Ist Es?" lay flat on a shelf as if someone had put it back recently. Ritter picked it up and read the back cover.

"Do you know it?" Ulrike asked.

"'Fraid not."

"It's about finding out what is it to be German, at least a modern German."

Is that what I'm doing? Ritter asked himself as he slipped the small book into his suit jacket pocket.

"He has someone after him, too," Ulrike said.

"Who?"

"The hero of that book….And he's from an old German family."

Ritter looked perplexed.

"The Springers go way back," Ulrike said. "I thought you knew."

"Not really."

Ritter continued to look through Wolf's books, flipping through the pages in case something had been hidden or forgotten inside. In his murder cases, he sometimes found useful evidence that way. At a minimum, the type of books a victim or suspect had helped him learn a bit about who the person had been.

"Yes. Very Prussian. Lots of military men….like your father."

"My grandmother, who raised me, was not very chatty when it came to my father. Her story was: 'He died in the war. Lots of people did. It's over. Move on.'"

Ulrike said Wolf had told her his father had been a high-ranking officer. She'd pressed him for details but never got much. She wasn't sure why.

"Wolf was very slippery when you tried to pin him down. If he didn't want to talk about something, he'd change the subject — or start taking your clothes off."

Ritter wasn't sure how to respond. Ulrike saved him by going back to the book Ritter had pocketed.

"In that book," she said, pointing, "the father of the main character was one of the few heroes in the war. He led a plot against Hitler and got shot for it."

"Sounds like a distinct minority."

Ritter took the book out of his pocket with new interest and opened it to the first chapter. After a moment he put it back in his pocket and said, "I thought about being a writer once."

"Hmmm. I wouldn't have guessed."

Ritter laughed.

"Not surprised. I can be a little rough around the edges, but back when I was in college, I actually started writing a novel."

"About what?"

"Small boy, big city, no parents, angry at life. A little autobiographical, like a lot of first books."

"I'd love to read it sometime."

Ritter thought she sounded like she genuinely meant it, but he had no copy of that aborted project and wasn't sure he wanted anyone to see where his head was back then, even if he had a manuscript.

At one end of Wolf's bookcases was a tall rack of stereo equipment, all tinted glass, smoky plastic and polished chrome. Ritter pushed a small, black button at a corner of the unit and a beveled CD door pinged open. Alongside the stereo was a storage cabinet jammed with compact discs and tape cassettes. As he had with the books, Ritter scanned the titles on the jewel-box spines to see what his brother's tastes were. The majority were symphonies. There was a clear preference for Germans: Beethoven, Brahms, Mendelssohn, Berg and Wagner, with a few Austrians like Mozart, Mahler and Lehar thrown in. Ritter noticed a majority of the discs and tapes had been published by Deutsche Grammophon and that many featured von Karajan and the Berlin Philharmonic.

"A bit of a German chauvinist, I see."

Ulrike shook her head.

"I think he just thought those Germans were the best. We've done some horrible things and some wonderful things as a people. No sense apologizing for the latter."

"Is that Wolf speaking?"

"That's a lot of Germans these days....especially younger ones."

Ritter continued his inventory of the apartment. On the walls were reproductions of Durer, Schiele and Klimt. At least he guessed they were reproductions. There was also a modern oil painting that was red and black on white canvas. To either side of it, mounted behind frameless glass, were some black-and-white photos of female nude torsos.

Ritter lingered over one photo and pulled out his magnifying glass, making a theatrical examination.

"Anybody I know?"

Ulrike shot him a coy smile.

"No comment."

The kitchen had Chinese-red cabinets and white countertops. The tile floor was black-and-white like a large swatch cut out of a harlequin's jersey. A small butcher's block stood in the center of the floor, with black-handled knives hanging from a magnetic strip on its side.

There were appliances Ritter had seen in magazine ads: a food processor, a coffee-bean grinder, a small version of a restaurant espresso machine and an Italian ice-cream maker. There was an array of cooking implements stored in a set of blue plastic cylinders: wooden spoons, wire whisks, spatulas and a few utensils Ritter didn't recognize.

"Wolf cook much?" Ritter asked.

"Yes. He was quite good, in fact. Simple stuff. But tasty. He'd attack a recipe, break it down, then play with it, trying variations. More like an engineer than a chef....Somewhat German, I guess." Ulrike paused. "How about you?"

Ritter shook his head.

"Just the basics. Pancakes on Sunday. Barbeques on the week-end….My wife did most of the cooking."

"Did?"

"We're separated….Guess Wolf and I had that in common. Couldn't make a marriage work."

"Separated not divorced."

Ritter hesitated.

"In my case, no real difference. We'll probably do the formal papers after I get back."

Ulrike looked embarrassed as if she'd asked one question too many. Ritter pretended not to notice and began rummaging through kitchen drawers for odd bits of note paper, receipts, match books — the type of things a man collects without thinking, clues that might tell where someone had been and maybe what he'd done. He found a few old supermarket coupons and some cash register receipts from a hardware store but nothing relevant. Under the sink, there was a collection of cleaning powders and liquids, sponges of various shapes and colors and a tool kit with the rudiments of an apartment workshop.

There was no bulletin board or pad hanging on the wall next to the kitchen phone. Ritter went into the main bedroom, where he hoped to find some place where Wolf might have written notes to himself. He thought he'd found what he was looking for when he spotted a small desk in a corner. But he quickly realized someone had probably gotten there before him. The papers and books on it were stacked too neatly, even for a German, Ritter thought. All the surfaces were completely clean, even of dust. Among the stacked items, there were no note pads or loose pieces of paper. Most of the things were foreign-affairs jour-nals with scholarly articles on current topics. There was an unfinished expense report of a trip Wolf had made to London for the foreign min-istry. But there was nothing really helpful.

"Wolf have somebody come in to clean?"

"Every Wednesday."

"So in theory, no one's been in here to clean since last Wednesday?"

Ritter had almost said "since Wolf was murdered," but he'd caught himself.

"I wouldn't think so."

Ritter put the stack of papers back in order.

"Was Wolf a neat person?" he asked.

"He was orderly. It's one of the things I liked about him. I'm that way, too."

Ritter thought about that but said nothing.

"How about you?" Ulrike asked.

More comparisons, Ritter noticed.

"My trains run on time." Ritter smiled. "My wife thinks I'm compulsive."

Ritter flung back the duvet on Wolf's king-size bed. He made a rather clinical inspection of the fitted sheet on the mattress.

Ulrike didn't look pleased at the personal intrusion.

"So these are the sheets from last Wednesday?"

"I suppose."

Ritter put the coverlet back, straightening it and smoothing out the wrinkles. He checked the closet next. It was a large one with bi-fold doors painted an off-white like the ceiling and the adjoining walls. There were some empty leather suitcases on the floor next to various pairs of brown and black dress shoes, some patent-leather opera pumps, and two pairs of athletic shoes. Next to them was a pair of well-oiled hiking boots and a set of green Wellingtons.

Above the rain boots was an assortment of ties, some of them solids in dull reds or blues, the sort of thing a diplomat might wear. Toward the back of the tie rack were sportier models, one in lemon with black polka dots. The suits were conservatively cut, some blues and grays, with and without pin stripes — standard foreign-service issue. And a notch-lapel tuxedo. The suits all looked expensive, but after examining the stitching, Ritter concluded they were off-the-rack, not bespoke. Beyond the suits, were a black leather sports jacket, two tweedy sport coats and wool trousers to match.

Ritter found a few German and Swiss coins, some three-month-old concert ticket stubs in the various jacket pockets, plus a pack of matches advertising a German beer.

Wolf's dresser top drawer had the usual treasures of a man's life: a pocket knife, a pair of well-used Zeiss binoculars with some brass showing through on some of the edges, an old Leica rangefinder camera, pairs of silver and gold cufflinks, a box of coins of various nations, a bankcard — perhaps a duplicate — and a current, nondiplomatic passport. Ritter pocketed the last two items before pawing through the drawer's remaining objects: paper clips, stamps, various owner's manuals for electronic equipment, a Sony Walkman and a roll of masking tape.

In the bathroom medicine cabinet, he found an open plastic bag of disposable razors, an aerosol cream, a pump of anti-tartar toothpaste, bottles of fancy shampoo conditioner and a slim tube of styling mousse. On the chrome rack he noticed two toothbrushes, one red, one blue, the only sign someone else might have shared the apartment.

"Wolf have a travel kit with a razor and shaving cream? Things like that?"

"He kept a small suitcase packed with some clothes.

"I didn't see it in the bedroom."

"There's another closet next to the front door.…I'll check, but I don't like all this snooping," she shouted over her shoulder as she walked to the front of the apartment.

"I don't think we're the first ones to go through his things if that's any consolation."

Ulrike found no travel bag in the front closet. When she walked back toward the bathroom, she encountered Ritter coming out of the kitchen with the tool kit, a roll of paper towels and an empty plastic bucket in his hands.

"What are you doing?" she asked.

"A little plumbing." Ritter noticed Ulrike's hands were empty. "No travel bag, I take it."

She shook her head.

Ritter took off his jacket, put the bucket under the exposed pipes of the bathroom sink and turned off the hot and cold taps from the master knobs against the wall. With a wrench from the tool kit, he had the trap section of the pipes open in short order and was rooting around the gunky mess inside with the pen he had found in one of Wolf's jackets.

"Wolf got any of those zippered plastic bags in the kitchen?" he asked from under the sink.

"I'll look."

She was back in a minute and handed him one.

Ritter continued to poke about under the sink. Ulrike finally asked: "What are you looking for?"

"Samples "

"Of what?"

"Hair," he whispered. "I was hoping to find a hair brush, but this will have to do….There's tweezers in the medicine cabinet. Would you get them?"

Ritter took the tweezers and pulled out some dark strands of hair from the trap. He crawled out from under the sink and stood under a heat lamp, which he turned on.

Ulrike looked confused.

"I want to make sure I'm getting black not brown."

"His not mine, you mean?"

"Yeah."

Ritter held up the strands to the 150-watt lamp.

"Black, wouldn't you say?" he asked, offering Ulrike a look.

"If you want to be sure, look for one with a little gray. He's got some gray at the temples — just like you." She paused. "I don't. At least not yet." Another pause. "But if I stick with you, I may get some before the week is out."

Ritter got back down under the sink and got some more hairs. He located one with a little gray. He came back out and sat a moment as if he'd gotten an idea. He went back to Wolf's desk and cut off a piece of cellophane tape from a dispenser. He walked back to the bathroom and put the tape over the razor, lifting up some beard fragments.

"This should help me make sure I got the right kind," he said, holding up the tape.

"Not likely anybody else used his razor." Ritter thought a moment, then asked, "You didn't shave your legs here did you?"

"No," she said, emphasizing the word.

Ritter put his handiwork in various bags and stuffed them in his jacket pocket with the passport.

"What do you intend to do with all that stuff?"

"It's a secret," Ritter whispered, pointing to the ceiling.

Ritter reconnected the sink pipes, wiped up the floor with the paper towels, washed his hands and put the tools away. He put his coat on and made one more pass through the apartment to see if he might have forgotten something. After a last-minute inspiration, he looked behind the prints and paintings on the walls to see if they hid anything — like a safe. Before he closed the door and locked it, he said to Ulrike: "One last thing. You notice anything missing from his clothes in the closet. A favorite jacket, a briefcase, some shirt?"

"Not that I can think of."

"What kind of clothes did Wolf keep in that travel bag?"

"A dark blue suit, double-breasted, khaki pants, light blue shirts, burgundy ties.

"Nice detail. You'd make a good cop."

She shrugged.

"I went with him sometimes on his trips."

"Lucky for us."

"How?"

"We probably know what he was wearing when he was killed."

9

Saturday, November 4, 11:45 a.m. Bonn

In the elevator, Ritter said he wanted to make a stop at Wolf's bank to see if he had a safe-deposit box and to check a few other things.

"This is Germany. No banks open on Saturday. Just the cash machines."

"Still worth a stop."

Ritter smiled and pulled out the bankcard he'd swiped from Wolf's dresser.

"You wouldn't know what his access code for this is, would you?" he asked.

"I do, but I'm not sure I want to give it to you."

"Do you want to find out if he's alive or dead and maybe who killed him?"

"Of course."

"Well, if we get into his account we might find that he wrote a check to somebody relevant."

Ulrike didn't offer the number.

"Look, maybe someone was blackmailing him because he was a double agent or because he was into something illegal."

"How can you say that about your own brother!"

"I didn't even know the guy!"

Ritter realized he was sounding more like a cop than a sibling. Ulrike turned sulky. Ritter switched to a more soothing approach.

"All I'm saying is we can't rule out any possibilities. Sometimes even the best people get mixed up in bad things. They may not want to, but they do. I see it all the time."

Ulrike continued sulking for a while then eventually added: "Wolf was an honest person. He had integrity. I just know that."

"OK. OK." Ritter held up his hands in mock surrender. "But maybe somebody was trying to do something bad to him. His bank records might show that."

Ulrike finally conceded the point, and they drove to Wolf's bank. It was on a busy street. She had to park around the corner. At the ATM, Ritter inserted the bankcard. It worked. A glass window slid up. A message welcomed him in German and asked him to punch in his code number. Ulrike stepped forward and hit the appropriate squares. Ritter took note.

The machine asked Ritter what service he wanted. He pressed "Balance" and got a choice of "Checking" or "Savings." He punched "Savings," got the balance, then hit "Checking." All told, Wolf had more than 600,000 Deutsche marks.

"More than three hundred thousand dollars," Ulrike said, making the calculation in her head.

"My brother a rich guy?"

"There was some family money. He made a good salary at the foreign ministry, and he had some investments."

Ritter found himself wondering if the money was his or Heidi's now.

The machine's options included a printout of transactions for the last 30 days.

Ritter pressed the button and out came three sheets. He scanned them as they walked back to the car.

"What's this?" he asked, pointing to an unfamiliar name, Aldi Einkauf.

"The supermarket."

Ritter handed the statement to Ulrike.

"Anything jump out at you on that list?"

Ulrike took a long look and finally said, "Not that I can see."

"I was hoping for some big amount and the name of a person."

"So what do we do now?"

Ritter thought a moment, then said, "I need to send someone a package."

Ritter had Ulrike drive him to a DHL office. She waited in a no-parking zone while he made arrangements inside. With time to kill, she paged through the photo albums Heidi Springer had lent Ritter. In the first, she came to Wolf's wedding pictures and snapped that album shut, turning to the older one. She was studying a picture of Ritter's father when he climbed back in the car.

"Find anything interesting?" he asked.

She shook her head.

"Not really, though I did learn your father was an *Oberst* in the army before the war."

"What does that tell you?"

"That he was probably someone important during the war. Maybe a general. There are some patches on his uniform, but I don't know what they are. "I'm not much of a military expert."

"What do you write about?"

"Politics mainly. The environment. Sometimes women's issues."

"Are you full-time?"

"No. Free-lance. Mostly for left-wing publications."

"You're left-wing?"

There was a surprise in his voice, and Ulrike paused a moment before answering.

"Not as much as I once was. I'm a Social Democrat now. Over here, that's very respectable. Roughly like your Democratic Party."

Ritter looked through the older album himself.

"So this is all new to you," Ulrike said, pointing to the photo book.

Ritter nodded.

"My grandmother was like the Sphinx on my father. She was his mother-in-law, so maybe there was some tension there because of the separation."

"Why'd your mother pick Chicago?"

"Not sure. Grandma Helga's family had moved to Milwaukee after The Great War, as she called it. Didn't want any part of what happened to Germany after that one. She made that pretty clear."

"So how'd your mother meet your father?"

"On a vacation in Germany in the 30s. In Berlin. They got married, and she stayed."

"But then she went back — with you."

"Yeah. They separated. I don't think there was ever a divorce. And then he died."

Ritter stopped at a photo of his mother and father.

Ulrike looked over.

"That's a nice one. They look in love."

Ritter lingered over the photo a while.

"That they do."

A police car pulled alongside Ulrike's car. The officer in the passenger seat gave her a stern look and signaled with his index finder for her to move on. She started up the car, turned to Ritter and asked, "Where now?"

Ritter thought about Davies's crazy plan for a moment, then said: "Munich, I guess. Maybe someone will recognize my face, and we can find out if Wolf really was down there. It's a long shot, but it's all we've got at the moment."

Ritter noticed he'd said "we." And Ulrike hadn't objected.

"How about a quick lunch first? I'm famished."

"Sure," said Ritter, thinking it wasn't much of a sacrifice.

Five minutes later, they were walking into a corner *Weinstube*. Rolf Müller, an elderly man, came out of the kitchen, an apron around his suit jacket, and answered the restaurant phone. His face lit up when he saw Ulrike. He signaled a silent, friendly greeting. Ulrike and Ritter sat down at a battered wooden booth in the back and began studying the one-page menu. After a few moments, Müller came over. Ulrike got up and gave him a kiss on the cheek. She introduced Ritter as Wolf's brother. Müller looked flustered.

"I, I thought you were Wolf," he said.

"Understandable, " Ritter said.

"And how is he?"

"He's…." Ulrike started to say.

"Out of town," Ritter interrupted.

Ulrike looked at Ritter and changed the subject.

"What do you recommend today?" she asked.

"The special is *Sauerbraten.* But first, a little soup."

"We're in your hands," Ulrike said.

After Müller had gone back to the kitchen, Ulrike mentioned that he'd been a soldier during World War II and might recognize the unit patches on the uniform of Ritter's father.

"We could show him the photo."

"Couldn't hurt."

Ulrike went back to the car and got the older album. By the time she was back at the table, Müller was pouring out two glasses of white wine from a chilled pitcher.

"Rolf, we were wondering if you could identify these uniform patches for us. It's an old picture of Matt and Wolf's father."

It was the first time she'd called him Matt, Ritter noticed.

Müller put the pitcher down and dried his hands on his apron. Ulrike opened the album and showed him the black-and-white photo, which was still crisp after all the years.

Müller took the book and said, "I'll see what I can do, but it's been a long time since I thought about such things."

Müller put the book down for a moment and pulled out a pair of glasses from his jacket breast pocket. He peered closely at the photo, putting it quite close to his eyes. Appearing to have some difficulty, he took the book to a nearby window, where the light was better.

He flipped through the book, looking at different pages. He finally stopped on one in particular. Then he returned to the booth.

"If I'm not mistaken, your father was in the *Abwehr*."

"What's that?" Ritter asked.

"Military intelligence. By his rank in 1938, the date of this first photo, he must have worked closely with Admiral Canaris."

Ritter looked puzzled.

"Head of military intelligence," Müller said.

"Well, that helps a little, I guess. We got separated before the war. I didn't know him very well."

Müller opened the album to the second snapshot he'd examined and handed it to Ritter.

"That one is very interesting too."

It was a photo of Ritter's father in civilian clothes, cropped from the chest up.

Ritter had seen it before but had skipped over it. He looked more closely this time.

"I'm not sure I get your point."

Müller bit his lip as if not sure how much he should say. He looked around to see who else was within earshot, lowered his voice, and asked, "See that pin in his lapel?"

"Yes?"

"It's a pin of the Nazi Party."

"Well," Ulrike broke in, "a lot of the military joined the party during the war just to survive. They had to. Isn't that right, Rolf?"

Müller looked at Ulrike and then back at Ritter.

"Yes, of course."

Ritter saw the look on Müller's face and said, "I get the impression you're holding something back. Don't on my account. I'd rather hear the truth."

"Well," Muller said and then paused, looking apprehensively at Ulrike. "Look at the date of the photo. December, 1934."

"Is that some famous time?"

"Not particularly, but it means your father was an early member of the party. A *very* early member."

10

S aturday, November 4, 1:00 p.m., Bonn

Ritter and Ulrike finished lunch quietly. They talked about the weather and German politics and about anything except what Müller had told them. A passage from Thomas Wolfe popped into Ritter's head, another memory from his college courses: "Which of us has known his brother? Which of us has looked into his father's heart? Which of us has not remained forever prison-pent? Which of us is not forever a stranger and alone?"

He was looking homeward too.

Ulrike asked Ritter at one point if they should knock off for the day and start fresh on Sunday. He said no. He didn't have a lot of time. He had to get back to Chicago, he reminded her. When they got back to the car, Ritter's mood had turn gloomy.

"You want to talk about it, Matt?" Ulrike asked.

His first name again, now some sympathy. It seemed like some turning point, but he wasn't in the mood to explore it. He just said: "Not really."

"You're just like Wolf! He'd never talk about what was bothering him either."

She waited a moment, then added, "It's not healthy, you know."

"I know. My doctor says I'm a candidate for an ulcer."

"Well, say something!"

"I will, but first I need to make a call."

"And Munich?"

"Let's put that on hold for the moment. I want to check something."

Ulrike drove back to her apartment so Ritter could call Günter Becker in West Berlin.

"I need to do a little historical research," Ritter told Becker. "Nazi activities before and during the war."

"Sort of a broad topic. Does it have something to do with your brother?"

"In a way."

Ritter was trying to persuade himself that looking into his father's past was as good a way as any of finding his brother's killers. He certainly hadn't done much good looking for clues in the present. But he knew his interest in his father was more than that.

"We have some very complete files on that era here in Berlin. The embassy should be able to help."

Letting Rick Davies in on his inquiries was not what Ritter had in mind.

"Anywhere else?"

"There's a professor at the University of Heidelberg — Kurt Meier. He used to work in the prosecutor's office in Ludwigsburg. It's the main Nazi-hunting operation in the country. He's got a lot of the historical material on computer disks."

"That it?"

"Well, the best place, of course, is at the National Archives in Washington. The Americans took crates of Nazis records back with them after the war. Plus quite a few Nazis. Especially if you knew something about rockets. Or intelligence."

Ritter glanced at his watch, thanked Becker and hung up. It was just after nine in Washington. He took out a small address book from his jacket and looked up a name. Ritter dialed the number of a building on Pennsylvania Avenue. After a lot of electronic beeps and clicks, an operator answered, "FBI." Ritter asked for Tom Sullivan, an agent in the Criminal Investigative Division. Sullivan answered, and Ritter reminded him that they'd worked together on a teenage kidnapping-murder case a year before.

"Of course!" Sullivan said. "How ya doin', Matt? And how's what's-his-name? Bernie?"

"Retired. Got a new partner. Still breaking her in."

"Her? That doesn't sound good."

"Not so bad. She's pretty sharp. In fact, I left her in charge of a big serial killer case while I'm over here."

Ritter explained that he was in Germany and doing an informal investigation of the death of his brother. Sullivan sounded sympathetic and offered to help if he could. Ritter said he needed to make a quick inquiry to the National Archives and figured a request from the FBI would go through faster than one with his name on it.

"This about your brother?"

"Indirectly. It's about my father. There's a lot I don't know about him. I'm hoping I'll find something out that will help me solve my brother's murder. I've run up against a stone wall on everything else, so this is kind of a Hail Mary play."

Ritter asked for anything on Rudolf Springer, an officer in the *Abwehr*. He gave Sullivan Ulrike's home number and his hotel details and hung up. He found Ulrike staring at him.

"You really think the Archives will help with Wolf's case?"

"No idea. I guess I'm just grasping at straws."

"And maybe a little curious about your father and the Nazi Party?"

Ritter crinkled his eyes at the remark, and finally said, "It's on my mind."

"We still going to Munich?"

Ritter shrugged and said, "I guess."

"You don't sound very enthusiastic."

"Well, it's the crudest type of detective work. We'll be going to hotel after hotel and knocking on doors blindly — hoping to get lucky. What we really need is something more precise. A place he was. A person he met."

"And you think checking out your father's past will be more productive than that?"

"Right now, it's as good as anything else. Besides, somebody else is doing the checking for me. It's not taking up my time."

In mid-afternoon, Ritter asked Ulrike to pack a bag after she gave him a ride over to his hotel. Back at the Bristol, Ritter found he had a message from Davies. Ritter called him.

Davies was charming in asking if Ritter had thought about his idea to pose as Wolf to get into his foreign ministry office. Ritter looked at Ulrike, who was sitting on his bed. He thought for a moment about the frustrating search that lay ahead of them in Munich. And about what he'd just learned about his father's past. Davies's idea was risky, but — on a hunch again — Ritter found himself saying, "When do you want to meet?"

"Half an hour."

Davies gave Ritter an address.

"New plan," Ritter told Ulrike. "Let's do Munich tomorrow. I got one more thing to do first."

Ulrike said she wanted to come along and made a scene when Ritter said no. She asked what he was up to. When he refused to tell her, she demanded to know why.

"'Cause I'd hate to see you wind up in jail."

After Ulrike left to pack, Ritter took a cab to Davies's house in Bad Godesberg. It was a stone mansion on a small, wooded lot.

"Being vice consul must pay well," Ritter said after he was let inside.

Davies smiled as if that answered why a supposedly low-level diplomat should have been assigned such luxurious digs. Inside, Ritter found a mock-up of the West German foreign ministry complex laid out on Davies's dining room table. Two men in suits were standing near the layout, which sat on a green baize cloth. Another man was seated in a corner, dressed in a white barber's tunic.

"This is the target," Davies said, pointing to a model of an unimposing building on the Rhine.

"Where's the entrance?" Ritter asked, though he hadn't formally agreed to go along with Davies's scheme.

"Over here on this little side street," Davies said, pointing. "Tempelstrasse. There's a security booth with guards for cars and pedestrians. We don't know where Wolf's car is. Probably somewhere in Munich. You'll have to walk in. Say you took the subway if anybody asks. There's a stop nearby."

"What else are they likely to ask?"

"Probably not much."

That sounded optimistic to Ritter.

"You'll be going in just before midnight — about an hour before the change of guard. The guy going off should be tired and eager to get home — not very sharp. You'll hand him this."

Davies gave Ritter a leather-bound foreign-ministry credential. Ritter examined the ID photo and shook his head.

"If he asks," Davies said, "tell the guard you just need to pick up something. But he probably won't ask."

"Couple of things bother me."

"What?"

The haircut's different in the photo. If the guard knows Wolf, he might notice."

"That's why Fritz is here. He's the embassy barber. I also took the liberty of buying you a dark blue suit, like the kind Wolf used to wear, and a proper topcoat. They're one size larger than Wolf's. Should work."

So everyone thinks I'm fat, Ritter told himself, thinking of Ulrike's more direct jibe. Ritter ignored Davies's implied taunt and asked:

"What about Wolf's not reporting to work for the last several days? Won't his name be on some kind of hot list?"

"We had somebody call and say he was feeling sick."

"I thought you said the Germans were in on this investigation. Why doesn't the foreign ministry know Wolf's dead?"

Davies flashed a tight smile.

"I said the Germans were in on it, not necessarily the foreign ministry."

If Davies had been a suspect, he wouldn't have gotten away with such a slippery response, but Ritter let it pass, wanting to see what else Davies planned.

"What's the drill once I get in the building?"

"One more guard in the lobby. Just show him your ID. Then use this key to get into Wolf's office if it's locked."

Davies handed Ritter a thick envelope. Ritter ripped it open and found the key as well as a building map that showed the location of Wolf's office. There was also a small slip of paper with the combination to Wolf's file cabinet of classified documents.

"Very thorough….You get this stuff from Wolf?"

Davies said nothing, putting on his poker face.

"You got another agent in there maybe?" Ritter asked.

Davies's eyes narrowed. Ritter sensed he'd hit home.

"What am I looking for?" Ritter asked.

"A file probably. Maybe a thick one. There may be some sort of agreement in it."

Ritter nodded.

"One other thing: When you present your credentials to the first guard, you'll have to sign in so you'll need to practice Wolf's signature."

Davies gave Ritter some samples. Ritter looked at them and laid them side by side with a notebook Davies provided. He took out a pen and scribbled out the signature a couple of times, the last one with a flourish.

Davies examined them.

"That's good. I'm impressed."

"Chicago P.D. Faking it comes in handy sometimes when you're investigating a crime. I can read upside-down too."

"Have to remember that." Davies paused, then added: "How's your German coming, by the way?"

"Better. Been watching TV and listening to the radio."

Davies told Ritter to sit down, and motioned for Fritz to get to work. Ritter did, the first overt sign he was going along with Davies's plan. As hair fell to the floor, Davies turned on a recording of the foreign ministry night guard talking with visitors.

"This is from Monday," Davies said.

"You bugged the foreign ministry?"

"Nah. Little shotgun mike in the lobby is all you need."

The tape finished just as Fritz did. Ritter stood up and brushed some hairs from his shoulders. He went over to the tape player, took the cassette out and put it in his pocket.

"I'd like to listen to this again before I go in."

He walked over to a wall mirror to inspect Fritz's handiwork. His hair was shorter than he'd had it for a long time. He looked younger — maybe even thinner.

"Why don't you try the suit and topcoat to see if we need to make any alterations," Davies suggested.

Ritter went into the bathroom and tried on the suit and the burgundy tie that came with it. His black wing-tips were scuffed from all his running around since he'd arrived. They didn't look right with the stiff newness of the suit's wool fabric, but he figured he could get a shine at the hotel before the break-in.

"Perfect," Davies said when Ritter came out of the bathroom. "Wolf's own wife wouldn't be able to tell the difference."

She couldn't before, Ritter thought.

Davies asked Ritter to try the topcoat on for size too. The fit was fine. Ritter walked over and looked at himself in the room mirror for a while. He thought the image looked like an enlarged photo of his brother or perhaps a self that might have been. Mattheus Springer. Officially highfallutin, as Bernie would have said.

*****

Saturday, November 4, 11 p.m., East Berlin

Before Ritter played burglar that night, a lawyer who had worked closely with the East German Politburo reported in on what he'd learned about the unrest plaguing the ruling body.

"I may have made my last Deutschemark taking our people for a walk across the Glienicke Bridge to the West."

"How many have you sent across?" asked a Politburo member, one of the few remaining after a group had been ousted that week.

"Prisoners and ordinary citizens? Maybe quarter of a million. A nice little earner for the state. Like kidnapping with no consequences."

"A quarter million? Used to seem like a lot. We had twice that today in Alexanderplatz." The Politburo member poured himself a shot of *slivovitz* and downed it. "Even our famous spymaster was there, calling for reform"

"I heard about that."

"You think he's gone over to the other side since he retired on a colonel-general's pay?"

"No one seems to know what he thinks. We never did."

"And the placards now say: 'We are *one* people.' That doesn't sound like what they want is a democratic East Germany."

"No thanks to our friends in Moscow. They seem to be backing that idea, which makes no sense."

"This all would make more sense if we had Wolf Springer in a hard room."

"You're sure the man in Bonn was Wolf and that wasn't his body that we grabbed in West Berlin?"

"Yes. We thought it might be him for a while, but with the visual at his girlfriend's house, that's over. Now we just have to grab him."

"It gets a little delicate when you kidnap in the West, particularly in Bonn under the noses of the government."

"Time to take chances. I don't care about the consequences any more. Make the call."

*****

Saturday, November 4, 11:50 p.m., Bonn.

Davies picked Ritter up near his hotel and gave him a last-minute briefing. He drove Ritter up Adenauerallee to the front of the foreign ministry. Ritter felt surprisingly relaxed. He'd listened again to the tape of the guard's patter and found a comforting sameness to the man's bored inquiries.

It was another cold Central European night. Like an insistent host, winter was making an early entrance. Ritter could hear the groaning of cargo barges slicing through the black waters of the Rhine three hundred yards to the east as they headed toward Kennedy Bridge and points north. Farther south was the river's legendary Lorelei Rock. But Ritter was too focused on the potential disaster that awaited him inside the foreign ministry to be distracted by any siren call that might lure him elsewhere.

Ritter entered the lobby and flashed the ministry ID at the guard, who was reading a paperback novel. The preoccupied man shoved a log book at Ritter. Ritter signed it, inking in his brother's section and room number as he'd been instructed by Davies. A jerk of the guard's head told Ritter he was cleared to go. Ritter offered a weary "*Guten Abend*" to a second guard, who looked up from his newspaper for a second, then went immediately back to the sports pages.

The corridor leading to Wolf's office was dimly lit. Down the hall, Ritter could hear the clacking of a ticker tape. He imagined some important telex coming in from a post in another time zone or a lower latitude. Maputo calling. Or Ouagadougou.

Closer to his target, Ritter noticed he was tenser than he'd been in the lobby. One thing he and Davies had talked only fleetingly about was the possibility that, once inside, Ritter would meet someone Wolf knew well. Davies had seemed unconcerned.

"Mumble something about feeling better and wanting to catch up on your work.

Wolf was a workaholic," he'd said. "It will seem perfectly natural."

Easy to do is easy to say, Ritter thought. What if some guy asks me about our last night out together or some project we're working on? And yet there he was, breaking more than a few laws in a foreign country, and the simplest explanation he had for his irrational conduct was that he had nothing else going in his unofficial murder investigation, and he might find something that would help. More to the point, if he was being honest, he might find out something about his father.

Wolf's office was dark and locked. Ritter had the key ready. He didn't want to spend any more time than necessary in the hallway. He shoved the key in, turned it and slid into the office quickly, flicking on the overhead fluorescent light. He'd suggested doing his skullduggery by flashlight, but Davies had pointed out that Wolf had every right to have his own lights on. Using a flashlight would just raise questions.

Ritter pulled out the piece of paper with the combination to his brother's filing cabinet and had it open in less than a minute. He scanned the folder tabs inside, drawer by drawer, looking for anything related to the Soviet Union, the United States or any heading that seemed pertinent. No relevant folder had any agreement. To be safe, he checked every file. By the time he'd finished, twenty minutes had elapsed, Ritter noticed by the time on his watch. It had seemed like an hour.

He used the handkerchief from the breast pocket of his provided suit to wipe down the outside of the cabinet. He'd learned from one of his cases that twins, alike in most ways, have slightly different fingerprints.

Ritter quickly checked Wolf's bookcase but turned up nothing of interest. The only thing left was his desk. Nothing in the drawers, but on top was a slim address book. Ritter skimmed through the pages. He found a listing in East Berlin for "Aunt Fredi." He put the book in his inside suit-jacket pocket. Not wanting to press his luck, he abandoned the search, turned off the light and made an uneventful exit through the lobby after signing out.

"Nothing," he told Davies when he met up with him at the rendez-vous around the corner.

"Shit!" Davies said. "You sure you looked everywhere?"

Ritter stared a Davies a moment.

"Yeah. I'm sure."

Davies drove back toward Ritter's hotel and let him off a block away.

"Be in touch," Davies said.

Ritter walked toward his hotel, feeling the wind on his face but not through the topcoat. A couple of blocks away, Davies was speaking into the hand mic of his car radio.

"He's coming up to the hotel," Davies said. "I want somebody front and back.

Make sure he doesn't slip out tonight without company. I don't trust that bastard. He said he didn't find anything, but I'm not so sure."

Inside the cozy warmth of his room, Ritter stripped off his coat and tossed his suit jacket on the bed. Were these his now? Or would Davies want them back like a rented high-school prom tuxedo? Ritter found he was having some uncharacteristically possessive thoughts of late. They seemed to have started about the time he found out how much his brother had in the bank.

Ritter unbuttoned his shirt and found he was clammy with sweat. Not quite as cool a burglar as he'd thought. Bare-chested, he walked over to the mini bar to get himself a drink. He found there was no ice in the room. Ritter didn't feel like calling room service or going down the hall to the floor's ice machine. He downed a tumbler of Scotch neat.

All I need now is a smoke, he thought, looking around the room. He was almost happy there weren't any. He sat down on the bed and looked at his watch. His FBI pal Sullivan might be at home on a Saturday afternoon with college football games on TV.

He started to dial the number, hoping Sullivan had had more luck with the National Archives than he'd had at the foreign ministry. He stopped in mid-dial, put his damp shirt back on and headed for the lobby. He asked the desk clerk to arrange a call at one of the phone cabins the hotel offered. Less chance that Davies or someone else would be listening in, he thought. Ritter apologized to Sullivan for the weekend interruption.

"No problem. I was going to call you on Monday anyway. I got a little something. Maybe not as much as you need, but it might help."

Sullivan said he'd gotten a pal to check the files. The friend had found something but hadn't wanted to talk about it over the phone. They'd met for lunch. The friend was very evasive at first but eventually told Sullivan what he'd discovered.

"Your dad's file is sealed and can't be opened without a very special classification clearance — which my friend doesn't have. But he does know one thing."

"What?"

"Your dad either worked for MI6 or the OSS during the war. He could tell that much from the file number."

"MI6?"

"British foreign intelligence."

"And the other one?

"The Office of Strategic Services."

"That was one of those wartime agencies wasn't it? "

"Yeah. It's what they used to call the CIA before there was a CIA."

11

Sunday, November 5, 6:30 a.m., Bonn

Ritter was in high gear early the next morning, his pace stoked by anger, his fists clenched as he strode into the gray air. Tom Sullivan's findings were still swirling around his head after a fitful night of sleep. An image of Davies's face was there too with a cross hair over it.

Ritter put his suit and topcoat back on and took a taxi out to Davies's house. He told the driver to wait. It was 7:00 a.m. by the time the cab braked to a halt in front of the place. There might be someone watching, Ritter figured, and if Davies had a minder, the guard probably had a gun, which Ritter did not. He'd factored in those points in adopting his casual demeanor as he walked toward Davies's door.

In a slight slip of cover, Ritter mashed Davies's doorbell and kept his finger on it a beat too long. A few moments later, someone checked him out through the front-door peephole. Lock tumblers clicked, and when the door opened there was Davies in gray pajamas, navy robe and brown leather slippers. His hair was ruffled, and he had a puzzled look on his face.

"What's up?" he asked, sounding sleepy.

"I had a brainstorm last night about Wolf." Ritter tried to sound eager. "I wanted to try it out on you."

"Can't this wait? I haven't even had my coffee yet."

"It's something I think we should get on right way. Only take a minute."

Davies yawned and said, "All right. Come on in."

Ritter closed the door and quietly flipped its bolt lock as Davis trundled toward the living room, his back to his guest. Before Davies could turn around, Ritter punched him right where he calculated one of his kidneys was. It was becoming a bit of a habit. Davies slumped to the ground again, curling up in pain. Ritter manhandled him into a straight-back chair, stripped the cinch belt out of Davies's robe and tied his hands behind him to one of the chairback's spokes.

"What the hell are you doing?" Davies asked, trying to yell but managing only wheezy gasps.

"Trying to get your attention. You've been lying to me again, and I want to know why."

"I don't know what you're talking about!"

"Suit yourself. I can do this all day."

Ritter spread his large hands apart on either side of Davies' head and slammed his palms into his ears. Davies let out a scream.

"You probably can't hear me, but I bet that smarted." Ritter said nothing for a while, waiting for the likely ringing in Davies's ears to clear. "Just looking for the truth, one way or another," he shouted into Davies's ears.

His hearing back to normal, Davies recoiled at the volume of Ritter's voice.

"If I told you the whole truth, I could go to jail. As it was, I said more than I should have."

"If you're already a criminal, what's a little more blabbing? Judges run those sentences concurrently most of the time, so you're not really risking anything, the way I see it."

"Go to hell!"

"Well, not there, but I might go to the kitchen. Kitchen implements are very popular interrogation tools, I hear."

"Is that what you do in Chicago?"

"Nah, we just use big phone books. They don't leave any marks. Not sure the Bonn phone book would be big enough for the job, though. Probably just stick to an ice pick or something."

"I told you all I can tell!"

Ritter smiled. He knew he wasn't going to torture Davies to get him to talk, as tempting as that was. He'd thought of a less violent way to get Davies chatting.

"You couldn't even tell me the part about my father working for U.S. intelligence?"

Davies said nothing at first, beaming pure hate at Ritter. His look alone told Ritter he'd hit home.

"Who've you been talking to?" Davies finally said.

"Friends with access to files."

"That's top secret!"

And confirmation about the OSS, Ritter thought.

"Not much of a secret anymore. At least not to me."

Davies considered that.

"I'll have to talk to someone. Maybe we could get you cleared for limited purposes. Since you're helping us out."

Ritter laughed.

"You're good. I'll give you that."

"Untie me."

Ritter did, turned around and left, his mission accomplished. As he got to the front door, he shouted back Davies's previous sign-off: "Be in touch."

Ritter had settled his bill with the hotel before he went to Davies's place and brought his suitcase with him in the taxi. He had the driver take him to Ulrike's, hoping she hadn't unpacked for the Munich trip. A few minutes later, he was at her place, his bag beside him as he rang her bell.

She came to the door, dressed in jeans and a red sweater that came to her knees. Her hair was in a single long braid again. She had a piece of toast in her hand as if he'd interrupted her breakfast. She blinked at the vision of Ritter in his new blue suit and topcoat, and her mouth dropped open.

"Don't faint or anything," Ritter said. "It's just me."

"Matt?"

"Yeah."

Ritter had an embarrassed smile on his face.

"But why?"

"I needed to look like this to pay somebody a visit." Ritter hoped that would be enough explanation. He didn't want to drag Ulrike into his second-story work. "And now that I do look a lot more like my brother, it might prove useful for some other things."

Ulrike took a bite of her toast.

"Like what?"

Ritter found himself wondering if she'd like him more if he got into playing the role of Wolf, clothes and all. That delayed his answer, which was: "Don't know yet, but I do know where we're going next."

"Munich?"

"No. East Berlin."

"Why?"

"To visit Wolf's Aunt Fredi. *My* Aunt Fredi."

"I didn't know Wolf had an aunt."

"It seems my family has a lot of secrets."

*****

Sunday, November 5, 11:00 a.m., West Berlin

As Ritter had hoped, Ulrike hadn't unpacked the bag she'd prepared for Munich. With a little scrambling and a stop at an airport cash machine, they made the ten o'clock flight. Ulrike had been unquestioning at first about going to Berlin. During the flight, though, she finally asked Ritter how he'd found out about his aunt.

"A guy at the embassy had her address in a file."

A guy named Wolf.

In Berlin, Ulrike suggested they check their bags at the Am Zoo, an older hotel whose main attraction was its proximity to a station of the S-Bahn, Berlin's above-ground rail system. Ulrike told Ritter the S-Bahn was the best way to cross into East Berlin.

"Less paperwork," she said.

Ritter could have gone over at Checkpoint Charlie, where most Americans crossed. But as a West German, Ulrike had to use another crossing, she explained. On the S-Bahn, they could go together. The train also made it easier to see if anyone was following them, she said.

Ritter and Ulrike got off at Friedrichstrasse in the west part of East Berlin and began a 30-minute wait in the passport line. It would have been even longer if Ulrike hadn't led Ritter by the hand in a short sprint from the train to the passport-control room so they could beat most of the crowd. In line, she held onto his hand a moment, then noticed and broke the link, looking a little embarrassed.

"We were lucky to get through at all," she said after they were on the street outside the station. "They've been closing it down on some days because of all the demonstrations over here."

"What are they demonstrating about?"

"They want to get out. Travel is easing up in other Eastern European countries. They want the same thing, but the government won't budge."

Ulrike and Ritter changed the required amount of Deutsche marks into East German marks at the inflated official rates and headed past the nearby stage that Brecht had made famous. The address in Wolf's book led them to a coffee house not far away. It was closed. Through smudged windows Ritter could make out black café chairs stored upside down atop marble pedestal tables, a spindly forest in the quiet dimness. The gray tile floor still had the detritus of the former evening's revelries: stamped-out cigarette butts, scraps of paper, a broken plate, the odd spoon and fork — a real life poster for a Marxist paradise.

Ritter craned his neck toward the building's second floor and saw a bay window with the curtains pulled back. To the side of the building he noticed a weathered door that appeared to lead to apartments up-stairs. There were buzzers next to the doorjamb. None had a name at-tached. Ritter pushed the first one. A few moments later, an elderly but spry man answered the street door and gave Ritter a wordless look that seemed to say, "Well?" Ritter explained in German that he was looking for Frau Frederica Kraus, the formal name in parentheses in Wolf's address book.

"Frau Kraus?" The man sounded confused. "Ah, Fredi. Come in. She's upstairs."

With the old man leading the way, Ritter and Ulrike mounted a set of wooden stairs, severely worn by legions who'd come before them. At the top of the staircase was a door with paint-chip hints that it had once been glossy black. Ritter and Ulrike were led into a large, well-lit room that appeared to have been frozen in time.

It was what must have been the epitome of a 1930s Berlin salon, Ritter thought. There were threadbare chairs and couches sitting on thin Persian rugs whose once-deep colors could only be imagined. In front of the bay window, a woman of fragile frame lounged on a divan. She looked old, but her clothes and demeanor spoke of a younger, racier time.

She had a lit cigarette in a slender holder in her left hand. Her right arm was elegantly outstretched toward the window as she contemplated what appeared to be the advanced stages of a chess game on a table before her. She had on black harem pants with red-jeweled slippers over the alabaster wrinkles of her feet. Her collarless blouse was black too. The top two buttons were undone, showing more age than sex. Her wiz-ened face was made up with an orangey rouge, creating an effect of a large, smiling apricot with fine white hair sprouting on top. On her lap was a Dachshund.

It was not until Ritter was halfway across the room, the old man padding before him, that the woman noticed her visitors. Her concen-tration broken by her companion's stagey throat clearings, she finally looked up. A smile broke out on her face. Without getting up, she said, in a gleeful voice: "Wolf! What a pleasant surprise. You should have called. I could have prepared something."

The woman spotted Ulrike standing behind Ritter and added: "And who is this divine creature? Is this the one you were telling me about?"

"Aunt Frederica," Ritter said, struck by how strange the words sounded. "I'm not Wolf. I'm Mattheus."

Fredi squinted at her new arrival in the diffuse light of the room. She swung her legs off the divan and put her feet on the floor. Her dog jumped from her lap and came up to Ritter, sniffing his shoes. Fredi rested her cigarette holder on the table with the chess pieces and motioned for the old man to help her stand up. He obliged, using his right forearm under her left armpit for support.

"Come into the light and let me take a look at you," she said, motioning impatiently to Ritter with her right arm. The old man moved out of the way as Ritter advanced. Ritter wasn't sure whether to give her a kiss or a hug until he was formally identified.

"Goodness," she finally said. "Where did you come from?"

She made a clumsy grasp of Ritter's right hand with her left before deciding she preferred an embrace. Ritter found it a bittersweet moment. For so long he'd thought he had no family. Then he'd learned about Wolf and suddenly there was Fredi, a marvelous eccentric showing him unquestioned affection.

Ritter tried to look happy, but what he felt was dread of the message he carried. Fredi broke off her hug and said in a cheery voice: "Let's all sit down and get comfortable." She patted her lap. "Spaetzle, you come back up here where you belong." She patted the dog's head after he'd gotten back into the place of honor. "When he was a puppy, all he would eat was Spaetzles. His name was Fritz, but I changed it."

Everyone sat down except the old man, who stood to the side, looking back and forth at Fredi and the chessboard.

"You can speak in English if you want," Fredi said. "I'm quite good at it. And please call me Fredi. Everyone does. Frederica sounds so counter-revolutionary, like some tsarina."

She laughed at her own joke.

"All right, Fredi," Ritter said.

Ulrike smiled but look pained and said nothing.

"Now, I want the whole story," Fredi said. "From the beginning, starting with how's your mother. I always liked Greta. Lots of spunk, that girl."

Somehow Ritter had never thought of his mother as a girl. She had died when she was thirty-two. That image of a grown woman was the one he'd always had.

"I'm afraid she died in 1945. Right at the end of the war."

"Oh." Fredi paused. "I'm sorry to hear that. That would have been about the same time as your father."

"I never heard much about him."

Fredi looked confused.

"My grandmother never said much," he said.

Fredi nodded and smiled.

"Oh, yes. Old Helga. She never really liked our side of the family. I'm afraid. She thought my brother — your father — was a Nazi, and since I was a Communist. Well, you can imagine."

She laughed and so did Ritter, though it was forced.

Ritter sketched out his life for Fredi — schools and becoming a policeman.

"A policeman. I don't think we've ever had one of those in the family. Plenty of military types, of course."

Ritter said he'd gotten married.

"Any children?"

"No."

Ritter thought about prattling on, because it put off the painful news he knew he'd have to deliver at some point. But Fredi brought the matter to a head.

"And just how did Wolf finally find you?" she asked. "He tried years ago but never did manage."

Fredi paused, looked around the room. As if suddenly disoriented, she asked,

"And where is he? Why isn't he here?"

"That's, uh, partly what I came to talk about."

Fredi looked at Ritter's face for a while, then said "You're holding something back, aren't you....Don't worry about me. I'm a tough old bird. Heroine of the revolution, you know."

"Wolf never did find me, Fredi. I came over here because I got a call that he'd been....killed."

"Oooh. " Fredi put her left hand to her heart as she drew out the word in obvious pain.

Ritter took Fredi's hand in his. She took a couple of deep breaths and said, "That's all right." She slipped her hand from under Ritter's and patted the top of it, as if he were the one who needed comforting. "I'm OK. Just let me catch my breath."

No one said anything for a while. Ritter looked at Ulrike, as if he hoped she knew what to do next, but she remained silent.

"Tell me what happened," Fredi finally said.

Ritter started with the call from Clyde D. Havermann. He left out nothing, including his waning suspicion that Wolf might even still be alive.

"You think there's hope then?" Fredi asked.

"If there is, it can't be much. I was hoping I might find something here that would lead me to him....or at least to the people who killed him."

"Here?"

"Yes. Did he leave a notebook or a diary — or even papers from work?"

"From work? Not likely. They didn't even know he came to visit me. I'm still a Communist, you know. Notorious, even at my age. He thought it best we keep our little visits a secret. He used to slip over on the S-Bahn."

"That's how we came."

"Is this a secret visit too?" Fredi asked, a twinkle in her eye.

Ritter laughed.

"Probably best we keep it to ourselves."

Ritter cast a worried glance at the old man.

Fredi saw it and said, "Don't worry about Karl. If he says anything, I'll refuse to play chess with him anymore. It's his only pleasure in life these days."

Fredi laughed at her threat, but the old man didn't seem to find it amusing.

"Oh, lighten up, Karl, " Fredi said after she saw his reaction. "He's just angry because I usually beat him."

"The game is not over," Karl said.

Fredi gave him a tight smile.

"Checkmate in three moves, my dear. Queen to bishop's four. Take a look."

The challenge silenced Karl, and he moved to check the board.

"So who might ask?" Fredi asked.

"I'm not sure."

"Well, not to worry. I've handled some pretty tough customers in my day. Revolutionaries. Nazis. I've been out of the action for some time, especially after things went the way they did during the riots back in '53. But I can still take care of myself."

Fredi took a deep breath, and no one said anything for a while.

"I knew Rosa Luxemburg,…There was a tough nut to crack. They had to kill her. Threw her in the canal. In 1919, I think. I was just a teenager."

Fredi let out a long sigh as the memories flooded back.

"I don't remember everything so well anymore. Except the old stuff."

Ritter hoped Fredi would remember some things he needed to know.

"You said Wolf tried to find me."

"Yes. Inge — your father's mother — told him about you. Not right away, of course." Fredi paused. "Inge loved Wolf, but she was cruel in her way."

"Grandma Helga didn't tell me at all. That call from the State Department was the first I knew. I didn't believe it at first."

"Ach. The war is still punishing people."

"And did you know?"

"About splitting you two up? No. Not till later. I was out of the country organizing things against Hitler when your parents made that decision. I couldn't figure it out. I learned about it from Wolf, who wasn't told till he was in his 30s — and then with no details about where you were. He didn't even know the country you went to as far as I know. At least he never said."

Fredi let out a short laugh.

"I was very angry when I found out about the two of you because your father and I were very close, and he never told me. It's not like he couldn't trust me. We worked together to get some Jews out of the country in '44 and '45."

"Jews?"

"Yes. The Communists were the main resistance, and Rudi called me one day out of the blue. He knew where I was. He was in the *Abwehr*, so that wasn't so surprising. He said there'd be this trainload of prisoners heading to a camp in Poland. He told me the train would be diverted and asked me to have some people ready at the spot."

"And you went along?"

"Yes. He was family. Of course, my comrades were wary. I didn't tell them where I got the information — just that it had come from an anti-Hitler source in German intelligence. Rudi made me swear not to use his name unless absolutely necessary. My colleagues thought it might be a trap, but they decided we couldn't risk letting a trainload of people go to their deaths without seeing if we could rescue them. We were very careful. As it turned out, there was nothing to be afraid of. The train was there. It only had a few guards on it. We dealt with them without any problem. About nine months later, he called again about another train, and we did it again. He took a real chance."

"Did the Nazis ever figure it out?" Ulrike asked.

"I don't think so. I never told anyone Rudi had been the source."

"But you did say it came from German intelligence?"

"Yes, but that shouldn't have been enough. There were plenty of people in the *Abwehr* who hated Hitler, especially at the end. All sorts of plots to kill him."

Ritter tried to put the pieces of his previously unknown past together. But as intent as he was about puzzling out the new information, his detective voice reminded him that the mission at hand was finding Wolf or his killers.

"Fredi," he interrupted, "I was asking whether Wolf might have left anything here, anything that might help us find out if he's dead or who killed him."

"You can look in the guest room. That's where he stayed when he came to visit. He seemed to have meetings over here and needed a base of operations."

"When was the last time he was here?"

"January. Around his birthday. He always came with a cake and we'd have a party. Just the two of us. Wolf and I were the last of the line, so to speak." Fredi slipped her hand out of Ritter's and took his hand in both of hers. "Now maybe it's just you and me."

Ritter stood up to check out the guest room. Fredi held onto him a moment.

"First you have to introduce me to your beautiful girlfriend?"

"This is Ulrike. Ulrike Fischer. Actually, she's Wolf's friend….Mine too now. We're working on this together."

"Did you know Wolf well?" Fredi asked.

"Yes. I met him about a year and half ago."

Fredi nodded her head.

"He did mention he'd met someone after he separated from that awful Heidi."

"He never told you my name?" Ulrike asked.

"No. But that's not unusual for Wolf. Telling me anything about his private life was an aberration. Like a clam that one. You, too, I suspect, Mattheus. You two are peas in a pod, I'll bet."

The guest room was furnished in the same period style as the salon but didn't have much in it. To the left was a single bed with a blue-and-white striped mattress stripped of bedclothes. Against the wall to the right stood a dark wooden dresser with nothing on the top of it. Between the bed and dresser, in front of a white-curtained window, was a simple table with a lamp on it. In front of it, pushed forward, was a hardbacked chair. A small rag rug, a jumble of dull reds, blues and blacks, provided the only adornment on the room's worn, wooden floor.

"Check the dresser drawers," Ritter said, motioning to Ulrike. "Pull them out, look underneath and then inside on the sides and back. Might be something taped in there."

Ulrike began, and Ritter rolled back the mattress to see if anything lay between it and the box spring. Under the bed he found only the motes and hairballs of disuse. A closet in one corner had nothing in it but a few bent wire hangers and two empty cardboard boxes on a shelf above the clothes rack.

"Anything?" Ritter asked, hoping that Ulrike had had better luck.

"Just some newspapers lining the bottoms of the drawers. From years ago."

Ritter turned to Fredi, who was leaning against the doorjamb to the room, watching the hunt.

"And there was nothing else Wolf might have left here?" Ritter asked her. "Something he asked you to keep in your room or somewhere else? An envelope, a small box, a book, maybe a key?"

"Not that I can think of. I forget some things, but I don't think I'd forget that."

Ritter let out a sigh of disappointment.

"Well, it was worth a try."

Ritter went over to his aunt, put his right arm around her and kissed her gently on the head. He looked back at the room for one more check. He was about to give up when he spotted something under the leg of the room's table. It was a piece of paper someone had put under the leg to get rid of a wobble. Ritter tipped the table up and picked up the paper. He unfolded it and found it was part of a piece of stationery that carried the name of the Hotel Adler with an address for Wengen, Berner Oberland. Someone had started a letter by dating it December 25, 1979, then stopped.

Fredi, thinking the search was over, had gone back to the parlor. Karl was at the chessboard, apparently unable to figure out how Fredi was going to beat him in three moves.

"This look familiar?" Ritter asked, handing Fredi the paper.

"Hotel Adler? I don't think so. Where did you get it?"

"Under a table leg in the bedroom. I thought Wolf might have put it there. Is that his handwriting?"

She examined the date on the paper.

"I can't say for sure. We Europeans all make our numbers alike. But that looks like one of Wolf's 'Decembers.'"

Ritter took the sheet and handed it to Ulrike. She examined it, nodded and said: "I think so."

"How about Wengen?"

"It's a ski resort in Switzerland," Ulrike said before Fredi could answer. "An old one. But Wolf didn't ski."

Ritter remembered the album photo of Wolf in ski gear. Another secret?

"He sometimes went to Switzerland just before he came to visit me for his birthday," Fredi said. "I don't know precisely where, but he spent a lot of Christmases there."

Ulrike looked angry.

"He told me those trips were for the ministry." Under her breath, Ritter heard Ulrike say, "Bastard!"

"Did he go there with anyone?" Ritter asked Fredi.

The question snapped Ulrike to attention.

"I don't know," Fredi said. "He never said."

Fredi got pensive for a moment, then added, "Wait a minute, now. Something is coming back, something about that town. I think your mother and father may have gone there on their honeymoon."

"To this hotel?"

"I really don't remember. It's so long ago."

"That's all right. You've been a big help."

Ritter pocketed the paper, gave Fredi a big hug and wished Karl good luck with the game. Ulrike tried to shake Fredi's hand, but got an embrace instead.

"Goodbye. It's a pity you can't stay. Such big things happening these days. "

"The protests, you mean?" Ritter asked.

"Yes. And all the travel. The Iron Curtain is leaking like a sieve. People are going east to get west. All you need is your passport or your identity card. Thousands have left already."

"How about you?" Ritter asked.

"Me? Oh, I'm too old to start over. Besides, I think these thugs in charge today are finished….Who knows? I may even see that damned Wall come down before I die."

After Ritter and Ulrike left, Karl conceded the game and said he was going home.

"Oh, don't take it so hard, Karl. We'll have another match tomorrow."

Karl just nodded and headed out the door. He went down the steps and made an immediate turn into the coffee bar, which had opened. He used the public phone to call an office on Normannenstrasse that never closed. But sometimes its phone lines were busy, which was the case for Karl's first attempt to call. Ten minutes later, after a cup of coffee, he got through to his contact.

"You said to call you if I heard anything about Wolf Springer."

"What do you have?" asked the Stasi officer on the other end of the line.

"His twin brother came to visit Fredi's apartment today. He said Wolf was dead."

After a long pause, the officer said, "There is no indication in Springer's file that he has any kind of a brother, let alone a twin….Is it possible they are on to you and want us to think Wolf is dead? That's already the story we were hearing last week."

"All I can say is that he looked like Wolf….I met him twice."

"How do you know it wasn't Wolf, that this whole thing wasn't a charade?"

"I don't….Look, I'm just passing on what I heard."

"And where are they now?"

"On the S-Bahn back to West Berlin, I would guess."

"Why didn't you call sooner? We could have stopped them on this side."

"I tried earlier, but it was busy."

"All right, all right. We have people on both ends. If we can't get them at Friedrichstrasse, we'll catch up to them over there."

*****

Sunday, November 5, 3:30 p.m. West Berlin

It was mid-afternoon by the time Ritter and Ulrike arrived back at their hotel in West Berlin. Ritter hadn't seen anybody following them but sensed somebody had been there. He mentioned it to Ulrike, who said he was just imagining things. Ritter needed to make some calls. He and Ulrike ordered sandwiches and drinks from room service. While they waited for food, Ritter opened his suitcase and took out Wolf's address book. He tossed it to Ulrike, who was sitting on the bed. He asked her to see if any of the phone numbers in it seemed to be from Berlin.

"Where did you get this?" she asked, examining the book.

"Somebody at the embassy. I think it was in his office."

Ulrike nodded distractedly as she looked through the book.

"You want me to call anyone in here?"

"Only if it's *not* clear who they are."

Ritter rummaged in his bag for the photo albums that Wolf's wife had lent him.

"What should I say when I call?" Ulrike asked.

"Pretend you're Wolf's secretary. Make something up."

Ritter started through the two albums to see if there was anything to link Wolf to the Hotel Adler. Wolf's having been there — if indeed the old piece of hotel stationery showed that he had been — may have meant nothing more than a nostalgic visit to a place that had been important to their parents. But why then hide such a visit from Aunt Fredi and Ulrike? That's what intrigued Ritter. Maybe Wolf had just been his usual secretive self, but maybe there was more to it. It was just another hunch, but Ritter had little else to go on.

In the newer album, Ritter reviewed the photos of Wolf and Heidi on what appeared to be a skiing holiday. In the shots, mounted on a page that had been stuck to another, Wolf was clearly in ski gear. Yet

Ulrike, who'd focused on the older album, had said Wolf didn't like skiing. Why had he lied to her about that? Had he wanted to avoid going skiing with her in case she might ask him to go to Wengen?

If so, why keep Wengen a secret? With no answer forthcoming, Ritter turned back to the older album. As he did, he heard Ulrike begin a call with the story she had concocted. He eavesdropped a moment.

"I'm sorry to bother you," she said. "But I've spilled some coffee all over Herr Springer's personal address book and blurred most of the writing. I'm trying to reconstruct the pages I've ruined. I wonder if you could help me out."

There was a pause as Ulrike listened to the party on the other end, a secretary, Ritter supposed.

"Well, the ink managed to miss most of your boss's last name and your phone number," Ulrike continued. "But the line with his company affiliation is blotted out. I wonder if you could tell me what sort of business he had with Herr Springer. I'm new here at the foreign ministry. Just filling in his till his regular secretary gets back from vacation. I'm going to be in a lot of trouble if I don't get this book straightened out before she returns."

Ritter smiled and went back to paging through the older album. There were wedding pictures of his mother in white. His father wore an immaculate dress uniform. In one picture they were passing under the sword-drawn honor guard of what appeared to be a large entourage of his father's military colleagues. In another, his father, a wry smile on his face, was cutting a five-tiered wedding cake with a saber. Greta, beaming, was at his side. A few pages later, Ritter found what he was looking for. In front of a tall wooden structure, done in the gingerbread style of a turn-of-the-century Swiss mountain hotel, stood his parents. His father was dressed in a tight-fitting Argyle sweater over corduroy knickers and rough walking boots. His mother had on a similar outfit. There was a sign with the name of the hotel at the top of the picture. The upper parts of the letters of the name had been cropped out by whoever took the picture. Ritter filled in the letters with a pen, making the assumption that they said "Hotel Adler." They fit.

Ritter smiled at his handiwork but wasn't sure why he felt so good. What had he proven? Would going to the hotel be just a wild-goose chase? Ritter closed the album and waited for Ulrike to finish her call.

"Anything?" he asked after she'd hung up.

"Not sure. There were only four numbers with Berlin exchanges. One is a midlevel bureaucrat in the West Berlin parliament. He's in charge of liaison with East Berlin. Things like running the S-Bahn or picking up the garbage."

"The garbage?"

Ulrike explained that West Germans paid East Germans to pick up West Berliners' garbage. The East Germans also run the S-Bahn, she said.

"It's all part of the government's plan to keep Berlin together — just in case."

"In case?"

"Reunification."

Ritter had a blank look on his face.

"The reunification of Germany," Ulrike explained in an exasperated tone. "It's part of our constitution. Haven't you been reading the papers lately? That's part of what all these demonstrations in East Germany are about. Not everyone wants it, but a lot do."

Ulrike launched into a mini-lecture on how the garbage and train deals were just one way West Germany maintained links with East Germany in an effort to keep the dream of a reunited Germany alive. There were economic development loans, money for East German highways that led to West Germany and an agreement to pay the pensions of any East Germans who wanted to emigrate west after they retired.

"Sounds expensive," Ritter replied.

"It is. And that's not counting the money we spend on all those émigrés who've come west since Hungary tore down the Iron Curtain in the spring."

"You find anybody else in the address book?" Ritter asked, trying to get back on topic.

"The director of a foreign policy think tank that specializes in East Bloc issues, a restaurant called Fofi's."

"I think I ate there. Then I got mugged."

"And someplace called The German Club."

"Did you call that one?"

"Yes. The guy who answered just said the members were interested in preserving German culture."

"Was there an address?" Ritter asked, getting that hunch feeling again.

"Yes. It's not far from here."

Ritter and Ulrike were on their way to the club by four-fifteen. It was in the Charlottenburg section of West Berlin, not far from the chateau where Frederick I and his queen, Sophie-Charlotte, had once lived. The club building was a tasteful three-story mansion on a deep lot. Most of its neighbors had been converted to commercial use, including two consulates, an insurance company and a law firm.

The club entrance was above street level, approachable by a set of large marble stairs that began about ten feet inside a black, wrought-iron fence topped with pikes. The front door was secured by a buzzer system that required one to be identified before being admitted. A discreet surveillance camera was installed overhead.

Ritter identified himself as "Herr Springer," hoping that whoever was inside would think Wolf had forgotten his key or passcard or whatever members used to get in the door. The buzzer sounded. Ritter grabbed the ornate brass handle and pushed the heavy wooden door open. He let Ulrike go in before him into a large mosaic-tiled foyer with a small reception desk at the side.

"Herr Springer," the desk clerk said. "Did you forget your key?"

"I'm Herr Springer's brother, Mattheus," Ritter said in German. He had decided this was not a place where he could get away with faking that he was his brother. Too many unknowns.

The desk clerk looked perplexed but made a quick call to the manager's office. A few moments later, a prissy man in what looked like a maitre d's uniform appeared.

"Herr Springer?"

He sounded tentative.

"Mattheus Springer."

Ritter extended his hand. He hoped his open manner and his dead-ringer looks would be enough to put the manager at ease.

"May I be of assistance?" asked the manager, who identified himself only as Heysel.

Ritter chose his words carefully.

"I hope so. We're not sure whether to be alarmed or not yet. Oh, excuse me, this is Wolf's fiancée, Fraulein Fischer."

Ulrike shot Ritter an irritated look, but Heysel seemed not to notice and shook her hand, looking no less nervous than before.

"It seems my brother has disappeared. The police have told us it's too soon to worry. Frankly they haven't been much help. We're checking all his acquaintances and friends. We wondered if you might have heard from him recently."

Heysel cleared his throat and said: "I can check the club register, if you like….Everyone who comes here signs in."

"Much appreciated. And I wonder if we could see if my brother might have left anything here at the club. Anything that might help us find out where he might have gone."

"He has a locker here. We have athletic facilities. Perhaps there's something in it. I can check it for you, if you wish."

"Very kind."

Heysel flicked his tongue to the top of his upper lip.

"I have to get the combination of his lock from my office."

Ritter followed him without invitation. Ulrike fell in behind. When Heysel discovered he was leading a parade, he looked surprised but didn't protest.

"Why don't you wait here," he said. "I'm afraid the locker room is off limits to non-members."

Ritter took a seat in a leather chair in front of Heysel's desk. Ulrike remained standing.

After Heysel left, she whispered, "I don't think he wants us looking around."

Ritter smiled.

"That's why we followed him here. Watch the door and tell me when he's coming back."

Ritter got up from the chair and began rummaging through things on the top of Heysel's desk. Nothing intrigued him, and he moved quickly to a tall, black filing cabinet against one of the office's walls. There was a hasp on the top cabinet drawer for a padlock. The lock lay on top of the unit. Ritter opened the top drawer and riffled through the folders, checking the categories indicated on each tab. Halfway down the well-packed drawer he found a file that intrigued him.

Mitgliedschaft. Membership, it said on the tab. Ritter pulled out the manila folder and opened it. Inside was some correspondence about back dues owed by various persons. However, there was no official membership list in the file. Ritter found that strange. At the back of the folder, though, as if someone had tossed it in without thinking, was a small pamphlet. The cover indicated it was about a club-sponsored conference earlier that year. The slim booklet showed which club members had been in charge of what sessions at the meeting, a two-day affair on East-West issues. A list of club officers was included at front of the pamphlet. Ritter kept the booklet in his hand as he closed the folder.

"Someone's coming," Ulrike yelled, rushing to a chair.

Ritter jammed the folder back into what he hoped was its proper place and slipped the booklet into his suit coat. He slammed the file drawer shut just in time to hear someone begin to turn the handle of the office's door. There wasn't enough time to get back to his chair. In one motion, he whirled around and leaned against the filing cabinet, taking what he hoped would seem a relaxed pose: arms folded and ankles crossed one over the other.

Heysel gave him a strange look when he opened the door.

"Find anything?" Ritter asked before Heysel could make any accusations.

Heysel looked at Ritter and then at Ulrike, who looked bored sitting in her chair.

"Not really. There are just some gym clothes and a squash racket in the locker."

"No papers of any kind?"

"Nothing."

"And the register?"

"The last time your brother was here was more than a month ago....I checked myself ."

"Too bad....Well, we appreciate you help, Herr Heysel."

Heysel made a slight bow of the head and said: "Of course."

Ritter and Ulrike left the club and walked back toward the busy road in front of the Schloss Charlottenburg to find a taxi. As they pulled away from the chateau, Ulrike asked what Ritter had swiped from the filing cabinet. He showed her.

"Do you think this club has something to do with Wolf 's death?" she asked.

"I don't know. But maybe somebody on this list does. I'm just treating this like a murder investigation. Following all the leads."

That was true as far as it went, but he knew his hunt was more than about crime solving. If he was being honest, at least a parallel mission had become to figure out who he really was.

Ulrike told the driver to take them back to the hotel, but Ritter said he could use a walk before they returned.

"Walking helps me think," he said.

"We could go through the Tiergarten."

"What's that?"

"It's like a big park. Starts over near the Zoo and goes all the way to the Wall. It's quite nice."

The cab took Ritter and Ulrike down Kaiserdamm. A couple of traffic circles later they found themselves in the middle of the Tiergarten, which sprawls for about two miles from the glitter of the Ku'damm to the gloom of the East.

"What's that?" Ritter said, pointing to a large arched structure ahead of them.

"That's the Brandenburger Tor. The Brandenburg Gate. It used to be the symbol of Berlin. I guess it still is except now it represents two Berlins. It's on the other side of the Wall."

Ritter leaned forward to get a better view through the windshield.

"Why don't we get out here and walk?" Ritter said.

He and Ulrike strolled quietly up June 17th Street, a large thoroughfare that divides the landscaped park. Ritter seemed to be running something through his mind, which had been miles away for most of the cab ride. Ulrike let him think. After they'd left the wide street and cut into a wooded section of the park, Ulrike noticed that Ritter had begun to check out the scenery: the broad walks, the lakes and the flower beds, where efficient landscape crews had already rooted up the last plants of autumn.

"Did you think of anything?" she finally asked.

"Yeah."

Ritter had his hands jammed into his topcoat pockets. Ulrike tried to make eye contact, but Ritter was studying his feet as they walked along a gravel path.

"What?" she asked.

"Wengen."

"What about it?"

"I think we should go there."

Ulrike nodded, breaking into a slight smile. Then she noticed their walk had taken them close to the Berlin Wall.

"How about a quick peek at the Wall first? As long as we're right here."

A few minutes later, Ritter and Ulrike were at the famous barrier, which Ritter found was covered with colorful graffiti in several languages, painted flowers and skeletons and several two-dimensional doors to nowhere. A tall staircase with an observation platform on top had been set up just west of the Wall, so people could see what was on the other side. Vendors were standing on either side of the staircase with souvenirs of Berlin displayed on small tables. One seller, the one farthest from the steps, had fresh fruits and vegetables.

"He's probably from Poland," Ulrike said, pointing to the stand. "They can make a lot of money selling their produce here."

Three U.S. soldiers were on the observation platform. They were the only tourists in sight. Ritter and Ulrike mounted the stairs, crowding in behind the GIs for a look east.

"Pretty grim," Ritter said after they'd looked across the mined "death strip" that divided the outer Wall from the East German guard towers.

"People forget how ugly it is sometimes. A lot of Berliners don't even come here."

Ritter turned and looked back toward the free sights of West Berlin. Something caught his eye to the right. Someone slipping behind a tree.

"What's the fastest way out of here?" he asked.

"Well, if you want a cab we should probably walk over toward the Philharmonic," Ulrike said, pointing left.

"Let's go," Ritter said, taking her hand.

"Are we in a hurry?"

Ritter maintained a calm look on his face and didn't look back.

"I think somebody is following us."

"The embassy people?"

"I hope so. They're less likely to want to kill us."

After Ulrike had picked up her pace, Ritter dropped his hand from her arm. He scanned the path ahead of them, noting that a smaller walkway shot off to the right about fifty yards ahead.

"When we get to next path, turn right," he said. "Keep the same speed we're going now till we're out of sight of this path, then run like hell till I tell you to stop."

They made the turn, then sprinted for about a hundred yards past two more path turnoffs before Ritter yelled, "In here!"

Ritter, panting from the run, ducked down behind some dense hedges and pulled Ulrike down with him. After a moment, they saw two men streak by the long path they'd been on.

"One of them has a gun!" Ulrike whispered.

Ritter put his right index finger to his lips to stop any more whispers. The man with the gun came back to the path that led to where Ritter and Ulrike were hiding. He looked down it, then turned back toward where he'd come from after hearing a shout from his colleague.

Nothing happened after that for several minutes.

"What now?" Ulrike asked.

"We head as fast as we can back to that street we came in on and hope we can find a cab."

They peered around the corner of the path that intersected with the one they were on to make sure their pursuers weren't visible. Coast clear, they hurried back toward June 17th Street. They got lucky and were able to flag down a taxi almost immediately.

"We can't go back to the hotel," Ritter said in the cab. "We have to assume they know where we're staying."

Ritter and Ulrike went over the travel possibilities to Wengen. They rejected the night train as too slow and decided to fly. They told the cab driver to take them to the airport. Before they got there, Ulrike changed the itinerary. She told the driver to drop them at the Zoo subway station and gave the driver an extra 20 marks, telling him to pick them up in a few minutes in front of the Deutsche Oper stop. Ritter looked amused.

"You do this often?"

Ulrike smiled proudly.

"I saw it once in a movie."

Ritter and Ulrike got out at the Zoo station. Ulrike fished six marks out of her purse and bought two subway tickets from an automatic dispensing machine. She and Ritter ran to the platform and just managed to make a train about to pull out from the station. The doors of the last car closed right after they had boarded it. No one was able to get on the train after they had. They got off at the opera stop and took the stairs two at a time, with Ritter puffing more than he would have liked. Traffic was heavy, but Ulrike rushed into the street anyway, followed by the piercing sound of screeching brakes. Ulrike, who had been focusing on locating the taxi, glanced right and realized she'd almost been run down by a bus. The stopped vehicle stalled traffic, and Ritter and Ulrike made a dash for the cab, which had been idling up the street.

"*Flughafen!*" Ulrike shouted.

The driver took off toward Tegel with enough acceleration to pin Ritter and Ulrike to the back seat, but it was clear from the look on the driver's face that he thought he was dealing with a couple of lunatics. Ritter and Ulrike looked at each other and burst out laughing.

At the airport, they bought tickets for the closest place to Wengen they could land, which turned out to be Bern. Ritter used Wolf's passport and bankcard. Most people with an interest in Ritter wouldn't be checking on the movements of a dead man, he figured. And those who might still be tracking Wolf would find no trail from Bern to Wengen — or at least none Ritter planned to leave.

About six, with almost 45 minutes to go before takeoff, Ritter called Chicago. It was just after noon there. He caught Doreen at home. She didn't sound thrilled.

"Malone is very agitated about tomorrow. He's sure it's going to be poison and then everyone will be on him — and now your wife is calling me."

"Anita? What does she want?"

"She's bounced checks all over town. Seems you said you'd put some cash in the checking account but you didn't. She's hoppin' mad."

"Shit!" In his haste to leave town, he'd forgotten. "The money's in my savings account."

"I'll tell her."

"Won't do any good. It's in a police credit-union account….in my name. She can't touch it."

"So what do I tell her?"

"How much does she need to cover the checks?"

"Couple a hundred."

Ritter thought about a solution, but he didn't like it.

"Could you spot me the money till I get back?"

There was a long pause.

"I guess, but when's that going to be?"

"Soon. Getting close now."

"Seems I heard that before."

"Yeah, I know, but things keep happening."

"One other thing with Anita, she wanted to remind you about the marriage counselor tomorrow."

"Crap. Can't make that either. When you give her the money tomorrow, tell her I'll have to take a rain check on that."

"Me? Why don't you call her?"

Ritter looked at his watch and thought about his flight.

"Just call her, would you? And I'll owe you double."

Doreen waited a moment, then said, "I know one way you can pay me back right now."

"Why does that sound bad?"

Doreen laughed.

"I got a plan I've been thinking about, but I need to use your new apartment."

"Not much of a place for a wild party, if that's what you're thinking."

"No. But it's a good place for a trap….And I'll need to issue a press statement in your name that will make our killer want to come after you."

"For what?"

"Belittling him. The FBI serial-killer expert says our guy is on a power trip and making fun of him will drive him nuts."

"I see you've been doing your homework."

"I had a little help from Bernie. I called him like you said."

"OK. Give it a shot. Since I won't be there, I guess I can't object, but you be careful. Don't go in there yourself."

"I won't, except to set up some cameras before we issue the release."

"While you're there, take the phone off the hook. That way he'll have to come over. If nothing else, you can get him on burglary, then you can search his place looking for other stolen goods, and if you find anything on the murder victims, you're off to the races."

Ritter had almost been tempted to say "*we're* off to the races." But he had a race of his own to run and Chicago had faded as the finish line since he'd arrived in Germany. Ritter started to say goodbye, but Doreen stopped him by saying "One other thing."

"What?"

"I was over at the lab this morning to check on those samples you sent, and they don't match. The dead guy at the warehouse was definitely not your brother."

Ritter hung up and went to find Ulrike. He weighed the pros and cons of telling her that the man she had loved might still be alive. All Ritter knew for sure was that the body stolen from the Berlin warehouse hadn't been Wolf's. The body might have been part of some cover-up. Wolf was still missing, and everything pointed to foul play. That was the cop in Ritter speaking. And like the famous TV detective, he was sticking to just the facts. Better to keep his mouth shut till he knew for sure, Ritter decided. Deep down, he knew that was bullshit. If he had the choice, he'd pick the Wolf-dead scenario. It just worked better for Ritter on a lot of fronts.

On the plane, Ritter took the window seat, rather than his usual preference on the aisle. He wanted to see if anyone unusual had an interest in the flight. The plane backed away from the gate, and Ulrike said: "We made it."

"Maybe." Ritter was looking out his window as he spoke.

"Oh, you're such a pessimist. Just like Wolf."

"I hope so, but I'm pretty sure I just saw the face of one of those guys who was chasing us in the park. The one with the gun."

*****

Sunday, November 5, 10:45 p.m., Wengen, Switzerland

It was dark by the time Ritter had rented a car at the Bern airport and got on the road to Wengen. There were no cars allowed in the ski town itself, which sits 4,000 feet above sea level, at the foot of the Jungfrau, one of the most majestic peaks of the Swiss Alps. Ritter left the car in a multi-story parking lot in Lauterbrunnen, a small village in the deep valley that Wengen and other nearby mountaintop aeries overlook. From there he and Ulrike took a cog-railroad journey up the steep slope to the village. Many of the large hotels weren't fully open, but the manager of the Adler, an elderly woman who spoke German with an Italian accent, was sitting behind the front desk when Ulrike and Ritter walked in the front door. She was atop a tall stool doing what appeared to be the books. A large Bernese dog lay on the floor beside her, sound asleep and snoring.

"Herr Springer," she said when she saw Ritter. "How nice to see you again so soon. I didn't realize you were coming."

"A last-minute thing," Ritter said.

"Well, it's a nice time to come. Still not many people in town. Perhaps you can get in some hiking tomorrow? The weather will be good."

"Perhaps. For now, we just want a good night's sleep."

The woman shot a glance at Ulrike, and asked: "Will you be wanting the usual arrangements?"

"Yes."

Ritter wasn't sure what that meant but didn't want to risk any questions.

"No. 10," the old woman said as she handed Ritter a key with a large, iron fob at the end. She didn't ask Ritter to sign in or provide the number of his passport on a registration card.

"No bags?"

"No. We were so tired, we left them in the car down below."

Ritter went toward the hotel's small elevator, hoping that the buttons inside would tell him which floor No. 10 was on. Before he got there, the manager yelled after him that he would have to take the stairs because the elevator was still broken.

"It's getting old, like me."

Ritter, trying to look like a veteran of the hotel, turned slowly and moved toward the broad formal staircase to the side of the front desk. Before he got there, the manager asked: "Will you be going to the bank in the morning?"

"Probably," Ritter said, hoping to hear more.

"I'll get your key then."

The manager went to a small office behind the front desk and came back in a few seconds with a small, stiff blue envelope. Ritter took it, and he and Ulrike went up the stairs, producing creaks from the wood beneath their feet as they did. After some confusion, they managed to discover that No. 10 was one flight up, and down to the left, the corner room on the floor. It was a large chamber with a full-sized brass bed and a distressed leather couch near a set of French doors that opened toward the mountains.

There was a connecting door to a bathroom that had a huge bathtub and a 19th Century-style sink with an antique mirror above it. A deep red Afghan rug covered most of the bedroom floor. Against one wall was a fireplace, stacked with wood.

"Very cozy," Ulrike said. "I wonder what 'the usual arrangements' means."

"Maybe Wolf slept on the couch."

"I doubt it, but that's where I'll sleep."

"No, you take the bed."

"Don't be ridiculous. You're too big for the couch."

Ritter examined the sleeping accommodations and decided Ulrike was right.

"We can ask for a second room if you want," he said. "Say we had a fight or something."

Ulrike shook her head negatively.

"Or that I've begun to snore."

She smiled.

"I would have asked for two rooms, but I didn't want to do anything out of the ordinary."

"Apparently you didn't." Her look turned angrier, then quickly cleared up. "You did the right thing. It's not you I'm angry with."

Ulrike crossed her arms and looked around the room.

"If he weren't dead, I'd probably kill him….I guess I never really knew him."

That makes two of us, Ritter thought as he sat on bed and took the bank key out of its envelope.

"Maybe this will tell us a little more," he said, holding up the key.

"Does it say which bank?"

"No. It just says '42.' But how many could there be in a town this size?"

"It may be the number of a safe-deposit box."

"That'd be my guess."

Ulrike ran her hand over the bed and said, "You know, I'm more hungry than sleepy. You think the manager could get us some food?"

"I think Wolf could get whatever he wanted at this hotel."

The manager came up with some roast chicken, a salad and two bottles of Swiss white wine on ice in a bucket. Ritter and Ulrike avoided the topic of Wolf as they ate. Ritter asked Ulrike why her English was so excellent. She said she'd done two years as a graduate student in Southern California.

"I can do some Valley Girl if you'd like."

"That would be, like, totally awesome."

Ulrike said she liked the free-wheeling life in the States. But she felt there was too much emphasis on consumption and wealth and not enough on social issues. They talked about music. Ulrike said she thought Americans and the Brits seemed to do rock best.

"German is a terrible language for rock and roll," she said. "French isn't much better, but they just won't admit it."

Ritter laughed.

She said she listened to "oldies" when she was relaxing at home: The Temptations, Four Tops, Marvin Gay, Aretha Franklin. Ritter said he was more inclined to listen to Wagner and Puccini.

"It doesn't sound like our tastes are any more compatible than yours and Wolf's were," he said.

"That didn't matter. He listened to mine; I listened to his....Tolerance is a big part of love."

"Plus compromise."

"And trust."

Ritter paused and said: "You don't know anything for sure."

"You don't have to defend him....He wouldn't have done it in your place. Too competitive. Always wanted to be No. 1."

Would he have told you I might not be dead? Ritter asked himself, thinking of his own competitive omission. After the conversation lulled, Ulrike finished off the wine by pouring herself a large glass.

"You're probably wondering how I could love a man like that," she said, glass in hand.

"Well, he was a handsome devil."

They both laughed.

"Love's not a rational thing," she said. "At least not in my vast experience with it….You look at a man, and he appeals or he doesn't. After you get to know him, you decide if there's something that makes it worthwhile to go beyond."

"That how it worked with Wolf?"

Ulrike shrugged.

"I liked Wolf at first because he was strong and handsome. And pretty smart, though not as smart as he thinks he is. Those all made for a good start — and good sex."

"Of all the things I don't know about my brother, my ignorance is unbounded when it comes to his sex life."

"Well, he was very good, in case you wanted to know."

Ulrike got up and wobbled toward the couch from the small table they were using for their dinner.

"Oooh," she said. "I forgot. Don't drink too much at high altitude. Goes right to your head."

She plopped on the couch and said she was just going to close her eyes for a moment. In a few minutes, she was asleep. Ritter took off her shoes and put a pillow under her head and a blanket over her body. He checked the locks on the room windows and closed the curtains, but not before making a careful scan of the illuminated hotel grounds. He locked the room door and decided he should stay alert for a while in case the man with the gun had managed to follow them somehow.

The room had a small bookcase with well-worn novels on it. Thomas Mann and other German writers. Ritter didn't feel like anything that heavy. He pulled out the thin novel he'd swiped from his brother's apartment. The really relevant parts for Ritter don't occur until midway through the book. He got only to page 10 before he dozed off. The next thing he knew, he heard a rooster outside the window. He bolted awake and found he had a stiff neck.

*****

Monday, November 6, 5:45 a.m., Wengen

Ritter cursed softly for having fallen asleep on the job. He hopped out of bed to see if he and Ulrike had any visitors below. He peered through the slit in the front window where the curtains met. The night-time grounds lights had gone out, but there was enough dawn to let him know no one was lurking below. Maybe he'd been wrong, he told himself as he headed for the bathroom. Maybe he'd seen the wrong man at the airport. Maybe their pursuers had only been able to track him and Ulrike to Bern. He said maybe, but he didn't really believe it.

He found a hotel kit with disposable razor, soap, toothpaste and a brush. He showered and shaved. When he finished, Ulrike was still asleep, deep in the arms of Morpheus or maybe it was Dionysus, given the amount of wine she'd drunk. He headed downstairs to see if he could get some coffee and maybe a little breakfast.

A dark-skinned woman was setting out dishes on tables in the breakfast nook. Only three tables were prepared, probably an indication of how many people were in the hotel, Ritter thought. He ordered dry cereal, yogurt, orange juice and coffee, getting back into diet mode. The woman told him in German that it would be ready in a few minutes.

Ritter dawdled over breakfast, reading a German morning paper he found in a bundle in the lobby. There were stories about the East German government's decision to allow travel to the West through Czecho-slovakia. One commentator said the move was the beginning of the end for the troubled Communist regime.

There was no sign of Ulrike by the time Ritter finished. It was still before seven when he went back into the lobby. He decided to take a walk. He told the woman in the dining room to let Ulrike know he'd be back soon.

He found the streets of Wengen deserted. Most of the shops and the only movie theater in town were closed until later in the month, signs in the windows said. The mountain air was cool and bracing on his skin.

It would have been a particularly enjoyable outing, Ritter thought, if he hadn't had to make it in a suit that constituted his only wardrobe or worry about somebody with a gun. The walk did have one benefit. He learned there were only two banks in town. Both opened at nine.

By the time Ritter got back to the hotel, it was eight-thirty. There was still no sign of Ulrike, so he went upstairs. He heard a hair dryer going in the bathroom. He went back downstairs to wait for her. There was a lounge off the lobby with lots of books and magazines. An upright piano, a black Bosendorfer, was against one wall. Ritter walked over to it and uncovered the keyboard. It was early. He decided on a something mellow. He worked through a tune, humming the words to himself in his head. Then another, a long one.

"Very nice," he heard Ulrike say behind him. "I didn't know you could play."

"'Play' may be too strong a term. I had some lessons when I was a kid. Grandma Helga insisted. Quite a few lessons, in fact. She was tough."

Ritter fingered another song. He smiled and asked: "Any hangover?"

She punched him playfully in the shoulder.

"I seem to recall you had some wine."

Ritter played on.

"What's that?' Ulrike asked, sliding next to Ritter on the piano bench. "Sounds familiar."

"I doubt it. It's even older than the Temptations."

Ritter winked at her.

"Very funny, grandpa."

Ritter played some more.

"You should know this. He's German. Left Germany even before I did."

"Hmm. I know I know that tune."

Ritter began the tune and rasped the first words.

"Oh, it's a long, long time...."

"September Song!"

"Yeah. Kurt Weill."

"I thought you were just into opera."

"Well, he wrote the Three Penny Opera, so he sort of fits. Did a lot of Broadway stuff, which isn't my thing, but I like this one."

Ulrike hummed along for a while, then asked, "Are we going to visit the banks?"

"Yes. Did a little exploring. There are only two in town, so we may get lucky."

Ulrike waited a moment.

"Did you put me to bed last night?"

Ritter nodded.

"You fell asleep. For the record, I just took off your shoes and put a blanket over you."

"That it?"

"That was it."

Ulrike smiled.

"In some ways, you are definitely not like your brother."

After Ulrike finished breakfast, she and Ritter tried the banks. The first was a one-story building with a board in the front window that showed the day's quotations of currency rates. Inside there were only two teller's cages, one of which was closed. Ritter moved toward the open one with a hundred-mark bill in hand. He planned to ask for Swiss francs, hoping that someone would recognize him. His back-up plan was to use the exchange operation to scan behind the teller for safe-deposit boxes. The teller didn't recognize him, and there were no boxes in sight.

In the second bank, which was larger, the layout was similar. Ritter thought he was going to strike out there, too, after getting another hundred changed without any sign of recognition. He did manage to notice a door behind the teller's area that might lead to safe-deposit boxes, but it was closed. He had just about decided to push Wolf's key across the counter to see what happened, when from behind him he heard: "Herr Springer! *Guten Morgen!*"

A man in a green loden coat, gray knickers, knee socks and hiking shoes strode over to Ritter after he'd turned around with the Swiss francs in his hand. The man, who had on an alpine hat with a feather in it, stuck out his hand to shake Ritter's. Ritter took it, asking in German how he was — *Wie geht's?*

"You're back in town so soon," the man said.

Suddenly the man was distracted by a rapping sound. It was the bank clerk banging a coin against the bulletproof glass of her teller windows and asking for instructions on some matter. The man excused himself and dealt with the clerk.

"Could be the bank manager," Ulrike whispered.

"That's not the correct procedure," the man said loudly to the clerk. "You know what to do."

"Yes, Herr Snell," the clerk said through the loudspeaker above the window.

Herr Snell returned to Ritter and asked: "Now where were we?"

"You were asking why I'd returned so soon, Herr Snell. I need to get something out of my safe-deposit box."

Ritter held up the key. He figured if Snell looked confused, he could pretend he meant a box at the other bank. Snell wasn't confused. He took Ritter and Ulrike through the closed door behind the tellers' windows. The room was small with only about fifty safe-deposit boxes. Most were tiny, except for some large ones across the bottom row. No. 42 was one of those.

"Please sign the register," Snell said, pointing to a leather-bound book that lay atop a wooden stand on a table in a corner of the room. Ritter did, using the phony signature he'd practiced for Davies. He asked to be left alone after Snell had inserted his key in the double-lock box.

The drawer was about half full. On top was a large ledger with a stack of old photos tied in a faded light blue ribbon. Under the ledger was a layer of new Swiss francs in packets still swathed in bank wrappers. Ritter pulled one out and put it in his inside topcoat pocket. He saw Ulrike staring at him.

"We may need some operating money," he explained. "Besides this may be mine now."

"I wasn't being critical. What's under the money?"

Ritter shoved a few more stacks of bills out of the way and saw there was a thick folder. He pulled it out.

"Paydirt, I would guess," he said, holding up the folder.

"I don't understand."

"I think this is what all the commotion's about," he said. "This is what they wanted to get from Wolf."

"What is it?"

"If we're lucky, some agreement. Something to do with the Russians."

"What's it supposed to say?'

"Don't know. We can take a look back at the hotel. I don't want to stick around here too long in case Herr Snell asks some questions I don't have the answers to."

Ritter gathered up the ledger, the photos and the folder. He picked up another stack of Swiss franc notes just in case. The bank wrapper indicated the packet held five thousand francs — about $2,500, he calculated, remembering the rate posted in the window. Ritter picked up one more packet for good measure.

He turned the key in his lock, hoping Snell wouldn't insist on coming back in the room to do his. He asked Ulrike to put everything but the money in the large purse she had slung over her shoulder. He pocketed the cash. They walked out into the main bank area. Ritter was pleased to see Snell was on the phone. He yelled out *Auf Wiedersehen,* and he and Ulrike beat a hasty retreat out of the building before Snell could protest.

The narrow street in front of the bank was deserted. Ritter and Ulrike saw no one until the lane curved past the train station, which was located about halfway back to the hotel. Sitting on a bench was a man in a ski parka reading a newspaper. He didn't look up as Ritter and Ulrike passed. Ritter took Ulrike's hand and pressed it hard.

"What's the matter?" she asked.

"Look straight ahead. That was one of the guys I saw at the airport."

12

Monday, November 6, 10:30 a.m., Wengen

After they passed him, the man casually got off his bench and trudged up the path behind them. Ritter staged a stop along the way pretending to look at the snow-capped Jungfrau as a ruse to get a view of what was behind them.

"He's following us," he told Ulrike, pointing to the mountain as if commenting on it like a tourist. "The other one is probably guarding the station."

"What do we do?"

"We can't let them get the folder. Without that we'll never find out what happened to Wolf, and our lives probably won't be worth a whole lot either."

"Maybe the hotel manager can help. She might know another way out of here."

When Ritter and Ulrike got back to the hotel, they affected a happy mood. The manager was again behind the desk, atop her stool. They exchanged pleasantries and Ritter opened a gambit he hoped would get him and Ulrike out of town safely.

"I wonder if you could help us. It's really sort of embarrassing."

"Of course. Anything, Herr Springer."

Ritter made up a story that some business people he knew had followed him to Wengen and that he was sure they wanted to buttonhole him about a government matter. He suspected they'd try to pretend to run into him by chance, then bring the matter up. He preferred not to have a confrontation and asked if there was a way to slip out of Wengen without taking the train down.

The manager said there was a trail from the back of the hotel that led to the village at the foot of the mountain. She warned it would be rough going and a little muddy in parts. The descent would take about an hour. The manager slid off the stool and went to a map on a wall in the lobby, showing Ritter where the path began and ended. Ritter paid the bill and apologized for cutting the visit short. With no bags to collect, Ritter and Ulrike went out the back way and found the entrance to the path.

"We're going to look like ridiculous hikers," she said. "You look so out of place in that suit and coat."

They made good time in the initial part of the path, which was only slightly inclined. They muddied their shoes and Ulrike slipped once, getting her right knee dirty when she broke her fall. After a switchback in the trail, Ritter told Ulrike to stop as he peered around the bend to see if they were being followed.

"I wish I'd brought my brother's binoculars."

"I have a knife if that helps."

Ulrike pulled out a black-handled knife from her purse and handed it to Ritter.

"It's a paratrooper knife," she said. "You just flick that lever and it drops down. Put the lever back, and it locks in place. There's also a spike on the other end."

Ritter laughed and tried it out. The blade dropped out of the handle.

"You continue to surprise me. You learn about this in school?"

"No, no. A gift from Wolf. He wanted to be sure I could defend myself."

"I have no idea why he was worried."

Ritter looked at the knife blade, which had a manufacturer's mark on it that read "Fallschirmjäger-Messer."

"They were designed to help you cut parachute cords if you got tangled up," Ulrike said.

Ritter tested the blade with his thumb and winced at the sharpness.

"Wolf said to keep it sharp."

"We call this a gravity knife. If you had this in Chicago, it'd be a crime."

"Well, it's a good thing we're not in Chicago, then."

They started down the path and took stock again of any pursuers when they got to a wooded part. They had to maneuver some more switchbacks. At the end of one, Ritter looked up at where they'd been a few minutes before. He kept staring.

"What?"

"I think I see someone."

Ritter grabbed Ulrike's hand and pulled her along the trail at a faster pace than they'd been going.

"What are we doing?" she finally asked, breaking free.

"Looking for the right spot."

"For what?"

"An ambush."

As the last switchback ended, the path went through a series of boulders. The rocks were big enough to hide a large homicide detective with a knife in his hand. Ritter asked Ulrike to back up a bit to see if she could see him. She couldn't, and he asked her to lie down on the path just past the rock he'd be using. He told her he wanted it to appear she'd been injured. He said his plan was for anyone who came upon Ulrike to have his back to him when the person bent down to see what was the matter with her.

"What if he has a gun," she asked.

"He's not going to shoot you if he thinks you're unconscious."

"Won't he wonder about you?"

"Maybe he'll think I abandoned you and ran, but I hope he won't have time to wonder about that….And I'm going to give him one more distraction other than you. Let me have your purse."

Ulrike slipped the bag strap over her head and handed it to him. He took out the ledger and told her to lie down. He slipped the ledger under her so half of it was visible from the oncoming path.

"I'll keep the purse and the folder with me — just in case."

"In case what!" Ulrike said, looking up from her prone position.

"Don't worry. I'll be right here. And I won't abandon you. Now close your eyes and lie still."

Ritter took his position behind the rock, put Ulrike's purse on the ground, opened her knife and took off his topcoat and jacket. The air was cold and he rubbed his arms to keep warm. As he waited, he noticed a good size rock on the ground. He decided it might make a good weapon too. He switched the knife to his left hand and picked up the rock.

A few moments later he heard the scrape of shoe on rock and got ready. The first thing he saw come into view was a pistol in a man's hand — a 9-mm fitted with a silencer. A man in a green parka stopped at the side of Ulrike's body and knelt down. He switched the gun to his left hand and pulled the book from under her. He put his gun on the ground next to him and began reading the ledger. Ritter threw the rock toward the back of the man's head. It was a glancing blow, but it made him drop the book and put his right hand to his head in pain. Before the man could turn, Ritter pounced on him, pinned him to the ground with his knee in the man's back and the knife against his neck. Ulrike lay still next to him, continuing to play her part.

"Don't think about going for your gun," Ritter said in German. "Or you're going to see a lot of blood."

The man froze where he was.

"Ulrike, grab the gun and point it at him, will you?"

Ulrike got to her feet, dusted off her trench coat and picked up the gun. She gripped it with both hands and took a stance with her legs spread. Ritter told the man to stay put, got up, looked at Ulrike and laughed.

"Where'd you learn to handle a gun like that?"

"The movies. You should go more often. It's very educational."

Ritter smiled and carefully took the gun from her. He told his stunned captive to get on his on his knees and put his hands in his pants pockets.

"Go back up the trail to the first bend and let me know if anyone else is coming. I need to have a little talk with our friend here."

Ritter told the hiker to take off his parka — very carefully. The man did as he was told, revealing an empty shoulder holster under his coat.

"Now turn your pants pockets inside out."

Out came some Swiss and German bills and a few coins. Ritter asked where the man's wallet was.

"Back pocket," the man with one cloudy eye said in German.

Ritter told the man to put his hands back in his pants pockets and walked around behind him, curious to see if he had another weapon stashed in his waistband. He didn't.

Ritter fished a wallet out of his back pocket while holding the muzzle of the pistol to the man's head. Ritter checked the parka's pockets and found car keys, sunglasses. He opened the wallet and found a driver license.

"Rudiger Hahn, " Ritter read aloud. "West Berlin. That your real name?"

"Go to hell!" the man said in English.

"Bilingual. Very impressive."

Ritter noticed Ulrike was coming back down the path.

"Someone coming?" he asked.

"No. I just wanted to see what was going on. Are you going to kill him?"

Ritter laughed at the suggestion.

"As attractive as that idea might seem, this is *not* the movies. Murder is such messy business. Bodies lying around and police asking all kinds of questions. I have a different plan."

Ritter went behind the man again, turned the pistol around in his hand, raised it slantways over his left shoulder and smashed the back of the man's head with the gun's butt. The man collapsed to the ground, and a familiar odor filled the air. Ritter brought the pistol grip to his nose.

"What?" Ulrike asked.

"Gelignite, if I'm not mistaken. I'm pretty sure I've run into Herr Hahn before."

Ritter wiped the pistol on one of Hahn's pants legs and handed it to Ulrike. He dragged Hahn by his feet behind the rock where he'd been hiding. He came back for Hahn's parka, laid it over his body and put on his own suit jacket and coat. He picked up the man's possessions and handed them to Ulrike to put in her purse.

"Without keys or ID, that might slow him and his pals down."

Half an hour later, Ritter and Ulrike emerged from the mountain trail at a clearing that led to the edge of the village where they'd parked their rental car.

"I'm guessing they're watching the car, so we need to get out of here another way."

"How about the train?"

"They may be watching that too."

"Maybe we can surprise them."

Ulrike opened her purse and took out a train schedule.

"Where'd you get that?"

"At the hotel. Thought it might come in handy."

Ulrike studied the timetable and looked at her watch.

"There is a train in seven minutes. We can stay out of sight till the last moment than run like hell and jump aboard."

"What if it doesn't leave on time?"

She smiled.

"This is Switzerland."

With seconds to spare, Ritter and Ulrike sprinted to the train and got on board just before it was set to leave. A stern-looking conductor with a trim moustache moved to the door and locked it behind them. After they were in, a burly man with a pockmarked face suddenly bolted out of the station's waiting room and ran toward the train, catching up to it as it began to pull out. He pulled on the locked door, and the conductor shook his finger at him, pointing to his watch. The man stared right at Ritter and Ulrike and banged a fist on the side of the train, producing an angry look on the face of the conductor, who took out a notebook from his coat and wrote something down.

"He's not going to be too happy with us either when he finds out we don't have a ticket."

The man trotted off toward the parking lot.

"That guy may try to follow the train by car, but I think we'll get there faster."

"He won't get there at all if the guy up on the path had the only car keys."

The conductor came by and gave them a lecture about buying tickets ahead of time because issuing them on board slowed him up on his rounds. They bought tickets for Bern.

"If we don't see any sign of those guys, maybe we should jump off earlier. They probably know we flew to Bern. I don't think we can go back to the airport."

The train pulled into Interlaken. Ulrike checked the schedule for departure time, and they jumped off at the last minute after not seeing any cars pull into the station from the direction of Wengen. They jumped into a taxi and told the driver they wanted to go to the center of Bern. Ritter pulled out a fistful of francs from Wolf's safe deposit box and handed them to the driver.

"It will be worth your while."

In Bern, Ritter had the driver locate an office of the same car-rental agency they'd used at the airport. Ritter pretended to be angry that the Renault they'd rented wouldn't start in at the parking lot in Lauterbrunnen. He demanded a new car and said he'd drop it off in Germany. He slammed the keys of the abandoned rental car on the counter.

"Next time, I'll demand a *German* car," he said.

The clerk looked irritated and said Ritter should have stayed with the car and called a garage.

"I didn't have time for that," he said, switching to English. "I've got to catch a plane back to the United States." He waived his hand dismissively. "If I need to pay a penalty, that's fine. I just need to get going."

The clerk didn't look any happier, but he gave Ritter a BMW. Ritter said he'd drop it off at the Bonn-Cologne airport. Ulrike drove because Ritter said he wanted to see what was in the folder he'd found in Wolf's safe-deposit box. She headed toward Basel, the crossover point to West Germany. From there she took the autobahn toward the capital, driving fast.

"Doesn't anyone drive under a hundred miles an hour over here," he said, recalling his trip to the U.S. embassy with Werner.

"I'm in the slow lane as a favor to you."

A Porsche passed them on the left and was quickly out of sight.

"See," she said.

Ritter went back to the folder, which contained an agreement stamped "draft."

"That's the Black Forest over there," Ulrike said after a few moments.

"Un huh," Ritter said, trying not to lose his train of thought.

Ritter read on for a moment, then looked up at the expanse of black-green forest on the eastern horizon. The car whizzed by a sign for Heidelberg, and Ritter got an idea.

"Get off here, would you?" he asked.

"I thought you wanted to go to Bonn."

"That was just a cover story for the rental agency. There's a guy I want to see in Heidelberg. As long as we're close, we should take advantage. Besides, I want some place where we can hide while I go over this folder and that ledger."

13

Monday, November 6, 4 p.m. Heidelberg

Ulrike wanted to buy some clean clothes, check into a hotel and clean up before visiting the German military expert Ritter had been told about by Becker, the West Berlin policeman. Given the late afternoon hour, he insisted they just go to the professor's office rather than risk missing him.

As it turned out, his office was in his home, a renovated town house on a side street just off Hauptstrasse. A small brass plaque to the side of the house's door said "Military Studies" in German and English.

Becker had told Ritter that Kurt Meier was the best academic source in the world on the German military during the Nazi era. From the wrinkles in his face, Meier appeared to be in his late sixties. But other things made him look younger. His close-cropped hair was a mixture of black and gray. Over icy blue eyes, he wore oversize red frame glasses that would have been appropriate for one of his students. He was in good shape, the boxer in Ritter noticed. He was lean and small of frame, radiating an intense, intelligent energy. He padded around his office in tatty bedroom slippers and had on a loose, navy woolen sweater over shiny pants that appeared to have once belonged to an elegant gray herringbone suit. Albert Einstein could have been his sartorial mentor.

Meier's office, lit by a single, flickering fluorescent overhead light, looked like some great pack rat's nest. Mounds of yellowing papers and dusty folders with curled-up corners were stacked everywhere, including a tottering pile in front of the room's sole window. The only clear space in the entire area was a worktable on which sat, a mint-new computer terminal and keyboard, the only indication Meier was as much a man of the present as the past. Meier, who had invited Ritter and Ulrike in after minimal introductions, apologized that there was no place to sit.

"I got your name from a police officer in West Berlin," Ritter explained.

"Is this a police matter?"

"Not really. More of a personal one. I'm looking for some information on my father. He was in the *Abwehr* during the war."

"Ritter, Ritter," Meier mumbled. "Doesn't ring a bell, but we can check the files….The *Abwehr* you say?"

"Yes. But my father's name was Springer. Rudolf Springer. I think he was a general."

"Ah….Springer!" Meier's eyes lit up. "That sounds more familiar." He became pensive, turning his gaze away from Ritter toward some unfocused spot on the tiled floor as he tried to make the connection. "A bit of a loose end, perhaps." He put his index finger in the air as if he had suddenly come upon a way to solve the puzzle. "Let's see what the computer says."

Meier called up his directory of files, which formed in green luminescent lines on the black background of his monitor. He put the machine's cursor on the command line to ask the computer to search its directory for any files on "Springer." The computer found two Springers. One was "Springer, A." Meier sounded as excited as an archaeologist on the hunt for ancient artifacts.

"Springer, Rudolf. General in the *Abwehr*. He was an aide to the departmental chief of military intelligence."

"Un huh."

Ritter wasn't sure what that meant.

"Your father's boss was anti-Hitler."

"And my father helped this guy?"

After Fredi's stories about his father, Ritter hoped Meier's answer would be the right one.

"Most likely, given his position in the *Abwehr*."

Meier explained there had been layers of opposition to Hitler in the *Abwehr* and other branches of the armed forces. One group merely wanted to keep Germany out of a war. After the conflict had begun and started to go badly, they just wanted to end it and have Germany enjoy what territory it had seized. A more radical group included Hans Oster, the boss of Ritter's father, Meier explained. They grew more vehement in their opposition as they saw what a madman Hitler was. Mostly professional soldiers, they wanted to oust him because he was a threat to the country — and to the military.

"They caught your father's boss," Meier said. "He was hanged in 1945."

"So you think my father might have been in this group that wanted a coup?" Ritter asked.

"Could be, but there was also a third group that wanted to shoot Hitler on sight — the sort of people who tried to kill him in 1944 with that briefcase bomb under the table. The von Stauffenberg group. The famous Valkyrie plot. Your father could have been in this group, but you have to understand, people didn't put these things on paper."

Meier told Ritter that the Allies had grabbed most of the files from the Nazi era right after VE day. He'd managed to get hold of his share, he said, flashing a proud smile. He noted that most of the originals of Nazi documents were in Washington and Berlin, but there were copies of many things. Through friends and associates from East and West, he said, he'd collected thousands of documents. Over the years, he'd also talked to many of the people who'd written the documents.

"The Allies couldn't lock them up with the files," he said. "Most of them are dead now, of course, but I have their statements right here."

Meier patted the computer monitor as if it were a loyal dog.

"One hundred megabytes of storage on hard disc and as much as I want on floppies," he said, picking up a small blue plastic square with a brushed aluminum center and clamp on it. "Research isn't what it used to be."

"What does the computer tell you about my father?'

Meier continued scrolling the text under Ritter's father's entry.

"Oh, yes, I remember now. I entered this one a long time ago — when I had my very first computer. A primitive thing, a little 64K job." He shook his head at the memory. "I don't know how I got along."

Ritter was getting impatient with Meier's long explanations and was about to ask him to get to the point when Meier leaned closer to the screen, scrutinized some details of the entry, then nodded his head.

"He committed suicide," he said matter-of-factly, as if recalling some famous date in history.

Ritter took in the words but said nothing.

"The story is that your father committed suicide while in the hands of the Gestapo. In 1945."

Ritter scanned his memory of the conversation with Aunt Fredi. She'd said his father had been arrested and had died in custody. She hadn't said how he'd died, Ritter suddenly realized. He'd assumed that she meant his father had been executed. Was his suicide one of those things she couldn't remember — or hadn't she known? Or hadn't she wanted Ritter to know? Was suicide the Gestapo's way of saying he'd died in their custody? He was surprised at the rage he felt over something that had happened nearly half a century before.

"No, I think he actually had a motive for taking his own life."

"What?":

"To protect someone."

Meier explained that Ritter's father had been working in a spy network with links to the Allies and that the Gestapo had managed by the end of the war to arrest most of its members. But in 1945, there was a young courier they were still looking for, he said. The courier was taking sensitive network messages out of the country to the Allies. People like Ritter's father, he explained, had wanted to slow Hitler down — and later to stop him altogether — so they leaked information on what Hitler was up to: troop movements, invasion plans, shortages of petroleum supplies, counterattack ideas. The Gestapo desperately wanted to shut that information outflow down, Meier explained. Hitler was frantic to complete development of his superweapons: his new V-series rockets, his heavy-armor tank, maybe even the A-bomb, Meier said.

"He thought they would change the course of the war, and he might have been right," he said. "But he never got the chance to find out. From what I've been able to discover, your father wouldn't tell the Gestapo who the courier was, and the damaging information kept getting out."

"I still don't see why he'd kill himself? Why not just refuse to talk?"

"You know the old joke." Meier laughed in anticipation of what he was going to say. "They had their ways of making you talk….Your father may have been worried they might make him tell. Torture or threaten members of his family. A lot of this is speculation, of course. But it's as good as anything you'll get."

"Anything else?"

"There is some data to suggest he helped some Jews escape concentration camps in '44 and '45. Nothing confirmed."

"Un huh." Ritter remembered Aunt Fredi's story. "What do you have on his working for American intelligence?"

"Maybe it was just *with* not *for*. His did communicate with the OSS, although my information is that he was initially an asset of MI6. They probably turned him over to the OSS as an asset. The British never did like walk-ins. Still don't. But the Americans didn't seem to mind. They were the new boys on the block in the espionage business and didn't have many agents of their own. They took whatever they could get."

"Do you know what my father did for them?"

"No, the Americans are not among my best sources."

Meier chuckled at his understatement.

"What about that courier he was trying to protect?'

"That's the loose end I was talking about. We never found out who the man was. He'd be about 70 if he were still alive. The only thing I've heard about him is that his codename was 'Patriot.' If that's true, he must have been a real agent — working *for* not just with — at least at some point."

Ritter thanked Meier for his help and left the professor's office looking tired. He and Ulrike strolled silently down Hauptstrasse. Eventually she asked what he was thinking. Ritter sighed and said he was wondering why the CIA kept his father's wartime file sealed.

"What could be so important after all this time?" he asked.

"How do you know it's sealed?"

"A friend."

"OK. Then it would have to be something he did that affects the present."

"That's what I was thinking."

"Like hiding some terrible thing the OSS did. Some atrocity."

Or shielding the identity of someone who's still alive and doesn't want it known he worked for the OSS, Ritter thought. Somebody important.

Ritter and Ulrike strolled into the Marktplatz, the main square of the old town. Closing time was near, so they darted into a clothing store and bought some shirts, sweaters, washable slacks and some walking shoes. With purchases in hand they went up a street looking for a hotel for the night. Ritter grinned broadly when he saw a sign that read: "*Hotel zum Ritter.*"

"Look at that," he said. He craned his head back to look at the building's Renaissance architecture.

"It's famous," Ulrike said. "In all the guide books. It's about 400 years old." "I don't see how we could stay any place else."

At the reception desk, he asked for two rooms and filled out a guest card. Wolf Springer still seemed the better name to use. If he checked in as Herr Ritter it would be too memorable an experience for the clerk. Besides, more people seemed to be looking for him at that point than his brother. The clerk asked him for a credit card to cover the mini-bar. He still only had Wolf's bankcard, so he offered to leave a cash deposit, changing Wolf's crisp Swiss francs for marks. The clerk looked at Ulrike and raised an eyebrow but took the money.

"The bellman will take your luggage up," he said, handing over two keys.

"We just have these," Ritter said, pointing to the shopping bags from the clothing store.

The clerk gave Ritter a look, then finally said, "Of course."

Ritter and Ulrike walked toward the elevator. She leaned her head toward him and whispered: "He thinks we're going to fool around."

Ritter's room had a king-size bed and a view of the old cathedral. They put down their packages. Ritter sat on the bed, and pulled out the folder with the draft agreement. He gave the ledger to Ulrike, who sat in a wing chair.

She noticed a complimentary bottle of German white wine on the room desk. She opened it with a plastic corkscrew that sat next to some crackers and white cheese. She poured herself a full glass and one for Ritter too. Ritter took it, but put it on an end table as he read. After a while, he stretched out, leaving the glass untouched as Ulrike emptied and refilled hers. A packet of photos lay at his side. From time to time, he asked Ulrike to translate a word, but mostly they worked in silence. Ritter occasionally glanced up at Ulrike and found himself thinking how natural their being together had become. She looked up once in a while too, taking a sip from her glass, and he wondered what was on her mind. He knew what was on his, and it wasn't a folder.

He finished reading the draft agreement. He wasn't sure what to make of it. Lots of words about Germany helping the Soviets with economic and technical aid. There didn't seem to be much quid pro quo for West Germany other than they'd get a big new market if the Soviets used the aid wisely and needed German exports. He went through the rest of the folder, which included a record of day-to-day operations — trips and reports with code names for people. It didn't make much sense to him other than his brother or someone seemed to have been running agents — for what purpose he wasn't exactly sure.

He tossed the folder on the bed and saw that Ulrike was done with the ledger. She was staring at him. When she saw he was finished, too, she walked over to the bed and they exchanged items. File in hand, she stood for a moment at the side of the bed, looking right at him, then went back to her chair.

Ritter leaned over and picked up the photos. He undid the ribbon and splayed the pictures across the bed. There were shots of his mother and father in the pack, including several individual ones from when they'd been students, long before they'd met and gotten married. There were several of his father in uniform. One showed him with his arm around a young officer in his mid-20s. The young man had the same shoulder patches on his uniform as Ritter's father. Ritter turned the photo over. On the back it said:

"Gen. Ritter and Lt. Biermann, 1944."

Ulrike got engrossed in the draft agreement, reading it much faster than Ritter had. From time to time, she spoke aloud, more to herself than to Ritter.

"Unbelievable," she said at one point after she flicked a page of the document.

Ritter found the ledger slow going. The front of it consisted of lined pages of numerical entries; he thought they might be payments of some sort. With pen and a scratch pad, he struggled to make sense of them. He finally gave up and flipped to the back of the canvas-backed book. Toward the end, the pages were blank, but the back flyleaf had some letters with numbers inscribed after them.

"What do you make of this stuff at the back?" he asked.

"Huh?" said Ulrike, still immersed in the draft accord.

"The numbers at the back of the ledger. Make any sense to you?"

"I think so…Just a second."

Ulrike finished the last page of the draft memo, then put it on her lap.

She took a deep breath, then said, "Phone numbers would be my guess….The numbers in parenthesis look like German area codes."

"And the letters are people's initials?"

She nodded.

"Must be Wolf's agents. That sneak was a spy."

"But for whom? I guess we have more phoning to do."

"Phoning? Who cares about who the agents are if this agreement is anything other than some fantasy dreamed up by Wolf. It's the answer to the perennial 'German question,' as the diplomats call it. Whither Germany and with whom?"

"Yeah. Looks like West Germany turns the Soviet Union into a high-tech wonder and gets East Germany in return."

Ulrike let out a harsh laugh.

"Well, that's one thing that would happen if this becomes official. But if I were sitting in Washington or Brussels, that'd be the least of my worries."

"I don't follow you."

"This arrangement would change the face of Europe. The face of the world really. This deal could lead to German reunification. Moscow has played the German card!"

"You mean like Nixon played the China card?"

"More than that. This says Germany becomes neutral, which means it's out of NATO, which is what has kept the West together — maybe even out of the European Community."

"Why would we need NATO? Wouldn't this deal end the Cold War?"

"Yes. If you could trust the Soviets not to use a neutral Germany to rearm and regroup as its economy grew."

"Gorbachev sounds peaceful enough."

"Gorbachev's in trouble. He may get tossed out by hardliners after he signs this, assuming he hasn't signed it already."

"You think the Germans would abandon their Allies after all this time?"

"Germany and Russia have a track record for going it alone. Remember the Stalin-Hitler pact?"

"Yeah. Rick Davies reminded me recently, but I still don't see the big deal. There'd be a lot of NATO countries left."

Ulrike gave him a disappointed look and laid out what a neutral Germany would mean: West Germany has the biggest and best armed forces of any NATO member. It's the front line of any new war in Europe, and it's where NATO keeps most of its nuclear weapons.

"The new front would be the Rhine, not the Elbe," she said. "France basically. And every NATO member, fearing the worst, would cut its own deal with Moscow. The U.S. would be on its own."

"Still seems a peace plan to me."

"Maybe. But for many, a united Germany just brings up the prospects of very bad things."

"Bad things?"

"Like World War I and World War II....On the other hand, the deal makes perfect sense for Gorbachev. He's in so much political trouble, so why not give up East Germany for West German economic help?"

"I guess that makes sense."

"If everything goes right, Germany helps the Soviet Union become an economic superpower. And we get 16 million East Germans, mostly young. There'd be eighty million Germans!"

"Give you a heck of an Olympic team."

Ulrike laughed.

"You know the beauty of this? The Allies have always said officially that they back reunification, so they'll have to back it publicly."

"If this deal is as bad as you say for the U.S," he said, "I don't see why our guys would let it happen."

"Maybe they don't know."

Ritter suddenly remembered Davies's remark: "The damned Krauts are up to something."

"And they may never know," Ulrike said. "This may be like a gentlemen's agreement. No signature but everyone follows the rules. No public announcement."

"I don't follow you."

" Remember Moscow didn't say a thing when Hungary tore down the Iron Curtain last May, even though it was obvious it would make East German escapes easier. And they haven't done a damn thing to stop all the East German protests in the streets."

Ulrike thought of another angle. "I wonder if this is our foreign minister's idea. He was born in the east and fled west. He's a Saxon — and pro-Soviet."

"So the government would follow his lead?"

"Well, the chancellor isn't pro-Soviet, but he needs the foreign minister's party to maintain the ruling coalition. And to be the first chancellor of a united Germany, that might have a lot of appeal, so he might not need too much persuasion."

Ulrike's analysis finally clicked for Ritter.

"What time is it?"

"Six- thirty."

Ritter scrambled to his feet.

"How late you figure the courier services are open?"

"Seven maybe."

"Be right back. See if you can find one open."

Ritter grabbed all the materials from the safe-deposit box and used a machine at the hotel's business center to make copies. He bought some large manila envelopes and stamps from the concierge. He was back in the room within half an hour.

"Any luck?" he asked.

"No. They all closed at six. We're very conservative about store hours here in Germany. People who work want to go home."

"Well, at least I can mail a couple of the copies. I'll save the courier one for tomorrow as the backup. I saw a mailbox in the lobby." Ritter looked at the case file and the ledger. "Maybe the hotel has a lock box. I don't want to leave this stuff in the room tonight."

"If those guys in Wengen know we've got this memo, they'll probably do anything to get it."

Ulrike dialed the front desk as Ritter scratched out a note to Doreen back in Chicago. He explained which newspapers and TV networks he wanted her to contact and what to tell them in case he didn't show up by the end of the month. Ritter wrote a similar note to Captain Malone and another to his lawyer, the one he'd consulted about the separation with Anita. On the latter two envelopes he wrote: "Open only in case of death." To the lawyer, he also included a one-page, handwritten will, leaving his car and savings account — the only things he and Barbara didn't own jointly — to his wife.

Ritter noticed Ulrike was watching him as he finished the will.

"You're taking this seriously, I see," she said.

Ritter shrugged.

"Hope for the best, plan for the rest."

"Very German."

"I guess....What did the clerk say?"

"They have a safe-deposit boxes, but he wondered why I was calling from your room.

Ritter flashed a smile.

"Maybe his suspicions were right."

Ritter gulped the wine left in his glass and went down to the lobby. He signed a form for a safe-deposit box. He gave one of the photocopy envelopes to the clerk, plus the original folder, the photos and the ledger. He put the other two envelopes in the lobby mailbox. Then he bounded up the stairs to his room.

"You hungry?" he asked Ulrike after he got back.

"Why don't we eat up here? I mean, as long as my reputation is ruined."

Ritter looked at Ulrike. He'd been putting the moment off for some time, for a variety of reasons. In Wengen, Ulrike had fallen asleep, then men had been chasing them, then there was the folder and other things to decipher. Even if there hadn't been obstacles, he'd been telling himself he should restrain what he'd felt since he'd first seen her in her doorway and wound up in her arms.

He'd been fighting some vague sense of responsibility to his dead brother not to fool around so quickly with the woman he'd loved. But all those excuses and noble thoughts suddenly got pushed aside as Ritter looked at Ulrike in the privacy of the hotel room. Their adventure had brought them closer. He wondered how close.

"That's logical," he said after waiting a few beats. He picked up the phone to order room service. Ulrike grabbed the receiver and put it back in the cradle. She began unbuttoning her blouse with her eyes on Ritter. He took off his sweater, and they both headed for the bed. Pulses raced. Lips met lips. In all the frenzy, no one bothered to turn out the lights. Dinner never was ordered.

*****

That same evening, a young aide to the East German Politburo named Detlev, whose family had dropped the noble "von" before its surname after joining the revolution, met with an elderly man named Gad, a Jew who'd managed to stay the entire war in Berlin thanks to a boyfriend with diplomatic connections. His job in the postwar Germanies was *Zeitzeuge*, an official storyteller. He told people about his life as a resistance fighter and the lives of others now dead to make sure people never forgot what the Nazis did. Given the claim of East Germans to have been the ones to vanquish Hitler and fascism, the old man was able to tell his stories on either side of the wall that divided the city he had so long called home. That made him a useful messenger for things that could not be safely transmitted over the phone, like the information Detlev wanted to send that night.

"The Politburo will say it's no longer a crime to flee to the West."

"What does that mean?" the old man asked.

"It means they are scared. Eight members of the Politburo have been ousted in the last month. The rest want to survive."

"So travel will be unregulated?"

"No. They're not *that* scared yet. People will have to apply for a passport at police headquarters, and they can only travel for 30 days."

"So what do I tell them on the other side?"

"Tell them to talk to the Soviets. Create more fear, and the Politburo will give in."

*****

Unaware of Detlev's message because it relied on a safe but very old fashioned method of transmission, the fat man who didn't like to be called Algernon reviewed an encrypted cable that was a response to a query he'd made earlier. He furrowed his brow as he took in the meaning and picked up a telephone to make a call to Munich. The executive took the call on a private line after saying no more than "Biermann." Usually he got a call from the U.S. embassy about defense procurement or short-range nuclear missiles or other military matters, but that day it was a more worrisome message.

"Someone has been checking out Rudolph Springer's file in Washington, Ernst."

There was a long pause in the conversation.

"I thought it was sealed, Gerry."

"It is, but there's an indication someone looked him up by name."

"Was the file looked at?"

"Not sure. It was someone from another agency who inquired, so we can't just come out and ask, but I figured I should warn you since your name is in it."

"Code name or real name?"

"Both."

"And do we know who inquired?"

"An FBI agent asked for the search, and some friends who listen to calls from that little fort over in Maryland say that agent took a call from Springer's son, Matt."

"Ah, yes, the twin. So what's he up to?"

"Looking for you, if we don't watch out."

14

Tuesday, November 7, 7:00 a.m., Heidelberg

One theory is that dreams are just random thoughts the brain tries to put into some sensible order while you're in deep sleep, even if the thoughts have no real connection. The thoughts themselves aren't so important, the experts say. It's how your brain puts them together that may tell you something.

Ritter had dreamed that fall night of many things. There were no trains going into tunnels or garden hoses not long enough to reach among the images that jammed his head. There were X-rated flashes of lovemaking and later faces of his father and brother. Even Rick Davies popped into view as if part of some bizarre strobe-light show. If there was some order or message to the images, Ritter's estimable brain did not discern it, any more than it had been able to make much out of the garbled clues about his brother that he'd tripped over in the previous week. What connections he did make evaporated a few moments after he awoke and found Ulrike nestled sleepily against him.

A line from Poe drifted through his groggy mind, the one that goes, "All that we see or seem is but a dream within a dream." But even that slipped away when Ulrike woke as he tried to slip quietly out of bed. They showered together and made love wet against the tiled wall. After the unexpected outburst of energy, Ritter found he had a ravenous appetite, and his new diet went out the window as he piled up his plate in the hotel dining room with cold cuts, dark bread, yogurt, cheese and other calorific delights of the breakfast buffet.

Ritter had just finished his fifth decade of life. Ulrike was barely into her fourth. After the events of the day before, they ate the meal in a pleasant mood, showing no signs of being moon-struck lovers. Like tourists on holiday, they lingered over their newspapers, which reported on more East German protests and another horde of émigrés going west.

"A new poll says the chancellor's coalition is only a few points ahead of the Social Democrats," Ulrike said, as the waiter poured her a second cup of coffee. "I wonder what a new accord with the Soviets would do to the numbers."

"Assuming they plan to announce it."

"Right. But they could announce something that would help him."

"Speaking of the agreement, I need to send that last envelope by courier." Ritter got up and handed Ulrike some cash.

"Pay for breakfast and anything else we owe. OK?"

Ritter retrieved the material from the lock box. He changed more Swiss francs so he could pay the messenger bill in cash. At the courier office, he filled in the "Sender" line of the bill-of-lading with just "Matthew" just in case someone might be checking whether he was sending packages or letters out of the country.

By 10:00 a.m., Ritter was ready to hit the road. With their dirty clothes in shopping bags, he and Ulrike retrieved the car, and she again drove. By ten-thirty, they were on the autobahn, headed for Bonn.

"I need to talk to a guy at the embassy," Ritter said as they passed the turnoff sign for Mannheim. "Probably better if you don't come along."

"Shall I wait for you at my apartment?"

"No. Might be somebody waiting for you."

"Those men from Wengen?"

"Among others."

Ritter pulled out the pistol he'd taken from Rudiger Hahn. He popped the magazine and saw it was half empty.

"Rudiger — or whatever his name was — must have been a busy boy before he met us." Ritter paused then asked: "Know anybody with access to 9-mm ammo?"

Ulrike paused, then said: "I've interviewed some people with armed radical groups."

"See what you can do while I get my little errand done."

A few hours later, Ulrike swung the car off the autobahn at the Bad Godesberg exit. She drove to a nondescript apartment building and got out. Ritter slid into the driver's seat and said he'd be back quickly. Ulrike looked at the familiar edifice. She mounted the stairs to the second floor and headed to a flat in the rear, where a fire escape provided a quick exit point if needed. She mashed the doorbell of 2C, which had no name of the occupant indicated. A woman about Ulrike's age, dressed in jeans and a gray sweatshirt, opened the door after peering through the peephole. She looked at Ulrike a long time.

"So did you come to your senses?" the woman asked.

"I came to my senses when I left."

The woman laughed and said, "I guess we have to agree to disagree."

"That should work, but I do need a favor."

The woman examined Ulrike a moment, then said, "Well, come in. We'll see what we can do."

Ulrike walked warily into the apartment, which was sparsely furnished with futons and boards set on top of cinder blocks.

"Still early hippie, I see," Ulrike said.

"We have simple needs."

"And still ambitious goals, I presume."

The woman stared at Ulrike.

"We know what we want. How about you?"

"I want a place to stay for a few hours. And a box of 9-mm ammunition."

The woman laughed.

"Are you back in the game?"

Ulrike shook her head.

"A different game. Can you help?"

"Not me, but I can call Markus. You willing to ask him?"

Ulrike paused, then said, "Yes."

"Must be pretty important then."

The woman made a call, and a man who called himself Markus showed up a few minutes later. He took off his coat and tossed it on the floor. He walked up to Ulrike and tenderly ran his fingers through the left side of her hair. She stared at him but kept her arms at her side.

"You've been missed," he said.

Ulrike waited a moment, then said, "It was time to move on….I was no good to you any more."

Markus, who was lean and about five inches taller than Ulrike, smiled.

"Maybe not to the group, but I wouldn't have minded if you'd stayed." He took a deep breath and kept his eyes fixed on hers.

"That was just sex."

Markus shrugged.

"Not the worst thing in the world."

"I've got a little more than that now."

"You mean your friend at the foreign ministry?"

"Not exactly." Ulrike thought for a minute and added, "Sort of the same, but something a little better, I think."

Markus showed a tight smile.

"Silly me. And here I thought I had all you needed."

"You do. It's 9 millimeters wide and comes in a little box."

*****

Tuesday, November 7, 1:00 p.m., Bonn

While Ulrike was renewing old acquaintances, Ritter parked the car a few blocks away from the place he'd left her and called Rick Davies from a street phone.

"Got something for you," he said after he'd gotten Davies on the line. "Wonder if we can meet somewhere."

"What do you have?"

"I think you know, and I don't think you want this discussed on the phone….And I want something in return. How about we meet at that hotel you put me up at. Maybe in the restaurant. I could use some food."

Ritter figured Davies would be leery of meeting him anywhere after their last encounter, and he hoped the hotel, which was likely under some sort of control by the embassy, would be a comfort zone for him.

Davies paused, then said: "All right."

Ritter guessed Davies wouldn't be coming alone, and he had a plan to deal with that. He raced over to the hotel so he could park his car on the street, out of sight. He didn't want Davies or his watchers to know what kind of vehicle he was driving in case he had to leave in a hurry, which was exactly what he expected to have to do.

Ritter was already in the hotel dining room when Davies arrived. He'd chosen a table in the far corner, close to the men's room. It took Davies a while to see him after he'd entered the room. Ritter rose from his chair to wave Davies over. He smiled broadly at Davies as if they were about to have some friendly business meeting. They shook hands. Ritter was nursing a glass of wine and had the remnants of lunch on his plate.

"I told the waiter we'd be taking the buffet. I figured we didn't want to be disturbed by a waiter."

"Good idea….Did you get what we were looking for?"

"Yeah. There's a draft agreement and more. I read the agreement, but maybe you'd better pull your chair in a little closer and lean in. I wouldn't want to talk too loudly about it. Dynamite stuff."

Davies pulled a face as if he thought Ritter's precaution was unnecessary, but he did as asked. After he had, he felt a hard tube against his testicles and noticed Ritter's right forearm was under the table.

"That's a 9-mm barrel with a silencer on it. If you don't want your balls splattered against the back of your chair, I suggest you give me a few answers."

"You're crazy! Davies said in a whispered yell. "You can't shoot somebody in a place like this."

"I'm worse than crazy. I'm a grieving brother who had an accident showing you a pistol some bad guys waived at him while he was on a mission for you — a mission you probably don't want to talk about to the police."

Davies seethed for a moment, then asked: "What the hell do you want?"

"Like the last time: some answers. And the truth, if it wouldn't be too much."

"What are you talking about?"

"For starters, my brother tried to find me and my mother at least twice. Came to the U.S. embassy for help. You guys knew she'd changed our name to Ritter. But you didn't tell him. Why?"

Davies licked his lips nervously with the tip of his tongue.

"That was long before I was ever stationed in Bonn, I can't be held responsible for what my predecessors did."

"But you never told him after you got here, and I think I know why."

Davies took a deep breath but didn't offer a defense.

"Because if he started poking into the past, he might have wanted to look at my father's OSS file. And you — or someone — wanted to keep that sealed. Probably because there's something in it you don't want Wolf or anybody else to know."

"Like what?" Davies said, sounding dismissive.

"Like the name of somebody who doesn't want it known that he worked for American intelligence. The name of one of my father's couriers."

Davies bit his bottom lip but said nothing.

"Does the name 'Patriot' mean anything to you?" Ritter asked.

The muscles in Davies' neck and face tensed.

"I don't know who you've been talking to. But you and your pals are in a lot of trouble."

"At least I'm not the one with a gun pointed at his balls."

Ritter took a quick glance around the dining room to see if he could spot any of Davies's bodyguards. He didn't see any and decided he didn't want to wait until someone showed up. He'd had his say and confirmed, as much as he could, what he had already suspected.

"Get up slowly," he said. "Keep your hands at your sides. Look normal. You're going to be on the outside facing the dining room. I'm staying on the inside. Me and the gun."

"Where are we going?"

"To the men's room."

"Why?"

"Maybe I gotta take a leak."

Ritter kept a calm pose as he marched Davies into the restroom. He'd been keeping an eye on it and hadn't seen anyone go in in a while. He hoped it would be empty, and it was. It was a small room with only three stalls and two urinals. It had no lock on the entrance door. But, as Ritter had learned on a brief reconnoiter before Davies had arrived, there was an attendant's chair to the side of the door, perhaps for formal dinners.

Ritter jammed the chair under the doorknob. He shoved Davies toward the farthest stall and pushed him inside. He made Davies stand with his back to the stall door.

"Look, if you must know, I was going to tell your brother about you and your mother. I figured I owed him at least that. He'd done good work for me."

"What happened? You forget?"

"No! Just about the time I was going to tell him, I started getting some disturbing information that he was working for the other side."

"Which side would that be?"

"The East Germans or maybe the Soviets. They're the ones in charge over there."

"You've lied so much, you've forgotten what bullshit stories you told me in the past. Last one was that the KGB killed him. So why would they kill their own guy — if he was their guy?"

"I said it was probably the KGB."

"Oh, excuse me. Big difference."

"We think they may have decided he was a phony double agent — working for us while pretending to work for them. That wasn't the case, but they may have thought so."

Ritter sighed after hearing the explanation.

"Rick, there is not much you could tell me anymore that I'd believe, so I'm just going to file that one under '*complete* bullshit.'"

Ritter punched Davies in the lower back. Third time's the charm, he thought. Davies crumpled in the stall and Ritter manhandled him to his feet. Ritter grabbed him under the left armpit, spun him around like a toy doll and planted him on the toilet.

"What are you going to do?" Davies asked, his voice creaking with pain.

"I was going to hit you over the head and knock you out. I need a little time to get away without any of your pals tailing me. But I got a better idea….Take off your pants."

"What?"

"Jockeys too."

Ritter got Davies down to his socks and shoes.

Ritter told him to close the stall door and lock it.

"I'll leave these for you right outside," Ritter said, wadding up the clothing in his left hand. "If I were you, I'd wait to be rescued. There are a lot of nice German ladies out in that dining room. They might not appreciate seeing you in all your glory."

"You are *sick*, Ritter."

Ritter smiled at Davies's discomfort and moved quickly to upend a tall waste can in a corner of the restroom. He put the can under a window on the outside wall of the hotel. He stood on it, undid the window latch, opened the window, threw Davies' clothes outside and heaved his bulky frame through the opening.

Four and a half minutes later, two men with drawn guns barged into the restroom, splintering the propped-up chair in the process. By then Ritter was a couple of kilometers away, hurrying to pick up Ulrike. Ritter figured that by the time Davies organized a search for them, he and Ulrike would be out of town. He didn't have a plan yet, but if Davies's men did manage to catch them, Ritter knew he needed one to be sure they didn't get the folder, the photos and the ledger. Those documents were his only leverage. Davies would likely want to make the deal public to scuttle it or figure some other way to kill it.

Everyone else who was after him likely wanted to keep it and all his copies secret. Even if Davies was the victor, Ritter had one consolation. He'd lied to him about leaving his clothes, which sat in a pile on the seat next to him.

*****

Ritter picked up Ulrike where he'd left her and let her drive.

"Where are we going?" Ulrike asked as she sped away from her friend's house.

"Don't know exactly. Depends on what sense we can make out of those initials and numbers in the back of the ledger." Ritter looked over at Ulrike. "By the way, did you get any ammo?"

"Glove compartment,"

Ritter took out a small, heavy package wrapped in brown paper, opened it and got Rudiger Hahn's pistol out of his topcoat. He filled up the pistol's half-empty magazine.

He checked the safety and put the gun back.

"You have to fund any terrorist groups to get these?" he said, putting the ammo box back in the glove compartment.

Ulrike shook her head.

"Just had to be nice to an old boyfriend."

Ritter's eyes widened, but he didn't press for details. He went back to the ledger and the numbers at the back. Ulrike noticed what he was studying and asked: "Shouldn't we make some calls before we go driving off to nowhere?"

"The best thing right now is to get away from Bonn. And ditch the rental car."

They dropped the car at the Bonn airport and took a shuttle bus to the terminal. They immediately grabbed a cab and took it to the outskirts of the airport complex where they rented another car from a small regional agency with no counter in the terminal.

Ulrike rented the car in her name to put off any pursuers looking for Ritter, who paid in advance for a week. With their new cover, they drove to a small town outside Bonn and used a phone in a post office to check out the numbers in the ledger. Ulrike played the role of secretary again, using a ruse of a wrong number to try to find out whose number she was calling.

"*Herr Fassbinder, bitte,*" she said after dialing the first number, which appeared to have an area code for Dusseldorf.

"There is no Herr Fassbinder at this number," someone at the other end of the line said.

"This isn't the number of Herr Henryk Fassbinder?"

"No, this is Herr Eickmayer's number."

Ulrike thanked him and hung up the phone.

"The guy's name is Eickmayer," she said to Ritter. "I couldn't get a first name."

"Looks like you were right about these being phone numbers. That number was for 'R.W.E.' The E is probably for Eickmayer. Try the next one."

"This looks like an East Berlin number. Why would Wolf be paying money to East Germans?"

"Don't know. We don't even know if this *is* a payment list, so let's stick to the West German ones for now. We can come back to the others later. We want people we can drop in on without a lot of trouble, which wouldn't include East Germans."

The second person Ulrike called refused to say whose number it was, but the third produced a result like the first.

"He said it was 'Herr Hoffmann's number,'" Ulrike said after she'd hung up. "Reinhard Hoffmann."

"R.P.H. no doubt," Ritter said after checking the ledger flyleaf.

"So do we go to Dusseldorf to see Eickmayer or Stuttgart to see Hoffmann?"

"I'd rather have a little more than just a blind confrontation. "

"Like what?"

"Like knowing why these guys names are on this list and what these figures connected to them are all about."

"How do we figure that out?"

Ritter thought about that a moment then said, "Let's check those initials against the names in Wolf's address book. See if anything matches. "

Ulrike took the address book out of her purse. Ritter called out the initials in the order they were written in the ledger to see if any names fit. Only one did: Ernst Biermann" was a possible match against "E . R . B ."

Lt. Biermann? Ritter asked himself, remembering the photo of his father and the young officer. One thing seemed wrong, though. The telephone number after Biermann's initials in the ledger was different from the one after his name in Wolf's address book.

"I've heard of this guy," Ulrike said. "He's an industrialist from Bavaria. Worth billions. He has a big private firm — defense, aerospace. Hates publicity. Rumor is, he's a confidential adviser to the chancellor. A journalist friend of mine tried to do a profile on him once."

"What'd he find?"

"She," Ulrike said, smirking. "She didn't find anything. He refused to be interviewed. She couldn't get anybody to talk."

"Might not be the same guy. The number's different."

"Maybe. Or maybe one's his office number, and one's a private line." Ulrike dialed the ledger number.

"Biermann here," a man on the other end said.

She was so surprised she hung up.

"He said 'Biermann,'" she said. "It's got to be the same guy."

Ritter thought of another way to verify the link.

"I wonder if he's a member of that club Wolf belonged to," he said.

Ulrike fished out of her purse the membership pamphlet Ritter had stolen from the club's filing cabinet.

"The chancellor is the honorary chairman, the foreign minister is the vice-chairman, and Biermann is the president. The name of his company is right here."

"Sounds like we need to pay Herr Biermann a visit. Where's his office?"

"Munich."

"Scene of the crime."

15

Tuesday, November 7, 5:00 p.m., Munich

By late afternoon, Ulrike had turned off the autobahn at the first Munich exit. Biermann's headquarters was in a small industrial park on the outskirts of town. A long gravel driveway led to a campus of low-rise, steel-and-glass structures, some architect's homage to the Bauhaus school. She parked in a visitor's slot, and she and Ritter marched toward the entrance.

"What are we going to say?" she asked.

It was a question she'd wanted to ask earlier, but Ritter had closed his eyes and actually slept during the trip. He'd awakened only shortly before she'd gotten off the autobahn. Rested, Ritter didn't seem nervous.

"I'll say I'm Herr Springer and see what happens. Technically I *am* Herr Springer. At least I was when I was born."

Ritter identified himself to the receptionist, who asked him and Ulrike to take a seat on the tan Barcelona chairs that were the only furniture in the vast reception area. A few minutes later, a well-coifed woman who identified herself as Herr Biermann's secretary came down the elevator and showed Ritter and Ulrike to his office suite.

"He'll be with you in a minute," she said, asking them to take a seat on the black, glove-leather couch next to her desk.

"So far, so good," Ritter whispered.

"Are you going to pretend to be Wolf?"

Ritter shrugged.

"I'm not going to say anything till Biermann does. If he thinks I'm Wolf, I'll go with that. If not, I'll play it by ear."

The secretary said Biermann was free and showed Ritter and Ulrike into his inner office. A slim, short man dressed in a nail-head wool suit was on a stepladder pouring live gold fish from a plastic bag into a huge aquarium that took up the entire side of the room. Inside two stingrays stirred from the fine-sand bottom of the tank and checked out their new neighbors.

The man backed down the ladder slowly and turned, snapping his head back slightly as if he'd been surprised by his visitors. He turned back to the tank and checked a temperature gauge before addressing Ritter and Ulrike.

"Adding to your collection?" Ritter asked, attempting to be cordial.

Biermann showed a tight smile.

"No. Just serving lunch."

The rays swooped in on the gold fish, and, in short order, covered and devoured them.

Biermann watched with obvious pleasure, and turned his attention back to his guests.

"I'm hoping to breed them. But everything has to be right. They are fresh water species from South America. The water has to be extremely clean, and heated to about 26 Celsius. They will tolerate frozen shrimp, but I find the live kill seems a more natural thing for them."

Biermann tossed the plastic bag into his chrome waste basket and wiped his hands with a tissue he pulled from a box enclosed in matching chrome. He silently gestured for Ritter and Ulrike to sit down in the guest chairs in front of his desk and took his own seat, which was a dark gray leather swivel chair with wheels under the legs.

He leaned back and put his clasped fingers together on the part of his desk closest to him. His steely gray hair was cut short, as if he'd prepared for an inspection in the Afrika Korps. High on his left cheek was a two-inch scar, perhaps a war wound, perhaps the remnant of a saber fight, given his likely years in the military, Ritter imagined.

Aside from the chrome, glass, leather and steel surfaces of the office, only a blue, red and orange Tibetan carpet spread on the brown parquet floor and a lavender orchid on a coffee table provided touches of warmth. Biermann said nothing, and with no obvious welcome for his brother, Ritter was forced to identify himself as Matthew Springer.

"What can I do for you?" Biermann asked coolly without getting up to shake hands.

"I think you know my brother, Wolf."

"Really?"

"Of the German foreign ministry. "

Biermann nodded his head a few times as if processing the name.

"Ah, yes. We have talked from time to time."

"Well, the reason we came to see you is that he's missing. And I and his, uh, fiancée…This is Fraulein Fischer.…"

Biermann snapped his head forward as if acknowledging her but did not get up to welcome her.

"As I said, he's missing, and we're talking to anyone who knew him, in hopes of finding him."

"Have you tried the police?"

"Yes, and they think the last place he was seen was in Munich. We noticed your Munich address in his address book, and so here we are."

"Munich?" Biermann's voice had risen, Ritter noticed. "Well, he didn't come to see me. I haven't seen him in some time." He paused. "Is foul play suspected?"

"It's possible he was killed, perhaps here, but we've found no body."

Biermann's eyes narrowed.

"How strange. But why would anyone want to kill your brother?"

"He was working on a sensitive matter at the ministry. Apparently some people wanted to get their hands on one of his files. That's what we've been told anyway."

"A file?" Biermann sounded only mildly interested as he picked out a cigarillo from a cylinder that looked like a sawed-off howitzer shell.

Ritter tried another tack.

"Actually a draft agreement in the file. I have the title page. I thought it might be familiar to you, given your business and government connections."

Ritter pulled out a single sheet of paper from his suit jacket and handed it to Biermann.

"Recognize it?"

Biermann lit the cigarillo first, then took the sheet. He looked at it casually and said, "No. I can't say that I do." He handed it back. "I take it you don't have the full document."

Ritter helped himself to a cigarillo and pulled out the white matchbook from the German Club. When finished, he casually tossed the book into a large glass ashtray on Biermann's desk next to the cigarillo holder. Ritter saw Biermann flick a look at what must have been a familiar item, but the executive said nothing.

"Let's just say I'm aware of what's inside it."

Biermann took that in and calmly added: "Anything else I can do for you?"

"What kind of dealings did you have with my brother? Anything that might put him in danger?"

Biermann shook his head.

"Not that I can see. Government things….Confidential things."

Ritter waited a moment to see if Biermann would offer any more details. After it was clear he wouldn't, Ritter said: "Well, thanks for your help. It was a bit of a long shot to come here, but if anything does occur, we'd appreciate it if you'd give us a call."

Biermann smiled.

"Where can I contact you?"

"We'll probably stay in Munich tonight. It's getting a bit late to drive any more."

"Do you have a hotel?"

"Not yet."

"I know one with an excellent restaurant. My secretary can arrange it for you if you'd like."

Ulrike and Ritter agreed and headed out. They didn't say anything to each other until they got outside.

"Talk about a cold fish!" Ulrike whispered when they were alone.

"Maybe more like those sting rays."

"I think we hit a nerve," she said. "Something's going to happen pretty soon…. And if we're lucky, we won't even get killed ."

Ritter was silent for a moment, mulling over a name and a face in an old photo.

Finally he asked: "Did your journalist friend ever find out if Biermann was in the army during the war?"

"Not that I know of. Why?"

"I'm pretty sure he served with my father."

Maybe as a courier to the Allies, Ritter said to himself.

*****

After Ritter and Ulrike had left, Biermann's secretary called him on his intercom.

"The Chancellor, Herr Biermann. On your private line."

"I'll take it, but get me Willy as soon as I'm done. Tell him I've got another little problem to eliminate."

The Kempinski was a lot more lavish than Ritter was used to. But he checked in anyway because he wanted Biermann to know where he and Ulrike were staying. He changed more francs to marks and gave the clerk a deposit on the room for the night. He put the folder, the photos and the ledger in a hotel safe-deposit box.

"At this rate, we're going to run out of Wolf's money."

Ulrike took his arm.

"At least you only have to get one room."

Ritter and Ulrike dined at the hotel that night, as Biermann had suggested. The restaurant was a very public place, its key appeal for Ritter. The food turned out to be good, too, as advertised. Ritter and Ulrike both had the *Kalbsfilet mit Trüffelsosse,* a recommendation Biermann's secretary had given them on the way out. A chilled German white made it a memorable meal.

"You didn't drink much wine," Ulrike said after they'd finished their coffee.

"One of us has to stay alert tonight."

"I can watch part of the time….I've handled a pistol before."

"Professional training?"

"More like unofficial."

"Those friends with the ammo?"

"When it comes to weapons, they know what they're doing. Ideology is another matter."

Ritter looked at the woman he'd come to know and found it hard to match her up with the crazies like the Red Army Faction or the Baader-Meinhof gang. But then he had to admit he was not the same left-hating young cop he'd been during the riots after the 1968 Democratic National Convention in Chicago.

"If we have to shoot somebody," he said, "Let me do it. I don't want you getting into any trouble."

Ulrike laughed.

"Trouble? Armed men are following us. They probably want to kill us, and you're worried I might get into *trouble?*"

Ulrike suggested they take a little walk to work off the food.

"The English Garden's just up the street," Ulrike said. "It's famous."

Ritter didn't like the idea at first. But the garden was a public place, though not as well lit as the hotel. He had to admit, though, that the whole purpose of visiting Biermann was to provoke some action, and the garden was as good a place as any to do that.

"Let's go upstairs and get the gun first."

A short while later, they entered the park on its south side. Autumn was hanging on in Bavaria, more than it had been in Berlin or Bonn. People in Munich seemed livelier, with more bounce in their step. The pleasant evening was a gift of the season, and the park was full of people out for a stroll, making Ritter feel a little more secure about the decision he'd made.

The meal had made Ritter feel full and comfortable, but he wasn't exactly relaxed. He tried in unobtrusive ways to glance left, and right and occasionally behind him to see if he and Ulrike were being followed. His right hand was on the pistol in his topcoat pocket. That gave him a comforting edge, as did the steps he'd taken with various mailings to make sure Wolf's handiwork wouldn't stay secret if anything happened to him and Ulrike.

"Let's keep on the paths closest to the streets," he said pointing toward Königstraße. "I'd like to have more people around in case we need to yell for help."

They walked at a good pace to make it clearer if someone was trying to keep up with them. They rounded a curve in the path, and Ritter noticed a juggler in shabby clothes performing under a dim lamp light. The performer, tall and lithe, had an audience of one, a man in a heavy peacoat. The lone patron dropped a few coins into a hat that sat on the ground in front of the juggler's feet.

The juggler bowed in thanks as the man in the peacoat pivoted and headed up the path toward Ritter and Ulrike. The man had turned away from the juggler so quickly that he had bumped into Ritter. He apologized profusely. It was not until too late that Ritter felt the familiar shape of a gun barrel in his back and heard a soft, determined voice of another man say, "Keep moving. Don't shout or the girl will be killed."

Ritter glanced at Ulrike, who had a frightened look on her face, a reaction to a pistol the man in the peacoat had stuck in her ribs.

"Do you have a gun?" the man behind Ritter asked. "I wouldn't want there to be any shooting. Someone might get hurt."

Ritter thought about pulling out his weapon, which he had in his grip, safety off. He glanced at Ulrike and decided not to. If the men had wanted to kill us, he figured, they could have dropped us right here. Somebody wants to talk to us, he decided. The man behind him poked him with the gun for an answer.

"In my right coat pocket," Ritter finally said. He pulled his hand slowly out of the pocket and felt a hand slip into it and relieve him of the pistol.

"Get moving," the man behind him said.

The juggler slipped into step in front of the group like a point man on patrol. The three men didn't take Ritter and Ulrike far. On Königstraße, the street that Ritter thought would provide some safety, a Mercedes limo with dark, tinted windows was waiting at the curb. The men shoved Ritter and Ulrike inside. They made them sit on jump seats while two of them pointed guns at them from the rear seat. The juggler got into the passenger seat and told a fourth man to drive off.

"Where are you taking us?" Ulrike said.

"You'll find out," the man in the peacoat said.

The Mercedes sped out of Munich toward the autobahn. The kilometers raced by without anyone saying anything. With the heavy tint of the windows, it was hard for Ritter to tell where they were going. But Ulrike puzzled it out.

"Looks like we're heading for the Black Forest," she said in a louder than normal voice.

"Shut up," the juggler said.

Half an hour later, the car skidded to a halt at the beginning of a gravel driveway.

The juggler got out and unlocked a gate. Once the car was through, he relocked it and got in. The car lurched forward up a hill. There had been no sign at the gate, not even a number for Ritter to guess where they were being taken. Ritter was certain it had to be somewhere connected with Biermann. The car finally pulled up in front of a rambling mountain chalet that was hidden from the road by a massive stand of pine trees.

"Get out!" the juggler said. He flicked a pistol in the direction of the chalet to show Ritter and Ulrike where to go.

"What do you think they'll do with us?" Ulrike whispered.

"Nothing till they find out what happened to that folder."

"No talking!" the man in the peacoat said.

He shoved Ritter toward the chalet, causing him to stumble. The huge house at the end of the path had stone steps, which weren't well lit. Ritter mounted them carefully, taking Ulrike's hand in the dark. The front door opened, and a shadowy figure appeared in the doorway, back-lit by a foyer light. The man was tall. At first Ritter thought it might be Biermann, but the man was too husky, more like Ritter's size. Exactly Ritter's size, as it turned out.

"*Willkommen,* Matt," the man said.

"Hello, Wolf."

16

Tuesday, November 7, 10:30 p.m., the Black Forest

Ulrike hadn't been paying attention. Head down, she walked in right behind Ritter and stopped in her tracks when she saw Wolf's face in the lamplight. If she had seen him a few days before, her reaction might have been like the one she'd had when Ritter appeared on her darkened doorstep and she'd mistaken him for Wolf. She shot a guilty glance at Ritter, then moved toward the man who'd been her lover.

"*Liebling!*" she finally said before embracing Wolf. "You're alive! I was so worried."

Wolf showed no notice of her mixed mood. He kissed her confidently as if her concern had been frivolous. Ritter winced imperceptibly as he watched what he hoped was a masquerade.

"I'm sorry I made you worry, I wanted to tell you what happened. But circumstances didn't permit."

"What did happen? You were supposed to…."

Wolf put his right index finger on her lips.

"We'll talk about that later. We have other things to attend to first."

Wolf held Ulrike at his side as he switched his attention to his brother. Ritter had thought a number of times about how he would greet his brother if he found him alive, and the likely response had changed as he learned more about his sibling from one day to another. At one time, he'd decided that a bear hug might be appropriate, even though he and Wolf had very little emotional past to justify such a gesture. When the moment of truth came, building on his curt "Hello" on the porch, he gave his brother a firm, correct handshake and a tight smile.

The man in front of Ritter had the same blood in his veins. But from what Ritter had learned of his sibling in his brief time in the two Germanies, he was as different from him as the two countries were from each other. In the old debate about nature vs. nurture, nurture seemed to have had the trump hand in what was left of Ritter's family.

Ritter wasn't sure what his brother had done to prompt the world's leading spy agencies to hunt him down, but he found that at that moment he felt very little for this man with his face, his voice and, for the moment, his woman. Knowing what he knew about Wolf, Ritter wasn't even sure he liked him. Wolf's arrogant, smug attitude that night did little to change Ritter's view.

"Well, I hope you've enjoyed your tour of Germany, " Wolf said after an uneasy silence.

"Switzerland was nice too. I may owe you some money — from the safe-deposit box."

Wolf's smile vanished.

"We found out a bit late about that."

"Those weren't your goons following us?"

"Unfortunately, no. You seem to have many people interested in your activities."

"Most of them thought I was you."

"You seem to have kept them very busy, " Wolf said in English that had a hint of a British accent. "You caused us no end of trouble, too, I'm afraid."

"Us?"

Wolf smiled.

"My friends and I. We had quite a time keeping up with you."

"Glad I could keep you entertained….Who *are* your friends anyway?" he asked, gesturing with his right thumb over his shoulder toward his captors. "KGB?"

Wolf took a moment to get it.

"KGB? Oh, I see you've been talking to Davies. How is he, by the way?"

"Naked the last time I saw him. "

Wolf gave Ritter a befuddled look but didn't pursue the remark.

"So who then — Neo-Nazis?" Ritter asked, hoping to provoke.

Wolf said nothing for a moment, then replied, "You disappoint me, Matt. I thought you might have figured it out better than that. You're supposed to be the detective."

"Well, I'm getting a little on in years, you know. Losing a step. Maybe you can help an old guy out."

Wolf laughed sarcastically.

"Nazis are going nowhere in this country. They'll never be more than an irritating little minority."

"All right. I'm out of guesses."

"We're just Germans. Germans who are involved in something important, and we're not going to let anything or anyone get in our way."

"Sort of has a Fourth Reich ring to it."

"Will you drop this stupid Nazi thing! You couldn't be more wrong."

"OK. Enlighten me."

"I will, but not now. Why don't we catch up on family matters tonight, and in the morning, when some of my associates arrive, we'll get down to more serious things?"

"Like what?"

Wolf showed a tolerant smile.

"You've stumbled onto some very complicated, important matters, things that have been developing for years, things you probably don't completely comprehend."

"Dying to know the details….or maybe *dying* is the wrong word." Ritter turned back toward the men who had abducted him and Ulrike. "You know, with the guns and all, I don't want to encourage anyone."

"Willy, Heinrich, put those things away," Wolf yelled at the two men who had guns out.

Ritter turned around and noticed the men took a while to comply.

"Could I get my purse back?" Ulrike asked, taking advantage of the slight ease in tension.

The man in the peacoat looked to Wolf for guidance. After Wolf nodded, the man reluctantly handed the purse back.

"Could I have my gun back?" Ritter asked, a mischievous smile on his face.

The peacoat man's eyes narrowed, his only response to the idea.

"Well, worth a try. I guess that shows where we stand. You don't really trust us."

Wolf let out a long sigh.

"I can tell you a little bit now. In the morning, after you've heard us out, I hope you'll see the wisdom of helping us — or at least of not interfering. Our project is something for the good of Germany. And at heart, I think you are a German. And Berliner like me."

"So I found out."

"Yes." Wolf smiled. "That must have been a surprise."

"How'd you find out about me?" Ritter asked.

Wolf flashed a smug smile.

"A little bird."

Maybe a courier pigeon? Ritter wondered.

"You mean you have someone spying on Davies?"

"Everybody spies on everybody. I spied on the Americans. I spied on the East Germans and even had a Soviet handler. And each of them thought I was on their side. But I was just working for Germany."

Wolf hesitated before his next revelation. He told Ritter that Davies had been told he was up to something with the Soviets.

"I got a little excited about a breakthrough and made a phone call I shouldn't have. I was cryptic, but apparently not cryptic enough. Sloppy on my part, and I paid by having to die." Wolf touched a gap along his gum line. "Lost a tooth in the process."

"So is that draft agreement a done deal?"

"I can't talk about that — or my network." Wolf paused. "Anyway, I knew it was only a matter of time before Davies or his goons would grab me, and I'd be in some dark room being deprived of sleep or some other kind of torture. To make it worse, some East Germans were getting nervous about me. Not sure what set that off. They are all so paranoid, so any little thing could have done it. And if the Stasi had grabbed me, I probably would have been tortured into telling all."

"How inconvenient."

"Exactly. So my officially dying was the only sure way to put everyone off the scent."

"Who did the arranging?"

Wolf smiled.

"Let's just say patriots."

"The people in your ledger?"

Wolf's eyes narrowed.

"It's best you just put those names out of your mind. People's lives are at stake."

Ritter dropped the name of the German Club, hoping to get a reaction from Wolf. Instead, Wolf ignored the reference and said: "Why don't we all go into the living room and make ourselves comfortable? And we can have a chat about the family."

The three of them took seats in front of the enormous stone fireplace that was the centerpiece of the room. Ritter flopped in an overstuffed armchair. Wolf lounged on a cloth-covered couch and patted the cushion next to him as a signal for Ulrike to sit. Willy and Heinrich stood at the door, arms folded, pistols in their holsters.

A tray of crystal snifters and a bottle of aged cognac sat on a table in front of the group. Wolf poured himself a drink and asked Ritter if he had any burning questions about their family. Ritter had a lot of questions — family and non-family — but he played it light, not asking Wolf directly about their father and the OSS.

"What can you tell me about dear old dad?" he started.

"Well that's a tall order," Wolf said, as if about to tell a bedtime story to a child.

"I don't know everything myself. But Grandma Inge did tell me a few things you may not have heard."

"I haven't heard much."

"The main thing, I guess, is that grandma was allowed to visit father for a brief period after he was arrested by the Gestapo in '45. She had powerful friends."

"That's what Aunt Fredi said."

"Ah, that's right. I forgot you met her. A lovely woman, isn't she?"

"I liked her. She about had a heart attack when I told her you were dead."

Wolf licked his lips.

"I would have loved to tell her the truth, but it was beyond my control."

"Guess you had your priorities."

"Yes," Wolf said, drawing the word out into a hiss. He gave Ritter an irritated look, then added: "Well, as I was saying, Grandma Inge got a few minutes with father. He told her about working with the OSS."

"So you knew about that before you went to work for Davies?"

"Yes, it actually made my recruitment more plausible. Son of a valued agent killed in the line of duty."

"Hasn't seemed to do me much good with him."

Wolf laid out the story behind their parents' separation: the OSS thought their father would be too vulnerable with his family still inside Germany, so they worked up a story about the marital split. Both boys were to go with their mother to the U.S. To trick any Gestapo watchers, their mother left the house for the train station alone. Grandma Inge was to bring the boys later. But, unwilling to lose both grandsons, she decided at the last minute to leave Wolf behind and offer their mother an ultimatum. One son in freedom or scrap a carefully planned trip their mother might not be able to duplicate for months. Inge won the gamble.

"Grandma Inge sounds like a piece of work," Ritter said.

"The whole family feared her. She was the matriarch of the clan, the one who had the money and the connections. Even father was afraid of her."

"And he didn't try to get you out later?"

Wolf explained that his father couldn't do that. The Gestapo found out quickly that their mother had left and put a permanent guard on Wolf in case she tried to get him too. As it turned out, the party was very sympathetic about what had happened. They offered to make a diplomatic protest about what they called the "kidnapping of a German citizen," even though Ritter had American citizenship through their mother. Their father, ever the professional military man, said it was a private affair that he'd handle without publicity. Unexpectedly, the party trusted him more than ever after the incident because he'd suffered this personal loss in their service, Wolf said.

"Very convenient for the OSS too."

"I suppose, but I don't think grandma was working for them, if that's what you're thinking."

"And after the war?"

"Inge and I looked for you and mother, but we couldn't find you. We looked everywhere for anyone name Greta Springer. We looked for Helga too. Her people were from Berlin, but they'd all been killed in the war. She just vanished. Living as Grandma Ritter, no doubt. That name change just stymied us."

"And the OSS?"

"They disbanded after the war, and the embassy here said they couldn't find anyone."

"Did father tell Inge any details about his spy network? Like who was in it?" Like Lt. Biermann maybe, Ritter thought.

Wolf hesitated, then said: "I hardly think that would be the sort of thing he'd pass on to her. She might have been interrogated by the Gestapo. The room they met in was probably bugged. He only told her about his OSS connection because the Gestapo already knew that."

"Maybe he just wanted us to know what he'd done and hint at why he killed himself."

Wolf thought about that.

"I've wondered that myself."

Ritter poured himself a good-sized cognac and took a strong swig. He glanced at Ulrike who hadn't said anything and looked very uncomfortable.

"Did our father say why he joined the Nazis?" Ritter asked.

Wolf brightened at the question.

"I do know something about that."

Wolf recounted how their father had been in disgrace back in the 1930s because, while still single, he'd had an affair with the wife of a superior officer. The affair had become public, which threatened to destroy his career. Then the Nazis came to his aid. At the time, they were moving up in power. They took in a lot of disaffected and disgraced military people into their ranks. People accepted their help before it became clear what the Nazis were really up to. Their father made friends with some of them because military life was all he knew, Wolf said. They put his career back on track. Later, he realized what madmen they were and started working secretly against them, Wolf said.

"So he wasn't a true believer?"

"No, no. He was like a lot of people who joined the party for a variety of selfish reasons. It's not a pretty story. But there are worse."

Ritter was formulating another query when Wolf seized his momentary silence to put his snifter down with a thud and say: "Let's call it a night. I'm bushed. You can tell me about Chicago later. But in the morning we have some other more pressing things to talk about after my colleagues arrive."

Ritter smiled thinly.

"Sounds like fun."

Wolf ignored the taunt.

"We have comfortable accommodations for you upstairs," Wolf said. "I'm afraid the view is a bit restricted. The shutters on the windows are already nailed shut for the winter. But you can't see much in the dark anyway."

Sounded a bit like a jail, Ritter thought. He wondered if the nails had gone in earlier that day, after he and Ulrike had visited Biermann.

Wolf stood up and said "Your room is at the top of the stairs, Matt. First one on the right. Ulrike, ours is at the end of the hall…I'll be up shortly."

Ritter and Ulrike climbed the stairs. Ritter opened the door to his room, which was furnished rustically like the rest of the chalet. He turned in the doorway and paused, his right forearm on the doorjamb, as Ulrike approached. She stopped in front of him, pressed her lips together nervously, then grabbed his left hand with her right.

"We have to talk," she whispered.

Ritter laughed bitterly

"Your explaining things to Wolf about us is the least of our problems."

"What do you mean?"

"He may be in charge right now. And he might not intend any harm to you or even me. But when the big boys arrive, there's no telling what's going to happen. Remember, these are the same guys who sent a corpse to Berlin to stage Wolf's death."

"You think they'd kill us too?"

"We know about their agents and the talks with the Soviets, which seems pretty important to them. They just might decide we have to die for the good of the project, whatever it is."

"Wolf would never allow that."

"He might not be able to stop them."

17

Wednesday, November 8, 7:00 a.m., the Black Forest

Ritter didn't sleep well that night. It should have been a happy occasion to have met his brother at last. But, given the circumstances, which included Ulrike, he sensed Wolf was about as fond of him as he was of Wolf. At first his anger about being used by Wolf and his pals kept him awake. Then came the yelling from Wolf's bedroom. He could hear the sound of Ulrike's voice but couldn't make out the words. Their meaning seemed pretty evident, though. And Ritter guessed that, come the morning, Wolf's feelings about him would be even less fraternal.

Ritter awoke to a fine fall day. The first sounds were the chattering of woodland birds, stragglers of the season, and the strong rush of autumn wind through supple pine needles. If he could have seen farther south, he'd have noticed the origins of the Danube, a river more associated with countries to the east. Out of sight too was the Feldberg, the highest mountain in the region. Tourists came to the area to visit the university at Freiburg or Calw, where philosopher Hermann Hesse was born, or the Triberg Waterfalls. They gorged on Black Forest ham for lunch or the area's famous chocolate, cherry and Kirsch cake for dessert when they weren't buying cuckoo clocks or wood carvings. The Brothers Grimm had made the Black Forest the setting of many of their epic fairy tales, but what happened to Hansel and Gretel or Little Red Riding Hood seemed like remarkably happy stories compared with what

Ritter saw ahead for him and Ulrike. Those fairy-tale characters survived their ordeals. Ritter wasn't so sure about his fate.

Below in the chalet, no one seemed to be stirring in the last moments of darkness. A few minutes later, the morning sun, rising above the dense tree line, poked its rays through cracks in the weathered shutters that were Ritter's prison bars. The wind picked up, and the hundred-year old forest grieved a bassy tune as trees bent and creaked against nature's implacable force.

Ritter planted his bare feet on the rough, planked floor. As usual, he'd slept nude and walked without dressing through the crisp air into a bathroom attached to his bedroom. As he'd found out the night before, while foraging for something to brush his teeth with, there was a shaving kit laid out for him, a nice, thoughtful touch that clashed with the danger he felt he and Ulrike were in. He wondered if it was just a courtesy given to a condemned man, like a last meal.

He showered and dressed. Even with the sun now higher in the azure sky, he could tell from the cold of his bathroom window pane that the morning air had a hint of frost to it. Ritter put on the shirt, sweater and khaki pants he had been wearing since he and Ulrike had left Heidelberg. He'd planned to do some more shopping after a night at the Kempinski, but that plan got changed in the English Garden.

In the hall, he glanced down toward the room where Ulrike and Wolf had spent the night. He thought about knocking to see if she was ready to eat. He was pretty sure she'd be glad to see him. But what if he'd misread the yelling in the night? The sound of rough voices below brought him back to reality.

One of the men who'd grabbed him in Munich, the one in the peacoat, was seated on a chair at the bottom of the stairs. He was eating pistachios and tossing the shells into a large ash tray at his feet. The man jumped up when he saw Ritter coming down.

Silently he pointed Ritter toward a morning room where a table had been set with dishes and flowers for breakfast. Wolf was already sitting down, sipping from a china cup as he read the morning paper.

"*Guten Morgen,*" he said, his only use of German since he'd met Ritter, other than his welcoming remark. "I trust you slept well."

"Under the circumstances, not too badly."

Wolf put the newspaper down and looked at his brother.

"Stop being so gloomy. My colleagues are honorable men. When you hear what we have to say today, I think you'll see that we have Germany's best interests at heart, and I hope you'll support our effort."

"You want me to join up?"

"No. Just don't get in our way.…You know some things that would be better left secret. We're just asking for a little time."

Before Ritter could respond, Wolf added, "By the way, I should have mentioned this last night when we were talking about the family. Grandma Inge had a small estate when she died. Nothing fantastic, but a sizable amount. She left it to both of us in her will. As no one knew where you were or even if you were alive, it went to me."

"Uh huh," Ritter said, sensing where Wolf was heading.

"The courts closed the estate long ago. But I want you to have your share — plus whatever would be reasonable interest from the time of her death."

"Forget it."

Wolf seemed surprised by Ritter's rejection of the money but pressed on.

"No, really," he said, "I've got plenty. I've made some wise investments. I assure you the money comes with no strings."

"You got to admit, it does sound a little like a bribe."

Wolf turned angry.

"Don't be stupid! You have the legal right to reopen the estate. I'm just trying to save you the trouble. If you don't want it, fine. I'm just trying to do the honorable thing."

"I'll think about it."

Wolf snorted out a breath.

"It'd be a tidy sum. Six figures — in dollars. You wouldn't be a millionaire, but you'd be on your way."

"That's been my life's dream. That's why I went into police work."

"Suit yourself. You're just being pig-headed, if you ask me."

Maybe he was, Ritter thought. With the alimony he'd have to pay Anita if things went as he thought, the money would come in handy. But he found it difficult to say yes.

Ulrike came into the room before any deal was set. Wolf rose in his chair.

"You look lovely this morning, *Liebling*."

She had fresh clothes on, a black wool sweater and charcoal slacks. She shot a quick look at Ritter then turned back to Wolf and gave him an icy stare.

"I hope the clothes fit. You know I always have trouble remembering your sizes."

"They're fine."

Wolf told Ritter he could borrow some of his clothes if he thought they would fit.

Ritter just said, "No thanks."

Wolf asked Ritter and Ulrike what they wanted for breakfast. Ulrike ordered eggs, bacon, toast and tea. Ritter, perhaps responding to Wolf's taunt about tight clothes, said he wanted black coffee and dry cereal with skim milk. Wolf got up and went out to tell the guard eating the pistachios, a man he'd called Willy, what the orders were. Willy didn't look pleased about being turned into a waiter. Ulrike and Ritter didn't have much to say after Wolf sat back down. Noticing, Wolf picked up his newspaper and created a conversation.

"Lots of news in here," he said, running his eyes over the headlines. "They're expecting a big rally today in East Berlin. Maybe half a million. The entire cabinet is resigning. The parliament rejected a new travel law.

Said it wasn't enough. And Mittig, that idiot minister from state security, even apologized for the Stasi 'overreaction' to those protests a few weeks ago. Everything is heading our way."

After breakfast, Wolf suggested Ulrike make herself comfortable in the chalet library while he and Ritter walked in the woods. Ulrike opened her mouth as if she wanted to come along. But Wolf had hurried past her and didn't notice. The first part of the walk was a monologue by Wolf on the flora and fauna of the area. He talked about the unique cattle and horses of the region, avoiding the topic that was clearly on both brothers' minds. Ritter wondered how long the warm-up would go on before his brother got to the point. After no particular preparation for the remark, Wolf asked Ritter what he thought of the arrangement with the Soviets.

"Seems like a pretty good deal for Germany. The Soviets too."

Wolf smiled.

"I'd hoped you'd see it that way. That's the way we feel."

"You and your pals in the German Club?"

Wolf stopped walking and turned to Ritter.

"I think it best you stop mentioning that association."

"Dangerous to my health?"

"This is a serious matter! It can end quite amicably, but it could just as easily get....messy."

"And they've left it up to you to determine which?"

"They let me talk to you first. You're my brother, and they owe me."

"But if I'm pigheaded...."

"Then I can't be responsible for what happens. So don't be stupid."

"And Ulrike?"

"She's German. She's not going to say anything. She'll like this idea."

"She already does."

"You've talked about it?"

"The other way around. She's the one who explained it to me. I'm afraid I missed some of the fine points the first time through, including that it might not be such a good deal for the U.S. That's my team, in case you forgot."

"You're at least half German."

"I'm an American. That's all I've ever been — or known."

Wolf got close to his brother face.

"There's nothing anti-American in the accord! At the worst, it would give America the good swift kick in the pants it needs."

Ritter didn't immediately respond, and Wolf backed away.

"I don't think Rick Davies sees it quite that way," Ritter said when the tension had eased a bit.

"That's because Davies, despite some intelligence, is short-sighted. America is in a slump. Historic trade deficits and debt. Drugs. Crime. Second-rate education. This arrangement would sound some alarms and make people get more competitive. Americans respond to competition."

"Yeah, I'd really look forward to that while you and the Soviets carved up the economic world."

"Don't give me that. We'd be doing you a favor. Americans like being the underdog. Tell them they're second-best or that they can't compete any more or that they're going to lose, and they come back at you. Twice as hard. Hitler found that out. And if they don't come back then they don't deserve to be a world power anymore."

"Like Germany, you mean?"

"Yes, like Germany! And what's wrong with that? We're tired of holding back, of being saddled with this war-guilt stuff. We created an economic miracle. On merit."

"Ah, yes, the *Wirtschaftwunder.*"

"Exactly! Half a century of penance is enough."

"People have long memories."

"They're just afraid of our capabilities."

"Maybe it was the last two world wars."

"We're done with that. This deal doesn't have anything to do with military power. We'll be a power, of course, given the size of our armed forces and our stockpile of weapons, but we won't have designs on anyone."

"So Biermann will continue to make a lot of money selling arms?"

"Even a neutral nation has to defend itself, but you're missing the point. The new war will be an economic one. And we plan to do well in it. Even with the shackles they put on us — taking half the country away — we export more than anyone else in the world and we have a bigger trade surplus. Bigger even than Japan's."

Ritter listened to Wolf's ardor and began to understand why people got so nervous about Germans.

"What you seem to be saying," Ritter interrupted, a smirk on his face, "is that all we have to do to respond to the new lean-and-mean Russia and Germany is to wipe out a trillion-dollar national debt, erase some multibillion-dollar trade and budget deficits, eliminate crime, stop drug use, get kids and parents to care about education, inspire everybody to learn foreign languages and figure how to make good products again."

Wolf laughed at the list and turned wry.

"I'm surprised at you, Matt," he said. "Whatever happened to Yankee ingenuity and that old can-do spirit?"

"I think the Japanese bought it."

They both smiled before Wolf turned serious again.

"Look, my job is not to make things easy for your country," Wolf said. "I'm working for *my* country. Maybe we'll do something stupid or even horrible again. But why can't we have a chance to show what we're really like when we don't have idiots or madmen in charge? Your country was wrong about Vietnam and a lot of other things. The Soviets were wrong about Afghanistan. And the French and the Israelis.. well, don't get me started."

Wolf reminded Ritter that at the end of World War II, the Allies had said that, if Germans became good democrats and capitalists, their reward would be to get their country back together.

"To many of us that's begun to look like a big lie. Later, we're told. It's always later, so we decided to make it happen on our own. I mean if somebody had kept a family apart for half a century…."

"Somebody did," Ritter interrupted, surprised that that part of the argument made some sense to him on a personal level.

Wolf smiled at the supportive remark.

"Precisely."

"It's not up to me to say…."

"It *is* up to you! You can tell Davies or somebody else about what you know or you can keep your mouth shut."

"He's going to find out eventually."

"Eventually is fine. By then, it will be too late. We just need a little time."

"So all I have to do is keep quiet?"

"Yes."

"And your buddies are going to let me walk out the door and take my word that I won't call up the White House or the State Department when I get home?"

"I think I can persuade them."

Ritter snorted as if he didn't buy it, but said: "I'll think about it. But if they aren't so understanding, you tell them for me that I've taken a few precautions."

Wolf got a worried look on his face.

"I hope you haven't done anything foolish."

"Not from my point of view. But if I don't get back to Chicago pretty soon, I suggest you take out a subscription to the New York Times or tune your satellite dish to CNN."

Wolf gave Ritter a look that seemed more one of concern than anger.

"That was very, very stupid, Matt," he said. "They want those papers you took from my safe-deposit box."

"I don't have them with me, as you can probably tell. Give me a few days and a ride to the airport, and I'll see if you can get them back."

"They'll never let you leave here without those documents."

"Letting me go is the only way they'll get them."

"You're willing to risk the consequences of not cooperating?"

"I don't give a damn about your deal! It was just something I stumbled across while I was trying to figure out who killed you. Now, I just want to get out of here….and I want Ulrike let go too."

Wolf looked at his brother.

"I see you have feelings for her….and she for you, if last night is an indication."

"Yeah, I heard the yelling….Sort of caught us both by surprise, if that's any consolation."

"Not much. And I'm not giving up on her. You should know that. I don't like to lose."

"So I heard, but the three of us is a separate issue. For now, I just want us let go, so you tell Biermann what I've said and let me know if we get a ride to the airport or have to stay here in jail."

18

Wednesday, November 8, 9:00 a.m., the Black Forest.
By the time Wolf and Ritter got back to the chalet, Biermann had arrived. He made no pretenses about cordiality. With an impatient finger, he signaled Wolf to come over for a tête-à-tête. Ritter noticed that Biermann's face, fixed on him, got redder as Wolf explained the situation. Biermann walked over to Ritter and said in English: "We will have a little talk."

Biermann chose the library as the venue. He positioned the guards, Willy and Heinrich, outside the door. He was surprised to find Ulrike in the library in a reading chair with a newspaper in her hands. He told her to leave, but Ritter insisted she stay.

"This is as much about her as it is about me."

Biermann thought about it a moment, then said, "As you like."

Biermann picked the largest chair in the room and gestured for Ritter to pick one close to it.

"Let's get straight to the point, Herr Ritter. Wolf tells me you've made some provisions to have his documents published. We cannot permit that. Lives are at stake. And something bigger than a few lives."

Ritter was tempted to tell Biermann his instructions didn't include publishing anything about agent identities, but he just said: "You don't have much to say about it. Neither do I if I don't arrive in Chicago pretty soon."

"But we do have you. And Fraulein Fischer."

Biermann smiled as if he had played a trump card.

"What do you plan to do?" Ritter asked. "Kill us? That might be a little hard to explain."

"For the time being, I think we might just keep both of you on ice, as you Americans like to say. How long did you say we have until your friends try to publish the documents?"

"I didn't," Ritter said, thinking he should have set the end of the week as the deadline, not the end of the month.

"No matter. I'm going to assume we have a reasonable amount of time." Biermann looked at Ritter as if hoping for some telltale sign that was true.

"Look, Herr Biermann, as I told Wolf, I really don't care that much about your little deal with the Soviets. I just want to stay alive."

"That can be arranged. All that we need to start are the originals of the documents you stole. Then if there are any copies, we can just say they're fakes….but I hope it won't come to that."

"Stole is such a harsh word."

"They're not your property!" Biermann said, slamming his right fist onto the arm of his chair.

Biermann composed himself, turned to Ulrike and said. "Wolf tells me that you, Fraulein, support our efforts and have no problems keeping quiet. Is that correct?"

"Yes."

"And you, Herr Ritter, I understand you haven't quite made up your mind even if we do let you go."

"Yeah, I find it difficult to think clearly when people who want an answer have guns ready to shoot me."

Biermann took a deep breath and pulled out a piece of paper from his jacket.

"Perhaps there is another way." He read the paper for a moment. "As best I can tell, you are not a rich man."

He handed over the paper to Ritter, who looked at it and grew angry.

"Did your friends at the CIA give you my bank statements?"

Biermann smiled thinly but ignored the remark.

"I have many companies. We have a lot of need for security. A veteran detective could be of extreme value to us."

"Especially if he kept his mouth shut."

"Keeping one's mouth shut is the essence of security."

Ritter laughed.

"This is the second time this week someone tried to bribe me to keep my mouth shut."

"Second?"

"Wolf offered me half his inheritance. Of course, legally I guess it's mine, but the timing was a bit suspicious."

"I'm not trying to be coy, Herr Ritter. A well-paying job. A nice life in Europe — or the U.S. if you'd prefer. We have units around the globe."

Ritter nodded.

"You know what I wonder?"

"I'm sure you're going to tell me."

"How did a lowly courier who worked for my father wind up a billionaire?"

Biermann's eyes narrowed.

"Don't stretch your luck, Herr Ritter."

"Luck has nothing to do with it. In those papers I left with friends is a little story. Maybe you know it. It's about a man playing footsy with the CIA while he is also advising the German chancellor and running a key defense company. How would that play out if the newspapers got a hold of it? You could claim my story about your agreement is a fake, but I think people would start asking some very hard questions about you."

Biermann looked at Ritter and calmly said, "I am trying to make you a rich man, and all you do is to try to provoke me."

"American training, I guess. I just never learned to follow orders."

Biermann stood up and paced around the room a bit, before saying: "I've been playing this game a long time and have learned to go with my gut feeling."

"And what does it tell you?"

"To keep you here and hope your deadline is later than mine."

"And after that?"

Biermann stared at Ritter a long beat, then said: "You are of significantly less value to me."

Biermann returned to his chair, looking smug about his decision. Ritter stood up and walked over to Ulrike, sitting on the arm of her chair. She put her hand on his back as if to show solidarity in the face of Biermann's implied threat. Her hand came off and then quietly slipped something into his right back pants pocket. Ritter stood up and put his hand into the pocket, finding he once again had her paratrooper knife, apparently retrieved from her purse.

No one was saying anything as Biermann's words hung in the air. Ritter headed over to the fireplace as if to warm himself and think about what to do. With his back to the fire, he took out the knife. He turned around and used his body to block his opening and locking of the 4-inch blade. He took the handle of the knife so it was in his fist with his wrists hiding the upward-turned blade as he walked over to Biermann. Ritter went behind the chair and leaned down as if to impart some confidence.

"I tell you what, Herr Biermann, how about if…." Ritter put the knife to Biermann's jugular, just as he had in his tussle with Rudiger Hahn in Wengen. "….you stand up slowly. The jugular is a very important vein. You cut it, and a person bleeds like a pig. Be a shame to mess up this pretty room."

Biermann did as he was told, and Ritter told Ulrike to stand behind him.

"Call one of your guards," Ritter told Biermann. "Keep it casual. Remember, I've got nothing to lose because it sounded as if you were going to kill me anyway."

"You misunderstood," Biermann said in a low voice.

"I'm taking no chances."

Biermann called for Willy. The muscular man, working the last of his pistachios through his teeth, strode into the room and stopped abruptly when he saw Ritter's knife.

He started to reach for the gun in his shoulder holster. Biermann shook his head. Willy withdrew his hand.

"Good," Ritter said. "Now walk over here and put your gun on Herr Biermann's chair. On the right arm, butt facing me."

Willy did and stopped, waiting for orders.

"Now get back over there near the door and get on your knees. And kneel on your hands."

Willy did as he was asked, and Ritter told Ulrike to get the gun from the chair and keep Willy covered. Ritter made Biermann kneel down, too, keeping the knife on his neck. He told Ulrike to move toward him. He took the pistol in his left hand and handed her the knife. He told Ulrike to stand behind Willy and put the knife to his back.

"If he moves, just shove it in. You won't kill him, but you will slow him down — and maybe make him think about moving in the first place."

Willy gave Ulrike a cold stare. She looked nervous about the plan, but she did as Ritter asked.

"Call in the other guard," Ritter told Biermann.

Heinrich came in. Ritter went through the same drill to disarm him. He gave Ulrike the second pistol, and she found herself with a weapon in each hand.

She laughed.

"I feel like some kind of commando."

Ritter looked at his two captives near the door.

"Who's got the keys to the car we came in last night?'

Willy said they were in his right jacket pocket. Ritter told him to fish them out with one hand and toss them toward him underhand.

"Now call Wolf in here, Ulrike."

Wolf came in drinking a cup of coffee and stopped in his tracks.

"Herr Biermann, Ulrike and I are going to take a little ride, Wolf. You need to stay here, so join the rest of the congregation. Kneel down and put your hands under your knees."

"This is crazy."

"I don't think so. Your boss seemed to say he was going to kill us."

"That was just talk," Wolf said. "A bluff to scare you. I assure you."

Wolf looked to Biermann for guidance but got none.

"I got all the assurance I need in my hand," Ritter said.

Wolf knelt down and Ritter, with his pistol trained on Biermann, frisked his brother.

"What are you doing?"

"Seeing if you have a weapon."

"Don't be ridiculous."

His search over, Ritter said: "OK, now Herr Biermann, you're going to walk to the doorway and shout to your other minions that the three of us are leaving and are not to be interfered with or followed. Understood?"

Biermann did as he was told, and the walk to the car proved easier than Ritter had expected. He'd worried that some unseen sniper might try to take him out even with the gun to Biermann's head. But after nothing happened, he decided Germans did indeed follow orders better than Americans.

Ritter made Biermann drive while he sat in the front passenger seat. Ulrike was in the back and kept her weapon pointed at Biermann, a slight smile on her face.

"Where are we going?" Biermann asked.

"Head back to the autobahn and drive north till I tell you to stop."

As the long car whooshed past the road signs, Ritter thought of a few loose ends he wanted to tie up as long as he had a captive audience.

"I'm curious. If we hadn't escaped and stood in your way of your grand plan, would you have disposed of us to save your grand scheme? You sounded that way back at the chalet."

Biermann took a while to answer before saying, "It's a hypothetical question."

"People answer them all the time."

"I don't."

"I ask because you guys do have a track record of killing people from what I know. Like that guy in the morgue in Berlin. The one with his head blown off."

Biermann was slow to answer.

"We didn't kill him."

"Who did?"

"The Munich police. He was a bank robber who died in a shootout with police. We arranged to take his body off their hands. We did do a little doctoring of the body, so it looked like torture….And your brother donated a good molar in the process so people would think it was him….We also lost two people trying to deliver that body to the East."

"Hadn't heard that."

"Davies's people intercepted our truck. They shot two of our men. A pity, but as it turned out the message we wanted delivered to the East got there after it was delivered to the West first. We made sure the Stasi got involved. They were the ones who grabbed the body at the morgue."

"And they killed two more people?"

Biermann nodded at the memory.

"We thought they'd just assign some burglars to steal the body, given that it was West Berlin. But they sent killers instead. More desperate for information than we'd thought."

"How about a guy named Rudiger Hahn? He was one of the guys who followed us to Wengen. He one of theirs?"

"Stasi. A thug. The East Germans thought you were Wolf at that point, I think. They wanted to bring you in for questioning. They're panicked about what's going on. As they should be."

"So what is it that would scare them so much if they knew. Wolf told me some of it, but I know there's more."

Biermann flashed a thin smile.

"He told you more than I would have."

"I already knew about the treaty."

"The draft agreement, you mean. That's all you could say — if you chose to say anything."

"If I did — and I haven't decided what to do yet — it'd still cause a ruckus."

"Indeed it would."

Ritter noticed a sign for a rest stop and told Biermann to pull off the autobahn. The facility offered bathrooms but not much else. One other car was in the parking lot, but it was pulling out just as Biermann braked to a halt. Ritter told Biermann to turn off the engine and hand him the keys. He motioned with his gun for Biermann to get out of the car. Ritter got out and inspected the toilets building. Ritter nodded his head as if satisfied. He told Biermann to give him his wallet and to turn his pockets inside out. Some paper marks and coins tumbled out and Ritter picked them up.

"You should be able to hitch a ride from someone and eventually find a phone somewhere to have your pals come get you. By then, we should be far away."

"No far enough."

"Maybe I should just shoot you."

"You wouldn't do that….I might, but you wouldn't."

Ritter rolled up the window and left Biermann in the dust, picking up speed till he hit 200 kilometers per hour.

"I could get used to this fast driving stuff," he said. "It's not half as scary if you're driving."

"Where are we going?" Ulrike asked.

"The airport."

"Won't they figure that?"

"I hope so. I want them to go there. Eventually. But not before we do a few things."

"Like make the treaty public?"

"Not necessarily. I'm not sure I'm against the plan from what I know about it. And if I blow the whistle on Biermann and Wolf, I just help Rick Davies and the Stasi, and I sure don't owe either of them anything."

"You surprise me."

"Well, as Wolf says, maybe we Americans need a swift kick in the pants."

"I don't get that."

Ritter smiled.

"Something he said."

That and what would you do if your family had been kept apart for half a century.

It was nearing sundown when Ritter pulled the car into the Frankfurt airport long-term parking lot. The afternoon sun was splashing a golden wash on the denuded trees along the airport's driveways. The air was invigorating and cool.

"Shouldn't we get rid of the pistols?" Ulrike asked.

"Good idea. In the trunk. Where we're going, we don't want to risk a personal search."

Ritter and Ulrike raced into the airport and paid cash for two tickets to Toronto, the next flight that was leaving for North America. With a little time before the flight was called, Ritter went to an American Express office and wired Doreen the money she'd given to his wife and a little extra. At a newsstand, he bought some newspapers and saw a postcard with a picture of Germany's fat chancellor on it. He wondered where he stood in all the intrigues. Staring at the card he asked himself: Are you about to be surprised too or are you an active member of the German Club?

Ritter handed Ulrike the newspapers and said: "I'll be right back."

"Shouldn't we go? The monitor says they're boarding."

"We have time. Go stand behind that pillar over there and try to stay out of sight."

Ritter went through security and eventually got on the plane. With ten minutes to go before the flight closed, he got off, telling the flight attendant he felt sick and would catch the next plane. He found Ulrike waiting where he'd left her.

"Where'd you go? I don't think we'll make it now."

"Change of plan. I handed in a ticket and got on our plane. People may think I'm on it when it leaves. Should buy us some time."

"For what?"

"Deciding what I'm going to do -- and postponing our deaths. I don't trust Biermann."

"What's the plan?"

"The cash machine for starters."

Ritter took out the maximum daily amount and paid for two tickets to West Berlin. He debated whether to use his own name or Wolf's. People in the West were looking for him. People in the East were looking for Wolf. He gambled and used his own passport. If Davies & Co. did manage to trace him where he was going, at least they'd be chasing him on enemy ground, and Ritter thought he'd have an edge there. And a close ally.

*****

At the rest stop, Biermann waited a few minutes to see if another car would pull in. His patience ended after a few moments, and he began jogging up the emergency lane, heading south toward the Black Forest. A road sign showed the next exit was five kilometers away. There'd be a gas station and a phone, he figured, and he settled into a steady trot, not unlike the runs he regularly made during the week to keep in shape.

He considered running across some of the farmland on either side of the highway. There was a farmhouse in the distance on his right, but the fields were muddy and had no roads through them, and there were no lights on or any signs of life like a parked car. He decided to take his chances with whatever he'd find at the exit.

Sweaty but not too fatigued, he jogged into a gas station only a few hundred yards from the exit ramp's end. There was a public phone. He slipped off his right shoe. From a compartment inside the heel, he pulled out five 100 Deutschemark notes and used one to buy some water. With the change, he called the chalet in the Black Forest and told an assistant named Rolf to send a car to fetch him and to get people looking for Ritter and Ulrike.

"He was headed north, but he's sneaky so check everything — airports, train stations, hotels. And report my car stolen. We might as well get the police to help us."

"What if he tells them about our plans?" Rolf asked.

"Tell them he's armed and dangerous. And a kidnapper."

19

Wednesday, November 8, 6:00 p.m., West Berlin

The plane landed at Tegel. Ritter had the cab drop them off at an S-Bahn station. A few minutes later, they were being processed by East German police, who looked not only at their passports but also frisked them.

"'Good thing we left the guns in Bonn," Ulrike whispered when they'd passed through the police checkpoint.

Passing Brecht's theater again, they noticed a small factory that had a sign that said: "Closed for Technical Problems."

"A lot of workers have fled the country through the east to the west," Ulrike said.

"Hungary, Austria, West Germany. It's like your underground railroad, but it's all above ground."

Another, a more honest sign farther up the street, said "Closed for Hungarian Problems."

"It must be driving the Politburo crazy," she said after seeing it. "But I don't think they can stop it. People are calling the reforms *die Wende.*"

"The turning?"

"Yes, and I don't think there's any turning back."

They walked to Fredi's apartment. She was ecstatic to learn Wolf was alive.

"*Wunderbar!*" she said.

Karl, her jealous chess partner, had a subdued reaction. His eyes narrowed when Ritter asked Fredi if he and Ulrike could stay the night. Karl announced he'd make them all some coffee and marched off to the kitchen.

"He's gotten a little too possessive," Fredi whispered after he'd left.

Fredi's TV was on as they waited for refreshments. The announcer said that the government cabinet had resigned and that the parliament had rejected a travel reform law that would have permitted each East German 30 days of travel outside the country every year.

"Too little, too late," Fredi said.

A leader of the dissident New Forum group said the resignations were a "first step" and called for legislators to consider a law permitting free elections, the news reader said. Ritter decided to take his great aunt into his confidence and told her about Wolf and his group's negotiations with the Soviets.

"So I can tell the world about it and blow it all up or keep my mouth shut and maybe you'll be living in one country again," he said after summing up.

"The last time didn't work out so well." She thought a while longer and said: "If I were in charge, I'd start all over again, and we'd have a real communist country, not this disgrace we wound up with. The revolution got sidetracked by criminals." She sighed. "But Communism is not too popular these days. People don't know what the real thing is. I'm afraid time has passed us by."

Ritter let out a small laugh.

"I was hoping for something clearer in the way of advice."

"You're the one who has to decide, not me. Do what your heart tells you."

"My heart and the rest of my tired body tells me to sleep on it."

Karl came back with the coffee and went back to the kitchen for some cookies.

"I don't think he likes me very much," Ritter said.

"He just wants to have me to himself. Chess and sex, that's all that's on his mind."

Ritter looked at Ulrike and both broke out into smiles.

"We'll at least he has good taste," Ritter said.

The discussion turned to the economic future and who would run what.

"Capitalism and the fat man in Bonn," was Freda's prediction. By the time everyone finished and some sardines and crackers and a bottle of cheap schnapps had been consumed, it was eleven. Karl, who had interjected his views only occasionally — usually to defend the reforms the government had proposed as good-faith steps — finally announced he was leaving.

He shook hands perfunctorily with Ritter and nodded a German goodbye to Ulrike. He kissed Freda, who was seated on the couch. Downstairs, he walked into the café, which had only a few patrons, and made another call to the Normannenstrasse office that paid him. Before dawn, a small paneled truck with two armed men inside appeared down the street from Fredi's apartment.

"Why don't we go in now?" the junior officer in the passenger seat asked.

"Orders are to wait till daylight to see if Springer shows up. He's the one we want, not his brother, but if the brother is all we get, we'll take him and maybe force Springer out of hiding."

"I hate overnight duty."

"Well, don't fall asleep. We still need to see if the brother and his girl friend come out. If they do, we grab them."

"Shouldn't be too hard," said the junior officer looking at the blue-prints of Fredi's building. "Only one way in and out."

Shortly after sunrise, Ritter was the first one up after a fitful sleep in the narrow guest bed with Ulrike at his side. He made some coffee, using the last of the grounds. Fredi came into the kitchen a while later with Spaetzle trailing at her ankles. She got out some crackers and fed him one.

"I need to get some food for him this morning."

"If you tell me where to go, I'll get some for you. Does he eat the dry stuff or the canned?"

Fredi laughed.

"Neither. Even if I could find real dog food, which is harder to get than fresh fruit, I don't think he'd eat it after all this time. He likes a good wurst. If I'm lucky, I'll find some."

Fredi got out a box of muesli and poured some into a bowl. She located a box of raisins and sprinkled some of the dried fruit on the cereal.

"A rare treat," she said holding up the box. "From my friend in high places."

After breakfast, Fredi pulled back the curtains in her living room and asked Ritter to open a balky window a little to let some of the fall air in. After he'd managed a modest crack, she went to the window to enjoy the coolness but soon got a worried look on her face. Ritter noticed and asked what was wrong.

"You see that panel truck down the street?" Fredi said.

Ritter took a look.

"It's what the Stasi use to transport prisoners to their headquarters."

Ritter considered the matter and said: "That might be for me."

"If they wanted you, they would have grabbed you by now."

"They may want Wolf. They may be waiting to see if he shows up."

"Well, they won't wait very long. Eventually they'll just grab you, toss you in a cell and make you tell what you know. And it won't be pleasant. I know. I was taken away in one of those once."

"What happened?"

Fredi smiled.

"My friend in high places got me out."

Ritter thought about his situation a moment and asked, "Is there a back way out of here?"

"Not really — unless you want to go up the fire escape and over the roof. I haven't been up there in a while, but there used to be a board you could walk across....Of course, that was a long time ago."

"How about down the fire escape?"

"It doesn't lead anywhere. Just an air hole. East German engineering."

Ritter woke Ulrike up and told her they needed to leave quickly. She got dressed, and he brought her a cup of coffee.

"We'll have to get some breakfast elsewhere."

Ritter came back to the salon and found Fredi on her divan, petting her dog.

"You'll need to come too, Aunt Fredi. If they come in, they won't be nice, given what they're after, and if you go back with them that would be the end of you."

Fredi stared at her great nephew.

"I haven't been out of this apartment in years. I'm not even sure I have a coat."

"You can borrow mine."

Fredi gave Ritter a look that seemed to say she wasn't going to cooperate. He didn't have time to argue, so he went a little nuclear with his arguments.

"If they grab you, there'll be no one to take care of Spaetzle."

Fredi got a worried look on her face and stared down at her beloved pet.

"I won't be able to get across the roof. I'll fall down."

"I'll carry you."

Fredi put Spaetzle on the ground and tried to stand up. Ritter had to give her a hand. He got his overcoat and put it around her, making her look like a shrunken doll.

Ulrike came out and looked surprise to see Fredi dressed in Ritter's coat.

"We putting on a play?" she joked.

"Fredi's going with us."

"Spaetzle too," Fredi said.

Fredi gathered up a few precious mementos of nine decades of life: an ancient black clutch purse, a cache of East and West German cash she'd hidden in some shoes in her closet, and a photo of a handsome man in his 50ss, dressed in a double-breasted suit. Ritter wondered if he was the friend in high places.

The trio made their way slowly out the kitchen window to the fire escape landing with Ritter handing his great aunt to Ulrike, like firefighters transferring a small child out of a burning building. Ulrike helped put Fredi on Ritter's back for a fireman's carry up the narrow fire escape.

"A piggyback ride," Fredi joked when she was aboard. Ritter went first. Ulrike carried Spaetzle. Two flights up, Ritter was puffing a bit. The gap between Fredi's building and the one behind it was about six feet. Ritter spotted a weathered 2 x 8 board next to the edge of the roof and slid it outward until it reached the next apartment complex.

"Glad to see it's still here," Fredi said. "I guess the Stasi don't know about everything."

Ritter tested the board and found it bent more under his weight than he would have liked.

"I don't think it'll take two," he said.

"It might if I was one of the two," Ulrike said.

Ritter nodded at the thought.

"Could work. You two go first. I'll hold the board."

Ritter put Fredi on Ulrike's back.

"Try it inch by inch," he said. "Nothing fancy."

"It'll be like a tightrope walk!" Fredi said.

"I hope it will be nothing like that," Ulrike said.

Ritter helped Ulrike get onto the board and get her bearings.

"Fingers crossed," he said.

"I feel better if you said a prayer."

"A little out of practice on that, but I'll see what I can do. If this works maybe I'll have to go back to church."

Ulrike edged across the board, taking deep breaths before each step. The board bent and swayed a bit under its two passengers, but Ulrike made it across. She turned back toward Ritter and let Fredi slip down onto the other roof.

"Your turn," she said.

Ritter got on the board and then heard a bark. He got off and picked up Spaetzle.

"You think Spaetzle could make it across himself?" Ritter asked.

"Unlikely."

"I was afraid you'd say that."

Ritter got back on the board with the dog. He inched across as Ulrike had. The board bent more than it had for her and Fredi. At midpoint it was so bowed the ends were a couple of inches off the two roofs, making a slight U out of the plank. Ritter stopped, worried it might crack.

"Ulrike, I'm going to toss Spaetzle over to you to make the load a little lighter."

"Don't hurt him!" Fredi shouted.

"If I keep him, it might be worse."

Fredi nodded silently in agreement. Ulrike got her arms ready for the catch. Ritter took a deep breath before making a shovel pass with the dog playing the role of a squirmy football. Ulrike made a good catch, but the force of Ritter's throw made the board crack, and instinctively he dived for the other side. He managed to grasp the lip of the far roof with his hands and forearms, all of which were aching from the impact as he dangled above the air hole between the buildings.

"You OK?" Ulrike asked, holding on to his wrists.

"Yeah," Ritter wheezed. "Just give me a minute."

Ritter got his wind back, then hauled himself onto the roof where his great aunt was petting her dog.

"That was fun!" Fredi said.

Ritter laughed and looked over the roof lip to the board below, which was now in two pieces.

"Well, at least no one will be following us."

*****

Around ten that morning, the Stasi officers in the panel truck were joined by Karl, who'd been ordered to appear for any assistance. Karl was told to stay in the café below Fredi's apartment after the officers decided not to wait for Wolf any longer. They headed upstairs, guns drawn. After they found the place empty, they came back down to the café and hauled Karl up to the flat.

"She can't be gone," Karl said. "She hasn't been out of this place in years. I'm not even sure she can walk."

Karl made his own search of the place to satisfy himself. He went to the kitchen and opened the window to the fire escape. He looked up and then down and spotted the board, not sure what to make of it.

"You stay here for now," the senior officer told Karl. "If she comes back, you call us. Sleep here if you have to. Tell her you were worried and so you stayed over. And say nothing about our interest in her."

Karl didn't want to stay, but he did what he was told. He thought there was little chance Fredi was coming back. She'd taken her dog and her cash.

20

November 9, 10:00 a.m., East Berlin

By the time the Stasi had discovered their prey had escaped, Ritter — his aunt in his arms and Ulrike with Spaetzle in hers — had made their way very cautiously away from the apartment, stopping now an again in a doorway or a lobby to make sure they weren't being followed.

"Do you know where we're going?" Fredi finally asked.

"Away," Ritter said, and all three laughed at their predicament.

"We probably can't go back on the S-Bahn," Ulrike said.

"My papers are in order," Fredi said, thwapping her purse.

Everyone chuckled again.

"If you're over 65, they don't bother you. In fact, they want you to go and have the West Germans pay for your pension. It's pretty nice from what I hear."

"If we get out of here, I think Wolf and I can do better than a pension for you."

"Let's figure it out over breakfast," Ulrike said. "That'll also get us off the streets."

Ulrike suggested the Hotel Metropol, which was lavish by East German standards. Located on Friedrichstrasse, it was tantalizingly close to the Wall and the S-Bahn station. They ate well, not sure of when the next opportunity would be. Fredi had pancakes and two fat sausages, some of which she fed to her dog. After breakfast, Ulrike said: "We can last maybe a day here if we check in late. The Stasi wouldn't likely get the report of our names from the hotel until morning."

"But they might be more efficient than that and wake us up at dawn."

Ulrike thought about that, then said: "What if we didn't use our names?" Ulrike smiled. "We could just pay someone to register for us and then get the key."

"Who could we trust, though? The Stasi seem to be everywhere."

"There are dissidents."

"You know any?"

"No. But I know where we can find them."

Before they left, Ritter went over to the concierge desk, took out a handful of West German marks and asked the man on duty: "Would the hotel happen to have a wheelchair we could borrow? We'll be checking in a little later, but we want to take a little walk with my….mother."

The concierge counted the money and said there might be one in the storeroom. He left and came back in a few minutes with a chair that squeaked as its wheels rolled and was covered with dust.

"Let me clean it up for you," he said.

"Maybe a little oil in the wheels," said Ritter, "and a blanket if you can manage."

The concierge performed his magic and got a little more money from Ritter, who installed his aunt in the chair and wrapped the blanket around her after taking back his coat. With a less conspicuous way of transporting Fredi than carrying her, Ulrike led Ritter and his aunt north to the Gethsemane Church, her intended sanctuary from Stasi pursuers. The Church walls were filled with notices from feminists, environmentalists, writers and homosexuals, calling for reforms from freer travel to free elections. Ulrike sought out a minister and explained the situation.

"If it's too dangerous for you, don't worry, we'll figure out something," she said.

The minister, originally from a rust-belt village west of Leipzig, smiled and said something might be arranged as quickly as that night — and they might not have to go back to the hotel.

"Just stay in the church during the day, and wait for word this evening. I'll have someone bring you sandwiches later."

*****

November 9, noon, Stasi Headquarters, Normannenstrasse, East Berlin

"So where is Ritter?" the duty officer asked.

"We don't know," the senior officer from the panel truck said. "We had him under observation at his great aunt's apartment, but when we went to arrest them, they were gone."

"Where?"

"Back to the west, I guess."

"I don't want guesses. Get some more men on this. Make this a priority unless you want to undergo some questioning downstairs by people who might want to know if you let them go on purpose."

"We'll check the crossings and the hotels first," the suddenly eager junior officer said. "We have their names out. And Springer's photo is everywhere so that helps get either one or maybe both."

"And we're sure this Ritter person is the brother and not Wolf Springer?"

"So it appears," the senior officer told the duty man. "He's saying Springer is alive, so that goes against the cover story."

The duty officer considered before saying: "I don't know what to think. But give me Wolf Springer in a cell, and we'll figure it out."

*****

November 9, noon, the Black Forest

"How many more calls do we have to make?" Biermann asked Wolf, who was sitting at a table with five telephones.

"Maybe a dozen, including our man in the Politburo."

"That's the most important one. If the press conference doesn't turn out the way we hope, people won't know to go to the Wall."

"I have the list. Bonhoeffer, our minister from Leipzig, is in East Berlin on a visit. The two New Forum people. Von Moltke, our man in Dresden. And the guard at the victims monument. Our German Club colleagues are also putting the word out without being too specific. We're just saying: expect big news on a new travel policy and watch TV."

"I wish we didn't have to move everything up like this," Biermann said.

"I know what you're going to say. You wouldn't have to if it hadn't been for my brother."

"And your little phone call from Moscow."

"Yes, guilty as charged, as I've said before, but I'm not so sure Matt is going to make our plans public."

"We can't take that chance." Biermann paused a moment as if deciding whether to say more. "Our arrangements with the Soviets were never going to be made public. We pitched a secret deal, so if he makes them public, that complicates everything. Especially because we were never going to honor the terms of that deal." Wolf's eyes widened.

"My draft accord was a total deception?"

"Not total. Maybe we'll work out something with the Soviets. Maybe we'll quit NATO, though I doubt it with this chancellor in charge. Whatever happens will be what's best for us. But first we need to create a little distraction that will set everything in motion. Or maybe not so little."

"So the chancellor doesn't know?"

Biermann smiled.

"We used one of his men in Moscow— our man really — to open a private channel and dangle the prospect of a neutral Germany in front of the Soviets to get them to allow the reforms we needed."

"A giant piece of theater then?"

"Diplomacy and politics *are* theater, but if your brother makes our plan public, then everyone would have had to deny it and take a hard-line stance on everything. And the play has a very different ending. We'd lose months of time. Years maybe."

Wolf let out a bitter laugh.

"And you couldn't even let *me* know?"

Biermann smiled.

"Need to know, as the spies say. If you'd known, would you have been as convincing about playing dead and trying to persuade your brother to keep silent?"

"Probably not."

Wolf's tongue touched the hole in his teeth where a molar was missing.

"I probably wouldn't have let you extract my tooth in the cause either."

Wolf looked at the list of the remaining calls he had to make.

"So what happens next with the Soviets?"

"Nothing tonight, I hope. The Soviets still have a lot of soldiers in the east, and the promise is to keep them indoors if there's any protest. After that, they'll just have to adjust the way the rest of the world will. We'll have two freer Germanies, and if the next elections go the way I hope they'll be, we'll be unified. Maybe this time next year."

Wolf crossed the first two fingers of his right hand and held then up.

"Speaking of luck, what's the latest on your brother?" Biermann asked.

"No word. He's not in any hotel that we can find. We got started a bit late on the search after we finally located your car and figured out he never left on that flight to Toronto. He's somewhere in West Berlin, as far as we know. We thought he might go back to get his luggage at that hotel near the Zoo. He left his suitcase there when he made his escape to Wengen. So far he hasn't showed up."

"If we can get through the evening without anyone hearing from him, we will have limited the damage considerably. But we still need to find him."

21

Thursday, November 9, 6 p.m., East Berlin

Dirk Jahr, a six-foot soldier from Saxony, got off duty after a muscle-wearying shift at the Monument for Victims of Fascism and Militarism, as the East Germans called their tomb of the unknown soldier. He and his colleagues did the *Gänseschritt*, the goose step, to their posts each day in the grey uniform of the *Nationale Volksarmee*.

The idea of the memorial, a restored version of Friedrich Wilhelm III's neoclassic New Guard House, was to bolster the illusion that the East Germany army was filled with cold-blooded Prussians who would march over you rather than be late for the changing of the guard. The image sought was one of *Kadavergehorsam* — cadaver obedience — but the reality behind the illusion of military invincibility was something quite different.

Jahr and his fellow goose steppers, none of whom had Prussian roots, trained outside East Berlin at a mockup of the monument and counted down every day of their boring 150-day duty. Marching like robots popped out of a cuckoo clock for every 30- minute shift was all they were fit to do should anyone ever invade their country. It was a boring job, but Jahr had another, secret employment that would get him killed should anyone find out about it.

Outside the barracks, a young woman approached Jahr, who carried his mushroom-shaped helmet under his left arm. She asked for a light. He pulled out a box of cheap East German matches and leaned in to shelter the flame. The woman took a puff, thanked him and said quietly: "The announcement should come tonight. Watch Schabowski's press conference. Then you know what to do."

"You have a preference?"

"Invalidenstrasse. They have a TV there in the booth. And the boys on duty are not so smart."

Out of sight of the memorial's barracks, Jahr took out a pocket knife from an outside uniform pocket, got out his regulation 150-centimeter measuring tape and cut another segment off to mark one more day of service. Ten centimeters of the tape were left. Ten days of duty to go. If his little protest were to be found out, he might spend some time in the stockade or lose some pay, but he was engaged in a much greater protest. If the plan worked out that night, there might not be any more inspections. If it didn't, he'd still probably end his service and just go home, like the 70,000 soldiers who had quietly taken off their uniforms and deserted the army in the months before.

*****

The widely publicized televised press conference at the International Press Center in East Berlin had been hastily called that same night. The room was filled with journalists from the West. The main speaker was to be Günter Schabowksi, who had become the acceptable face of the Socialist Unity Party of Germany, or the SED, as the communists were known. He'd been put out front by the Politburo after party chief Erik Honecker had been forced out for his hard-line stance and his replacement Egon Krenz had been booed in public for acting too slowly to lift travel restrictions and propose free, secret elections.

Just before the conference, a young man named Detlev, wearing a gray suit that sported a party pin in its lapel, handed Schabowski a note.

"There were some changes after you left the Politburo meeting. I took some notes."

The party leader took the notes and put them in his jacket pocket. He entered the steamy room, heated by the lights of East and West

Berlin TV stations, which were preparing to broadcast his remarks. Detlev, seeing that Schabowski had entered the room, sidled up to a journalist about to follow the party leader into the conference.

"He has news about the travel policy. Press him. You'll get some interesting answers."

Schabowski, the former chief editor of the party's newspaper, took the podium and droned on for about an hour about what the party had discussed that day. Television lights, fully switched on, made the wood paneled room seem even more cramped than it was, as the noise of clicking cameras provided a backbeat to his remarks.

Schabowski, a beefy man who had turned 60 that year, said he'd take a few questions. About 7:00 p.m., an Italian journalist, who had arrived late and took a seat on the stage where the podium was, asked about the travel policy. Schabowski, pulled the notes out of his pockets and said that East Germans would be allowed to cross the border "without proof of eligibility, reasons for travel or family ties."

Three journalists asked follow-up questions at the same time, including an American. In the confusion of the cross-talk, some journalist in the front row of press seats asked: "When does that go into effect?"

Schabowski, not having much information at his fingertips, looked at the young man who'd brought him the note for some guidance. Detlev tapped his watch with his right index finger several times.

"As far as I know *sofort, unverzüglich.*" Effective immediately, without delay."

"Does that include crossings into West Berlin?" another journalist asked.

Schabowski said yes, unaware the regulations approved in his absence called for East Germans to get permission in an orderly fashion and not right away, a fine point left out of Detlev's notes.

In West Berlin, Willy, back in his beloved city from the chalet in the Black Forest to search for Ritter, smacked his right fist into his left palm after hearing the answer on TV and said *"ausgezeichnet."* Excellent.

"Now all we need is a bit of luck," said the man next to him, the manager of a patriotic club in West Berlin.

"I don't think Herr Biermann is leaving it to luck, Frank."

*****

At the Invalidenstrasse crossing, Dirk Jahr, who had walked down Unter den Linden from his monument post before heading north, arrived at the guard station shortly after the press conference had begun. He'd asked if he could watch the proceedings on the guards' TV.

"Mine's broken, and I can't get the part I need."

"Try Hungary," one of the guards said.

The others laughed as Jahr turned up the volume on their set. Two of the guards kept their eyes on the no-man's land in between the inner wall fully in East Berlin and the outer wall that bordered on West Berlin. After Schabowski made his "effective immediately" remark, Jahr asked the guards, "Did you hear that? He said the wall is open."

"I heard it," the corporal in charge said. "I'm not sure I believe it."

"I can believe it," Jahr said. "What's the point of a wall if you can go west by just going around it to the east?"

"We have no instructions on this," another guard said.

"The last instructions we had were to shoot to kill, but those got rescinded," said another.

"You just got your new instructions," Jahr said. "From the voice of the party. I'm going home to change out of my uniform and cross over."

"Why change?" one guard asked.

"I don't want the Wessies to think we're invading them."

The guards laughed. After Jahr left the booth, he ran into a young couple out for an evening stroll.

"Did you hear about the Wall?" he asked. "Schabowski announced it was open. You can go to West Berlin if you want."

The man of the couple said that couldn't be true.

"If you don't believe me, just ask the guards at the crossing over there. I was just there."

Jahr went off intent on staying in uniform and having the same conversation with every person he ran into. As he walked out of sight, the young couple discussed it. They decided to give it a try, asking for permission from the guards to cross in their most humble way. The head guard looked at their identity cards, recorded their names, and waved them on, not even asking for a passport.

"If there's any trouble," the second-in-command said, we'll say we were just following orders. Schabowski's."

On the other side, the couple told their crossing story to the first West Berliners they met. The story spread like wildfire. A few hours later, it was broadcast on West Berlin TV, which East Berliners were able to watch.

Slowly but surely the new reality, quite different from the actual travel plan of written permissions and visas, spread, and thousands headed to the wall. At the Bornholmerstrasse crossing, by about 9 p.m., the guards began letting everyone across on the condition that their passports be stamped invalid. Two hours later, they gave up even that formality, and the crowds from the eastern part of the city streamed freely across on foot or behind the wheels of decrepit Trabants and Wartburgs.

Others came over the Bosebdrücke Bridge, and, in a scene that would capture the historic moment, Germans from east and west scaled the shorter wall near Friedrich Wilhelm II's Brandenburg Gate and celebrated under it in an area that had been off limits since the Antifascist Protection Wall had gone up in 1961. Champagne flowed, Wessies gave Ossies Deutschemarks to spend. The poorer cousins snapped up chocolates and even bananas, which were generally unobtainable on their side of the city.

A few hours earlier, a church deacon had sought out Ritter, Fredi and Ulrike and took them to the rectory to watch Schabowski's press conference. They heard his remarks about the timing of new travel policy. The young man turned to them and said: "That may be your ticket out of here. If we're lucky, by midnight, there will be pandemonium at the Wall. We're taking a crowd to see if we can get through. You're welcome to come with us."

"Count me in," Fredi said. "I love a party."

About 11:30 p.m., they arrived with the church group at the Bornholmerstrasse crossing. By then, the guards had lifted the border barriers and were taking pictures to capture the moment. In line, in front of Ritter, Fredi and Ulrike, was an elderly man with an old book under his left arm. In the celebration of the moment, he turned to Ritter and said he was using the opening of the wall to return the volume to the library.

"It's overdue," he said.

Ritter nodded and asked how long.

"Thirty years," the man said, laughing.

A few steps into West Berlin, Ritter and Ulrike noticed a man, sweat pouring off his brow, was attacking the graffiti-coated side of the wall that faced his part of the city. In the air, fireworks were exploding across the night sky. Behind him people were drinking champagne from bottles. The man stopped a moment to rest, and spotting Ritter, asked if he wanted a turn.

Ritter looked at Ulrike, who said: "This is history. Might as well be part of it."

Ritter took off his coat and took a couple of whacks at the wall, chipping off colored pieces of concrete from the graffiti clad structure. Ulrike picked up three and handed one to Fredi. Ritter took about a dozen more swings at the wall before giving up and handing the sledgehammer back to the man.

"I'm getting too old for this," he said.

They made their way to the Kurfürstendamm, Berlin's Great White Way, and inched down it among blaring trumpets and the spraying of sparkling wine. East Germans, identifiable from their cheaper clothes and shoes, were seen grinning from ear to ear, with bags from West Berlin shops in their hands.

"I'm going to get drunk tonight, but I have to be at work over there at seven," one of them said to no one in particular. "What else can I do?"

West Berlin's Mayor Walter Momper passed in front of them in a police radio truck, welcoming East Berliners while urging them to go home after the celebrations.

"He's worried they'll all want to stay the night at the Kempinski," Ulrike said. "And the bill will be on him."

"Speaking of hotels, maybe we can go back to ours and get our suitcases — and a shower."

Ritter, Fredi and Ulrike made their way down the famous thoroughfare and headed to the Am Zoo, pushing Fredi's wheelchair at a good clip. They checked in, asking for two adjoining rooms with connecting doors.

"I think you may have some bags of ours," Ritter said. "We had to leave in a hurry a few days back."

A bellman took their bags up and returned to the lobby to make a call to a chalet in the Black Forest.

"They've arrived," he told the person on the other end of the line. "Room 407."

Ritter turned on the TV for Fredi to watch the festivities, which were dominated by the crowd on top of the Brandenburg Gate. He helped her into bed after she'd brushed her teeth and washed up. In their room, Ulrike claimed the shower first. Ritter turned on his own TV and soaked in history in the making.

A few minutes later, the room phone rang.

"Are you watching it?" Wolf asked his brother.

Ritter let out a small laugh at his brother's ability to track him down.

"Oh, yeah. I was down there for a while. Made the crossing myself."

"From the east?"

"Yeah. Long story. Brought Fredi over too."

"Really?" Wolf said, sounding somewhat astonished.

Wolf thanked his brother for not making the German Club's plan public.

"I can't take much credit for that," Ritter said. "I was still thinking about what to do when I suddenly had the Stasi on my tail."

Ritter filled Wolf in on what had happened after his visit to Fredi's.

"Glad it worked out. Biermann couldn't take chances. He moved our plan up."

"Not surprised. He's survived a long time playing all sides against each other."

"He's not the only one. A lot of people helped."

"I think I met one of them at a church."

"Entirely possible. Even I don't know everyone involved."

"Maybe it'll be in the newspapers when they write this up."

"None of this will become public — unless you talk. Our little band might have to do it all over again, and we'd prefer to stay in the shadows."

"What about the Soviet deal? Surely that will have to be explained."

"It won't. Turns out, the whole arrangement was a ruse by Biermann to get them to encourage reform and then stay out of the rebellion in the east. Some of it may come true, but no promises. We'll just do what's best for us."

Ritter decided the situation gave him some leverage.

"Tell you what. You tell Biermann I'll keep my mouth shut for now about him and the CIA and your little club, but I want him to leave me and Ulrike alone. If something happens to either of us, I'll make sure everything comes out."

Wolf let out a slight laugh.

"You've become quite the operative, Matt. I could have used someone like you in my network."

The remark reminded Ritter of the case file and the ledger he'd left in the hotel in Munich before being nabbed in the English Garden by

Biermann's hoods. He told his brother he ought to get them out before someone else did.

"Shouldn't be much trouble. It's in my name, and you look just like me. Worked for me the other way around."

"Very funny."

Ritter told his brother he was curious about one thing: "Was the government in on the masquerade?"

"I wish I knew. It wasn't until recently that I realized how little I did know about *our* plans. Biermann says the chancellor wasn't in on it. Or at least he didn't say he was in on it, now that I think about it. But the chancellor is already talking reunification, which is part of the plan. And the chancellor just happens to be in Poland tonight. That's convenient if he needs to deny anything we did last night."

"I'd love to tell Rick Davies what an idiot he's been, but it probably works out better if I just keep my mouth shut."

"How so?"

"I've got something else in mind for him."

Wolf asked what Ritter planned to do now that the whole affair was coming to an end.

"Go back to Chicago. I've got a murder to solve or I'm going to get fired."

"Sorry you can't stay for the party. I suspect it will go on for a couple of days. I'm flying to Berlin myself in the morning. Maybe we could have lunch. Brothers should get to know each other."

"We'll do that. Not tomorrow. But I'll be back."

"Great. In the meantime, since it can't seem so much like a bribe any more, I'm putting your share of the inheritance in a bank account in your name."

"I don't know about that."

"I'm not asking for permission. I'm doing what I think is right. If you don't want the money, give it to charity for all I care, but my slate will be clean."

"Still wanting to be in charge, I see."

Wolf laughed.

"A national trait. Speaking of that, I can take care of Ulrike while you're away."

Ritter smiled.

"I won't be needing any help in that department. She's coming to Chicago while I sort things out."

There was a pause before Wolf said: "She'll be back."

"Yeah, but if she comes, it will be with me."

Ritter wasn't sure what that bit of bravado meant other than he'd decided he wasn't letting her out of his sight, whatever it took.

After the conversation, Ritter dialed Doreen at the office. It was late afternoon in Chicago. If she were working late, she might be at her desk, he thought. Ulrike came out of the bathroom with a towel around her body and another around her hair in a loose turban. She sat on the bed as Ritter gave her a shush sign while he waited for the call to go through.

Doreen was out, but the switchboard put the call through to the captain. Ritter tried to stop the transfer, but Malone barked a "Yeah?" before he could.

"Checking in, sir. Ritter."

"Really? I thought maybe you'd retired or something. I have the papers to put you on unpaid leave on my desk. I was just about to sign them."

Ritter doubted that. It was likely just more of Malone's bluster, but he found he wouldn't be that upset about some leave if it came to that, even with the serial killer still on the loose. Mentally, he'd turned that matter over to Doreen a while back.

"I'm on my way back, Captain. We can talk about that when I get there."

"Yeah, yeah. I'll believe that when I see you walk in the door."

Ritter waited a moment then asked Malone the status of the murder case.

"Getting' there. Thanks to Doreen. She flushed him out. He got away, but now we have photo of him and an APB out. Maybe you can help mop up if you ever do get back from your European vacation."

Ritter laughed at Malone's theatrics, finding he wasn't really that worried about his career anymore. He still liked police work, but he had some other options — and some money in the bank if he decided to use it. He suddenly had a family, including a beloved great aunt and a jealous brother. And, best he could tell, he had a girlfriend.

"I can probably get a flight out tomorrow — or actually this evening — it's already the 10th over here. Though it is a little crazy with the Wall coming down and all."

"The Wall?"

"The Berlin Wall. Didn't you see it on TV? Probably means the end of the Cold War."

"TV? Some of us have been working, you know."

"Well, in any case, I can be back there pretty quickly now that I got things cleared up here."

Ritter thought about telling Malone that his brother wasn't dead after all, but he imagined the likely response and left that out. He hung up and, like a good homicide detective, considered some other murders. He could think of at least four people killed in West Berlin. Rick Davies was likely involved with two of them — and most definitely David Price. He wondered if Rudiger Hahn had used those missing bullets in his pistol on the other two. Maybe Günter Becker and the German police would be interested. He had some calls to make.

With Ulrike listening, he called the concierge and asked him to make a reservation for two to Chicago on the evening flight. That left several hours to kill, and he turned to the most pressing matter at hand, the woman who was seated next to him. He tugged on the towel around Ulrike's torso, and it fell behind her.

*****

Wolf briefed Biermann on his call with his brother, more serious in mood than the upbeat tone he'd used with Ritter.

"Call our men off at the hotel for now," Biermann said. "But keep him under surveillance."

"And if he goes back to Chicago like he said?"

"We have people there. If he talks, there will be consequences. If he keeps his mouth shut, we'll see."

*****

About the same time, in Moscow, a Kremlin aide nicknamed Faddey, thinking of his Volga German ancestors on that historic night, called a certain club in West Berlin and reported in.

"They didn't wake the general secretary to tell him," he said.

"Why not?" asked the club's manager.

"They decided the Wall's fall was a good thing, not a crisis, so it could wait till the morning. They didn't even schedule a Politburo meeting. They bought the whole story. I have to say, I know that was the plan, but I'm surprised."

"Well, in the morning, they'll get two surprises of their own: the wall is down and that agreement is worth nothing."

"If they found out about me, that would be three surprises, Frank. Maybe it's time for me to move my family home."

"How long have they been there?"

"On my mother's side, since Catherine the Great."

NOTES

AFTERWORD

Some of the events in this novel are historically true, from the Kremlin decision not to wake Mikhail Gorbachev to tell him about the Wall's fall to the questions at Günter Schabowski's Nov. 9 press conference and the surprise impact of his answers.

Some give credit to a German or an Italian journalist for asking when the new policy went into effect. Others say it was Tom Brokaw, the veteran NBC anchor, who was at the conference. Perhaps he, not Ronald Reagan, should get the credit for bringing the infamous wall down.

Markus Wolf, the famous head of East Germany's foreign spy operation, the HVA — and the model for LeCarre's Karla — did appear at the Nov. 4 Alexanderplatz protest rally, opposing the Politburo with his own reform proposals. He died in 2006 — on the anniversary of the fall of the Wall.

Thousands of ethnic Germans, including the Wolgadeutsche or Volga Germans, did live in many republics of the Soviet Union before the Wall's fall, partly the result of the encouraging policies of Catherine the Great, the German-born Russian empress.

Communist hero Vladimir Lenin was one of them. Many returned to live in the new Germany after reunification, which occurred in 1990 after free elections. Previously thousands had moved to the U.S. Midwest, including the northern neighborhoods of Chicago, such as Jefferson Park, the fictive home of Detective Matthew Ritter.

Some of the characters, such as Dirk Jahr, the guard at the East German tomb of the unknown soldier and Gad, the elderly Jewish storyteller, are based on people I wrote about as a journalist in the period right after the Wall fell.

For those who paid special attention to all the German names I used, General Hans Oster of the Abwehr did indeed lead a plot to kill Hitler and helped Jews escape the Nazis' clutches, not unlike a certain General Springer. So did Dietrich Bonhoeffer, a Lutheran pastor. Helmuth James Graf von Moltke was part of the Kreisau Circle, which backed the ouster of Hitler. All three were executed in 1945 for treason. Von Moltke's wife Freya spent her life educating the world about a peaceful Germany. There was a Herr Biermann, but he was just an East German dissident singer expelled to the West.

George H. W. Bush was the U.S president when the Wall fell. Vernon Walters was the U.S. ambassador to West Germany. Both were former U.S. Directors of Central Intelligence. They had no employee named Rick Davies in Bonn or David Price in Berlin that I know of. Like Davies and Price, General Rudolph Springer and his two sons Matt and Wolf are just the product of an active imagination as was the German Club.